tangled ROOTS

A Kendra Clayton Novel

ANGELA HENRY

sepia™

TANGLED ROOTS

ISBN 1-58314-608-3

© 2006 by Angela Henry

www.kimanipress.com

Printed in U.S.A.

Acknowledgments

I would like to thank:

God, for giving me strength

All of the readers, reviewers, Web sites, book clubs, booksellers and libraries that have embraced Kendra.

My editor, Glenda Howard, for her awesome editing skills.

My agent, Richard Curtis, for taking care of the details.

My family, for their support.

Prologue

Inez Rollins lifted her heavy mass of braids with one hand and fanned her sweaty neck with the other. She spied a piece of hair she'd missed on the floor and aimed her broom underneath the stretch of counter. Soon she'd have her own shop and she'd pay someone else to do this mess, she thought. The cleaners her boss, Bruce Robins, employed to clean the shop only came every other night. When she had her own shop she wouldn't be working this late at night, either. People would have to make their appointments around her schedule and not the other way around. Bruce and the other stylists were nice enough but she'd been working in someone else's shop since she graduated from cosmetology school. It was high time she had her own place.

She'd sat down with a calculator during her lunch break and figured she only needed a few hundred dollars more to put a down payment on that little building over on Sinclair

Street that used to be a candy store. She'd have had the money by now if that bitch Renita Franklin hadn't been stealing her supplies. She had to shell out extra money reordering supplies that she knew damn well Renita had taken and hidden in her station. So what if Renita had written her name on the stuff? Inez wasn't stupid; she knew that stuff belonged to her. It was a good thing Bruce had fired Renita's ass before there was an even bigger problem.

Her ex-boyfriend, Vaughn Castle, had offered more than once to give Inez the money she needed for her shop. But she didn't want to take a dime from him, especially since she'd recently found out where the money really came from. It made her sick just thinking about it. How could she have been so stupid about him? And the way she'd found out still hurt like hell.

Her father had also offered, but she'd told him to go to hell and to take that skank he was married to with him. She wasn't going to salve his guilty conscience by taking his money.

The only person she could ever count on was her mother, and she was dead and gone now. Inez didn't need anyone's help to get where she was going, never had and never would.

She daydreamed and planned some more as she bagged up the trash and dragged it to the back door. She opened the door and was startled by the person standing still as a statue in the dark alley.

"You scared me! I thought I told you I had nothing to say to you. What are you doing out here in the dark?" she asked, stepping outside and looking around.

When she saw the gun she had her answer and minutes later, when it fired, she barely had time to blink, let alone think how quickly one's plans and one's life could change…or end.

Chapter 1

I always thought that I was the type of woman who wouldn't let a little gray hair bother her. I'm usually the first one to notice when a celebrity's face looks a little younger and tighter than before. I'm usually the first one to smirk and roll my eyes when a person won't admit how old they are. So you'd have thought I'd be unfazed upon seeing *my* first gray hair—wrong. Instead, I sprinted to the phone with a quickness that would have made Flo Jo proud and made an appointment for some color. Bruce Robins, my hairdresser—or stylist, as he likes to be called—convinced me that highlights would be much better. Well, whatever it takes. Funny how things change when it's you and not someone else.

But when I arrived at the shop that Saturday morning, there were police cars and an ambulance blocking my entrance to the parking lot. I parked down the street and walked back to join the small knot of people that had formed across the street.

"I think somebody's dead," said an older woman, who I remembered seeing in the shop from time to time, though I didn't know her name.

"Who is it?" asked another woman I'd never seen before. No one seemed to know anything more than the fact that someone had died at the shop, a.k.a. B & S Hair Design and Nail Sculpture.

It wasn't until later that morning when I'd gone over to Estelle's, my uncle's restaurant where I hostess part-time, that I got the lowdown from Gwen Robins, my uncle's girl-friend for the past eight years. Gwen is a statuesque five ten and she wears wigs to suit her many moods. She's also the aunt of Bruce Robins, owner of B & S Hair Design and Nail Sculpture. Today she was wearing a short blond number that made her look like a female impersonator, though I wasn't about to risk my life by telling her this. Besides, she looked like she already had the weight of the world on her shoulders.

"You heard about Inez Rollins, didn't you?"

I shook my head, not fathoming that Inez was connected in any way to the death at the shop.

"She's dead. Somebody shot her last night."

I almost fell over. "I was at the shop this morning to get a haircut. I knew someone had died but I had no idea it was murder. What happened?"

"All I know is she was the last one at the shop last night. She was closing up and somebody shot her as she was taking out the trash." Gwen shook her head sadly. I understood just how she felt; it was such a horrible shame.

"Was it a robbery?"

"Girl, who knows? Bruce found her about seven-thirty this morning when he went to open up. I've never seen him so upset. He really liked Inez."

A lot of men had really liked Inez. Besides being beautiful, she'd been a nice person. If she'd been a bitch it would have been easy not to be envious of her effortless charm and model looks. I guess I had no reason to be envious now. Inez had worked at the shop for about six months. She specialized in braids: intricate, unique designs that almost made me give up my short no-nonsense do and start sporting some. But it had been economy and not fashion that had led me to my current style. Braids are beautiful but they can cost an arm and a leg, especially when you had someone as talented as Inez doing them.

"She was shot in the face, poor baby. I just don't know how anyone could do such a thing," Gwen said. "I talked to Bruce about ten minutes ago. He said he's closing the shop 'til Tuesday. He had to notify Inez's father."

I only hoped that it had been quick and she hadn't known what hit her. I'd been on the opposite end of a gun myself quite recently and didn't have to imagine how scared she would have been. I was just now beginning to sleep through the night.

I sat down at a table near the hostess station and Gwen brought me a cup of coffee. I put four heaping tablespoons of sugar in it and a good measure of cream. Gwen laughed.

"There you go again, ruining a perfectly good cup of coffee. By the time you get done loading it down with sugar and cream, it ain't coffee no more."

"Hush, I'm not like you. You drink it strong enough to put hair on your chest." I took a sip and then added more sugar, ignoring Gwen's frowning face. "Poor Bruce. I bet finding Inez this morning really freaked him out. Did he find her inside the shop?"

"No, he said he found her outside by the back door. The back door was still open when he got there this morning. He went in through the front door. He was in the shop for almost twenty minutes before he went in back and saw the back door wide open. He thought they'd been robbed. He saw Inez lying on the ground when he went to shut the door. Said she was just lying there like a rag doll somebody threw on the ground. Blood was all over the brick wall." Gwen shook her head like the mental image of Inez's body was too much for her to bear.

"So nothing was stolen, then?"

"Girl, don't get me to lyin'. All I know is Bruce said he didn't notice anything was wrong until he saw that the back door was open. So, to me that means nothing was stolen, but who knows?"

"If it wasn't a robbery then it must have been personal. Who in the world would want to kill Inez? She was a sweetheart."

"Yeah, she seemed nice enough. But who knows what she had goin' on in her life? I didn't know her like I know most of the other stylists. She kinda kept to herself. But I do know a lot of folks who smile and act like they don't have a care in the world and they have the most god-awful messes goin' on in their private lives."

The bell above the door tinkled and we both turned to see Joy Owens, one of the other hostesses, walk into the restaurant. She looked at us, rolled her eyes, and headed back to the locker room to change into work clothes for her shift.

"And then there's Joy," I whispered, watching her retreating back, "who acts like smiling is hazardous to her health no matter what's going on in her private life." We both laughed.

★ ★ ★

I had dinner that evening with my best friend, Lynette Martin-Gaines. She and her fiancé, Greg Hull, had finally set a wedding date. I had gone to help Lynette pick out a wedding dress and Lynette told me she'd take me out to dinner afterwards to cheer me up. Carl Brumfield, the man in my life for the past four months, was in Cleveland on a family emergency: his brother-in-law had suffered a massive stroke and he had gone to be with his sister, Monica. He'd asked me to go with him but I couldn't get away from work. Besides, I knew his parents would be there and Carl's mother, Martha, and I hadn't exactly hit it off. She thought I was un-ambitious. I'd overheard her talking about me during a cookout at their house one Saturday not long ago.

"Is she planning on being a waitress all her life?" I heard her ask Carl.

"Ma, you know she isn't a waitress. She's an English teacher with a GED program. She hostesses part-time at her uncle's restaurant. Remember? We ate there last month."

"Waitress, hostess, what difference does it make? Anybody who has a degree should have a full-time job. She must not be looking very hard. Maybe she should go back to school and get her master's degree." I heard her say something else but was too disgusted to stick around and hear what it was.

Just because Martha Brumfield had overachiever fever and was working on her Ph.D. at age sixty while working full-time and volunteering for Planned Parenthood and the Sal-vation Army, didn't mean that was for everybody. I loved my work at the literacy center and nothing else I'd done thus far had given me so much satisfaction. I also loved working at Estelle's. And the fact that I'd mysteriously started receiving graduate school catalogs from every college within a fifty-mile radius of Willow hadn't exactly endeared the woman to me, either. I'd just have to grin and bear it, though. Carl's mother came along with the package, and I cared for him much more than I disliked his mother.

And I missed him much more than I thought I would, although I didn't want him to know just how much. I'd been trying to do all the right things and strike the right balance of togetherness and space in my relationship with Carl. Most of my past relationships had had the shelf life of a milk carton left sitting out on a countertop. I usually hung on to them long past the expiration date, pretending I didn't notice the smell when it went bad. I wanted things to be different with Carl. I was planning on welcoming him back from Cleveland in a major way that involved skimpy lingerie, whipped cream, and a hot bubble bath for two, not necessarily in that order.

The Red Dragon, my favorite restaurant in town after Estelle's, was crowded as usual. I was grateful when we were finally led to our table after a thirty-minute wait. Lynette had dragged me around to every bridal shop in town. Believe it or not, Willow had five. They outnumbered our grocery stores by two. All five did a booming business. Lynette had managed to be drawn to every expensive and figure-hugging dress that she saw. She'd been saving for the dress for a long time, so money was no object. However, as much as I love my best friend, I just didn't have the heart to tell her that she didn't quite have the figure for the type of dress she was so hell-bent on owning.

After three hours of watching her try on dresses that made her look like she'd swallowed a tire, my good humor was running out and I thought my face would crack from so much phony smiling. But the last straw came when she showed me the maid of honor dress she'd picked out for me. I laughed when I saw it 'cause I figured it had to be a joke. Then I saw the look on her face and realized it was for real. The dress was a sequined, Smurf-blue nightmare that made me look like I'd shit a large bow. It also scratched me at the neckline. I almost cursed when I saw how much it cost. Lynette informed me in a tone that was *quite* funky that it was going to be her day and when it was *my* turn she'd gladly wear whatever I chose.

Welcome to wedding hell, I told myself. I thought it was an urban legend, something I'd heard about for years but never thought I'd experience. My best friend had lost her damn mind and her good taste. I'd always suspected that as soon as women became engaged and started planning their weddings, they plotted to make every other woman in the bridal party look like a clown. Now, I had proof. And just how I was supposed to sit comfortably during the wedding reception with a big bow on my ass was anyone's guess. Boy, I couldn't wait until it was my turn to get married for no other reason than being able to pick out something poofy, promlike, and hideous for Lynette to wear. Visions of yards and yards of neon pink tulle and bugle beads danced through my head on the way to dinner.

The tension between us was thick as we sat in the restaurant. After we sipped our mai tais for a while we mellowed out and started acting like friends again. Lynette broke the ice first.

"It's such a shame about Inez. She was so beautiful. I still can't believe it." Lynette had had her braids done by Inez. Inez had been very talented, indeed. Lynette's hair looked great.

"I hope they catch whoever did it and put them *under* the jail." We both drank to that and then focused on our food. I took a bite of my cashew chicken and sighed in contentment.

"Did you know her father was Morris Rollins?" Lynette asked.

"You're kidding, right? Reverend Morris Rollins? You mean the one that has that big church, Holy Cross?"

Morris Rollins was the ultimate prosperity preacher with designer clothes, luxury cars, an expensive mansion, and rumors of enough illegitimate children to start his own small country.

"Yeah, that Morris Rollins. Didn't a lot of people from St. Luke's leave and start going to his church?"

"Mama said the Ivorys left for a while but came back," I said.

"I bet your grandmother wished they'd stayed."

Actually, Mama had been quite upset. Though she didn't pretend to have any fondness for Donna Ivory, she hated to see Donna and her husband Delbert being taken advantage of by Reverend Rollins. It seemed the Ivorys had forked over quite a bit of their retirement money to Reverend Rollins, all in the name of the Lord, of course. Mama had been happy when they'd returned to St. Luke's a little poorer but wiser.

"Abby and Dave went to a couple of services over at Holy Cross," Lynette went on. "They weren't too impressed. Of course, Abby isn't about to come up off any money, especially not 'cause any flashy preacher tells her to." Dave was Lynette's brother and a follower of anything that sounded remotely fulfilling. At age thirty-five he was still searching for himself. Surely his wife, Abby, hoped he'd find himself soon. She'd already had to endure his stints as a Muslim, an Amway salesman, and a vegan. I was surprised Reverend Rollins hadn't dazzled him.

"I think Dave would have gone back but Abby put her foot down," Lynette said as though she'd read my mind. "They just don't have the money to bankroll Reverend Rollins and put another fancy car in his garage."

"I was running the channels the other night and saw him on one of those local cable access channels. Does he have a talk show?"

"Yep. It's called something like *Light the Way* or *The Light of the Way*. It's kinda low budget. Looks like it's taped in the church basement or something. Reverend Rollins is the host and they talk about religious issues. And of course, at the end there's the usual plug for donations for Holy Cross Ministries. I've only watched it once."

"Doesn't sound like I'm missing anything." Lynette and I both laughed.

"What about Inez's mother?" I asked.

"Oh, she died a few years ago. He's got another wife now, some little young thing Inez's age. I don't think Inez and her father were close."

"How do you know so much about her?"

"Sitting in that chair for hours on end getting my hair braided. It works both ways, you know. I spilled my guts, but she spilled hers, too. She was saving to get her own shop. Told me she was just a few hundred dollars shy of a down payment."

We ate in silence for a few moments. Neither of us needed to comment on how incredibly sad it was that Inez had saved all that money in vain.

Chapter 2

The Clark Literacy Center, where I've worked for the past four years, was housed in what used to be an elementary school. Clark Elementary School closed due to low enrollment back in the mid-seventies. Besides the ABLE/GED program that I worked for there was also an ESL—English as a Second Language—program, parenting classes, aerobics classes, and an after-school latchkey program.

We were well into the new school year. It was October and the leaves were beginning to turn. Fall is my favorite time of year. This school year, however, had a different feel to it. For one thing, my friend and coworker Bernie Gibson, our program's tutor trainer and coordinator, had decided to take the year off to travel and pull herself together after experiencing some major drama in her life—a situation that I'd managed to get myself involved in. But that's another story. Anyway, the woman who took her place had become a burr in my behind.

Noreen Reardon was a retired kindergarten teacher with the appearance of a sweet little old lady and the personality of a piranha. I was already getting complaints from the literacy tutors over Noreen's "my way or the highway" working style. We were only a month into the school year and she and I had already bumped heads on several occasions.

I looked up from my desk, where I was grading some essays, and saw Noreen across the room laughing with Rhonda Hammond, our program's math teacher. It seemed that Noreen had charmed everyone in the program except me and the literacy tutors that she trained and supervised. Everyone else thought that butter wouldn't melt in the woman's mouth. Well, we'd see about that.

"You want me to pass out those essays, Kendra?" asked Shanda Kidd. Shanda was a senior at Kingford College who'd opted to do her mandatory community service at Clark Literacy Center. In order to graduate, all Kingford College students had to complete eighty hours of community service.

"Yeah, thanks, I'm finished with these," I told her, handing her the stack of papers. I looked around the room and smiled. Every seat was filled. Our enrollment had almost doubled since last year.

I watched Shanda pass out the essays and offer words of praise and encouragement to each student. The girl was a natural teacher; all the students loved her. However, she was a marketing major and had no interest in teaching as a profession. I was hoping her time at the center would change her mind. When she reached a young black man sitting in the back of the room, she bent down and whispered something in his ear. One of her braids fell forward and brushed his cheek. Timothy Milton looked up at Shanda and smiled. When they saw me watching they looked away, embarrassed.

I'd suspected that something was going on between them and didn't quite know what to do about it. I'd known Timothy Milton since he was a little boy. His late father, Jesse Milton, had been my uncle Alex's best friend. Jesse committed suicide five years ago, leaving a void in the lives of all those who had loved him, especially his sons'.

Timmy's a former crackhead. He'd been clean for about a year now. I was happy when I found out that he and his mother had moved back to Willow from Detroit. Life in Detroit had not been kind to the Miltons. Timmy's older brother, Dell, was in prison for armed robbery. Timmy had managed to turn himself around and was working towards his GED. He just needed to brush up on his geometry and he'd ace his exam. Alex had even given him a job at Estelle's. Shanda, on the other hand, was bright, pretty, and a big flirt. It was none of my business but I couldn't help but feel their involvement was going to end up with one of them getting hurt, probably Timmy.

"Kendra, you need to keep your workers on task," said a prim voice. I hadn't noticed Noreen walk up beside me.

"What?" I asked, not bothering to hide my irritation.

"That girl, Shanda. She shouldn't be talking to the students. They're here to study and she shouldn't be distracting them with chitchat. Workers who can't stay on task aren't organized, which leads to wasted time. These students don't have time to waste." She looked at my barely organized desk and shook her head.

I looked up at her. She stood by my chair dressed in her gray tweed suit and black lace-up oxfords. Her white hair was pulled into a thick topknot that added two inches to her height. Big silver hoop earrings dangled to her shoulders and silver bracelets jangled at her wrists. She looked like a fortune-teller crossed with a librarian. I tried hard to contain my anger and smiled sweetly.

"Noreen, as you've so astutely pointed out, Shanda is *my* worker and if and when she does something inappropriate, which she hasn't, I'll certainly let her know. Now, why don't you go back to *your* area and stop distracting me from *my* tasks."

"Kendra, you would be wise to try and benefit from constructive criticism. It can only make you a more productive teacher and help your students," she said, glaring down at me.

"Well, when you start signing my paychecks, maybe I will." I tried to keep my voice even and a smile on my face so the students wouldn't know what was going on.

"Stranger things have happened and I'd watch my step if I were you," she said with a mysterious smile as she turned and walked away.

What the hell was that all about?

"I see you two are at it again," said Rhonda, sitting down at her desk, which was next to mine. "You really shouldn't let her get to you, Kendra. She's a nice woman when you get to know her. She's just from another generation."

"You mean another planet, don't you?" I hissed. "Planet Anal Retentus, you know the one, located just past Uranus and shaped like a tightly clenched ass!" I was more than a little put out that Rhonda was taking up for Noreen.

"She's made it clear that she doesn't want a friendly working relationship with me. The only time the woman speaks to me is when she wants to criticize me, Rhonda. She needs to chill and take care of her own business," I whispered angrily.

Rhonda sighed and turned her attention to one of the students who'd come up for help. I needed to calm down so I took a break and went outside to the playground. While

I was out there swinging on one of the swings, a few students came outside to smoke. Timmy was with them and when he spotted me, he came over and joined me. He was a good-looking kid, a little on the skinny side, but tall and handsome like his father had been. It wasn't hard to understand what Shanda saw in him.

"How's it going, Timmy?"

"All right."

"How's your mom doing?"

"Fine."

Sometimes pulling conversation out of Timmy was like pulling teeth. He was quiet but very observant, which he proved with his next question.

"What happened with you and ole girl back in the classroom?"

"Oh, just a difference of opinion. I need to stop letting her get under my skin."

"You want me to beat her up for you?"

I looked over at him and saw that he had a smile on his face. I hoped he was kidding; with Timmy you can never tell.

"It's nothing I can't take care of." But I couldn't help but wonder what Noreen had meant by her last statement to me.

"I see you and Shanda have become friends," I said casually.

"Yeah, she's been tutorin' me in geometry," he said, looking down at his Nikes.

Yeah, I'll just bet she has, I thought, and looked away so he wouldn't see me smiling.

"I just want to make sure I'm ready. You think I'll be ready for the real test soon?"

The anxious uncertainty in his voice almost broke my heart. "The only thing you really need to work on is your geometry," I told him honestly. "I'd like to see you score two hundred and fifty points on your next practice test. Once you've done that, you should be good to go."

I was rewarded with a big smile that instantly eclipsed my encounter with Noreen and reminded me of why I loved my job so much.

Too bad I wasn't able to hold on to that feeling after our staff meeting later that afternoon. Dorothy Burgess, the literacy program's director and my boss, announced that she was taking an emergency leave of absence. Her elderly mother, who lived in Michigan, had broken her hip and needed someone to care for her. Dorothy would be out for at least six weeks, possibly longer. Because of her thirty years of teaching experience, Noreen Reardon would be in charge in Dorothy's absence.

Oh, hell no!

"Kendra, you better not let that old white woman run you out of a job you love!" said my grandmother, Estelle Mays, over dinner that evening. I had stopped by to have a quick bite to eat with the woman I've always called Mama. Not Granny, Grandma, Grandmother, and certainly not Estelle…Mama. She wouldn't answer to anything else even when her own children addressed her.

"I just know she's going to try and make my life miserable." I wound a forkful of spaghetti and took a bite, savoring the tomato and basil sauce. I'm a woman who enjoys her food.

"Can't you talk to Dorothy about her? Tell her what's been going on?"

"No, Mama," I said adamantly. "She's gone already, and besides, I'm not going to go whining to Dorothy over a clash of personalities. It's not my style."

"Oh yeah, I forgot. Your style is to say nothing, keep everything bottled up inside, and seethe in silence until things get so tense you're ready to burst a blood vessel. You're gonna end up making yourself sick if you don't learn to express your feelings, girl."

"Well, I don't think Noreen would like how I express my feelings for her. It would probably involve me bringing a gun to work."

Mama stopped eating, fork midway to her mouth, and stared at me in shock like I'd just sprouted an extra limb.

"That ain't funny, Kendra. Especially in light of that poor girl getting shot Friday. And if I recall, it wasn't too long ago that you were staring down the barrel of a gun. Don't you let anybody hear you talkin' like that either or you won't have to worry about that woman at work 'cause they'll fire your butt!"

She was right, of course, and I shut up and finished my food.

Later that night, I was soaking in a hot bubble bath when the phone rang. I reached for the cordless sitting on the floor next to the tub.

"Hello."

"Hey, baby." It was Carl. Things were looking up.

"Hello, there. I was hoping you would call. I miss you. How's John?"

"No change. It's not looking too good for him. I'm really worried about Monica. She's a mess." He sounded tired.

"I'm so sorry, baby. I wish I could be there with you."

"Me, too. How are things going with you?"

"Just fine," I lied. I didn't feel like ruining our conversation by mentioning my problems at work. I knew that I should confide in him. The one sore spot in our relationship was my inability to share my problems with him. Carl had hinted on more than one occasion that he felt like I didn't need him. It wasn't true. It's just that I'd never been good at crying on anyone's shoulder.

"So, tell me how much you miss me," he said. I proceeded to tell him in great detail, using my softest, sexiest voice and not failing to mention that I was wet and soapy.

"Damn, baby, I wish I was there," he said breathlessly.

"And if you were here what would *you* be doing?" I asked. I lay back in the hot, fragrant water and let Carl's deep, husky voice carry me away from my troubles.

Chapter 3

With Dorothy gone, Noreen took full advantage of her newfound authority. We were now required to give her copies of our lesson plans for her stamp of approval, which she only gave after lengthy revisions. She had weekly staff meetings planned. We also had a list of tasks we were supposed to complete during the two-hour break between the morning and afternoon sessions. Gone was the laid-back atmosphere we were used to under Dorothy's supervision. Suddenly, Noreen didn't seem so nice and old-fashioned to Rhonda. I was relishing this as much as I was resenting Noreen's micromanagement. Rhonda also felt that she should have been left in charge since she'd been working at the center for almost ten years. But Dorothy was gone before anyone could protest her decision.

"Give a person a little power and they just don't know how

to act," said Rhonda bitterly. We were cleaning out the supply closet, one of our tasks.

"What happened to 'She's really nice when you get to know her. She's just from another generation.'?" I couldn't resist rubbing her nose in it a little.

"Oh, shut up," she said, tossing an eraser at me and missing.

"Well, I'll tell you this: Cleaning this closet out is one thing. But if she thinks I'm gonna start sweeping floors and dusting, she can forget it. Nowhere in my job description does it say I'm supposed to clean this place."

"You got that right," said Rhonda.

"Attendance seems to be down a little these past few days," I commented.

In fact, I hadn't seen Timmy Milton in class that morning, which really surprised me. He'd taken his practice test the day before and I knew he was anxious for his score. He'd scored two hundred and sixty-five points. More than the two hundred and fifty points that we required in order for students to take the real GED exam. Shanda had also been absent. I just hoped they hadn't had a lovers' spat and stayed away to avoid each other.

"Noreen's probably scaring them away. Can you believe she's trying to keep the students from interacting with each other and from talking to us if it's not school-related? This isn't kindergarten. These are adults. Next thing you know she'll be trying to get them to take naps and have snack time," Rhonda said.

We both laughed.

"Excuse me, ladies," said a voice behind us. I turned around and found myself looking straight into the eyes of Detective Trish Harmon. Talk about someone I never figured on seeing again.

Trish Harmon and I had become acquainted several months ago during a murder investigation. To say Detective Harmon and I didn't see eye-to-eye was like saying people in hell were a little warm and thirsty. Her mannishly short graying hair, severe black pantsuit, and neutral expression instantly brought back memories I'd been trying to forget about for months. I noticed what looked like a flake of dandruff on Harmon's lapel. So, she was human, after all. Well, just barely. Her partner, Charles Mercer, was standing behind her. Detective Mercer was florid, overweight, terminally rumpled, friendly, and as opposite from his partner as he could get. I nodded at Mercer and received a smile in return.

As much as I wanted to ignore Trish Harmon completely, Mama's a stickler for manners and I knew she would put a foot in my behind if she got wind of me being intentionally rude to a member of the law enforcement community. So, with great effort, I flashed a friendly smile at the odd couple.

"This is a surprise, Detectives. What can we do for you?"

It was Harmon who answered. "Miss Clayton, we're here to ask you a few questions about one of your students. A young man by the name of Timothy Milton."

"Timmy? What about him, is something wrong?" I felt the bottom drop out of my stomach.

"When was the last time you saw Timothy Milton?" asked Mercer, walking up to stand beside his partner.

"He was in class yesterday morning." I looked from one to the other but neither of them was giving away a thing.

"Was he in class this morning?" Harmon's laser-like stare unnerved me.

"No, he wasn't. Will you please tell me what this is about? Is he in any trouble?"

"We just need to ask Mr. Milton a few questions regarding a murder investigation. If you see him please have him contact us." Harmon held out her card, which I snatched out of her hand—so much for my manners—then she turned and walked out of the room. Mercer followed her after giving us an apologetic smile.

"Boy, she has all the warmth and personality of a day-old corpse," said Rhonda.

I didn't comment. I was too worried about why the police were looking for Timmy Milton and why he hadn't come to class.

I headed over to Estelle's after I got off from the literacy center. I thought I remembered seeing Timmy's name on the schedule for that afternoon. Estelle's was bustling with its usual mix of students, staff and faculty from Kingford College, each group keeping a watchful eye on the others. Secretaries took note of which administrator had how many glasses of wine with lunch; instructors noticed which students hadn't come to their class but were hanging out at Estelle's; and everyone watched who was there with whom. Since the day it had opened almost six years ago, Estelle's was the place to be. What once was a dress shop and dance studio had been transformed into a stylish restaurant complete with exposed brick walls and black-and-white tiled floors on the first floor, and a bar that had live music on the weekends on the second. My uncle Alex had opened the restaurant after being laid off from his factory job after twenty years.

This afternoon, Joy Owens was hostessing. Joy was not the hostess with the mostess. If you were looking for service with a smile, Joy was not your girl. She was all of four foot eleven and looked like a kid. But Joy was twenty-one and a senior art major at Kingford College. She was very talented even though, to me, most of her work looked like something out of a schizophrenic's nightmare. In fact, she had a new painting on display in the restaurant. This one showed a creature with the body of a winged, white horse and the head of a bull with a dead cat in its mouth. It was hanging, appropriately, in the men's restroom, causing countless men who'd had one too many to miss the urinals as they stared at it. Alex was about to move it to his office because the cleaners were complaining about cleaning piss off the walls.

I watched Joy seat a young couple and waited for her at the hostess desk. She was walking with a slight limp, testament to a serious accident she'd had four months ago. She didn't look pleased to see me waiting for her. But then again, Joy never looked pleased. She smoked a pack and a half of cigarettes a day, cursed like a sailor, and had all the social grace of a doorknob. I guess you could say Joy had issues.

"Have you seen Timmy, Joy?" I never bothered with niceties with Joy.

"Nah, I ain't seen the muthafucka. And if you see him, tell him to get his ass in here! I don't appreciate havin' to do his job for him!" She grabbed a rubber tub from a cart behind the hostess station and started busing a vacated table. I watched her haphazardly toss plates, glasses and cutlery into the tub and halfheartedly wipe the table off, leaving crumbs and debris behind, and I cringed.

I walked back to the kitchen in search of Alex and encountered Grace Douglas, who cooked at the restaurant part-time, instead. She smiled when she saw me. Grace was a sweetheart most of the time but if you tried to give her grief, she'd cut you a new butt hole. She was the only person I knew who scared Joy.

"Hey, girl! What's going on?"

"Nothin' much, Grace. Is Alex around?"

"I think he and Gwen went to the market. Anything I can help you with?"

"Have you seen Timmy around?"

"Sure haven't. Saw him in here last night, though, with some cute little black girl with braids. They looked real cozy."

It had to have been Shanda. Maybe she knew where he was. I could have just called his house but I knew his mother worked third shift at a factory and slept during the day. I didn't want to bother her, especially with something like this, until I had talked to Timmy.

"Do you know if he called in?"

"Not that I know of, honey. Is everything okay?"

I sure hoped so.

I headed over to the registrar's office at Kingford College. I knew that Shanda lived at home instead of on campus. I didn't know her address, but knew who could tell me. Myra Hampton was Gwen's best friend and had worked in the records office at Kingford College for twenty years. If anyone could tell me where Shanda lived it was Myra.

Kingford College was a small liberal arts college with an enrollment of about fifteen hundred students. The tuition was so high it was no wonder Shanda lived at home. The records office was located in Tyler Hall, a gray three-story stone building that used to be the college president's house back in the thirties. It now housed the records, counseling, and cashier's offices.

It was a beautiful day, so I ditched my car and walked over to campus. Students were taking advantage of the sunshine and were camped out on blankets on the college green studying and socializing. I watched a group of students headed into Floyd Library, which was right next to Tyler Hall, and spotted Shanda heading down the library steps. I called out to her and she looked over at me for a second before turning on her heel and quickly walking off to the parking lot. I almost went after her but decided it might be better to try to catch her at home. She obviously wasn't sick. So, why hadn't she come to class and why was she avoiding me?

It had been a long time since I'd been in Tyler Hall but it hadn't changed a bit. The same cracked blue linoleum on the floors. The same narrow halls and beige walls covered in bulletin boards, and the same smell of coffee, disinfectant, and stale cigarette smoke even though no smoking was allowed in any of the buildings on campus anymore. I found the records office and went in. Myra sat behind a long, age-scarred wooden counter and had the phone cradled against her shoulder as she frowned at her computer screen. When she looked up and saw me, she gestured for me to wait a minute while she ended her call.

Myra Hampton had been Gwen's running buddy since high school. But where Gwen was statuesque, loud, and fun-loving, Myra was more reserved, petite, and almost prissy. She wore her hair in the same short, feathered seventies flip she had worn in high school. Gwen tried repeatedly to bring her best friend's fashion sense into the nineties without much success. And if Myra knew Gwen let it slip to me that she had met her new boyfriend, nicknamed Bone, no less, through the prison's pen pal Web site, she'd die of embarrassment.

"Well, ain't this a surprise. You here to register for a class?"

"Oh, no. Not me. My college days are behind me and I want to keep them a fond memory." I knew Carl's mother had a different opinion but she could stick those graduate catalogs she was having sent to me up her behind.

"You still working at the literacy center?"

"Yes. Actually, that's why I came by. I needed to ask you a favor. Is it possible for you to give me the address of one of the students here? She's one of our volunteers at the center and I need to talk to her."

"Sounds kinda serious. Who is it?"

"Her name is Shanda Kidd."

"Shanda? What's little Miss Perfect done?" Myra asked with a raised eyebrow.

"You know Shanda?" I was a sucker for good gossip and Myra looked like she could give good gossip.

"Not her so much as her mother. I went to high school with Shanda's mother, Bonita. We used to be friends 'til she got involved with that church, Holy Cross. She changed after she started going there. Suddenly I wasn't good enough for her. Got real uppity and would only spend time around people from her church. Even married one of the deacons. She never let Shanda play with other kids, thought she was too good to be around just any old kids. She was only allowed to be around relatives or kids from the church. You havin' a problem with Shanda?"

"No, nothing like that. I just wanted to check on her. She wasn't at the center today."

"Well, I wouldn't be surprised if Bonita talked her out of working there. I know she couldn't be happy with Shanda being around people she probably thinks are sinners and losers. Here," she said, handing me a slip of paper. "This is the address, but don't be surprised if Bonita won't let you through the front door."

I went back to the restaurant to get my car and mooch a sandwich from the kitchen. Timmy still hadn't turned up. Gwen and Alex were back from the market and arguing, as usual.

"Okay, Alex, if you want to serve your customers these little hard-ass plums, you go right ahead. Just don't come cryin' to me when someone sues you over a broken tooth!"

"There's nothing wrong with these plums, Gwen. They're for the plum sauce, not to eat as is. You'd know that if you knew how to cook." Alex never raised his voice. He was much too laid-back for that. He managed to make his displeasure known by the way his nostrils flared. When he got mad he looked like a pissed-off horse.

"Well, I may not know how to cook in the kitchen, but I know how to whip up a feast for your skinny behind in the bedroom! And let's see how long it is before you taste any of this again!" Gwen smacked her own behind and stormed out of the kitchen. None of us was fazed, especially Alex. Scenes like this were a regular occurrence where Gwen was concerned. I'd always thought Gwen would have made a great actress. She had an overdeveloped flair for the dramatic, not to mention enough clothes, wigs, and makeup to outfit an entire theater troupe.

"You working tonight?" Alex asked.

"Nope. Just came by to see if Timmy was around. You seen him today?"

"Why? Has he done something?" Alex had been more than willing to give Timmy a job at the restaurant provided he walked the straight and narrow. But if there were any indications that he was using again, he'd be out of a job. I didn't know what was going on, so I kept quiet about the police coming to the center.

"No. He passed his practice test and I know how anxious he is for his score. I just wanted to let him know the good news, that's all."

"He didn't show up today. Olivia called and said he was sick."

"Oh, well, I guess I can tell him when he comes back to class." I figured Harmon and Mercer had been by to see Olivia Milton and I wondered if she was covering for Timmy because she didn't know where he was, either.

"So, he's doing all right then?" Alex asked with just a hint of concern.

"Oh, yeah, he's ready to take his GED and if his practice test is any indication he should have no trouble passing."

"Glad to hear it. That boy's given Olivia enough grief. It's time he started giving her a reason to be proud of him. I think if he started using and getting in trouble again it would kill her."

I leaned back against the counter and watched Alex walk back to his office. I sure hoped Timmy wasn't about to break Olivia Milton's heart again.

Chapter 4

I parked in front of a two-story house with gray siding trimmed in white and checked the slip of paper Myra had given me with Shanda's address. This was the house all right. It was four o'clock and I hoped I could catch Shanda at home alone. I saw her little black Honda Civic in the driveway so I got out and headed up the driveway. The lawn was immaculate. Two large clay pots filled with geraniums flanked either side of the front door. I could hear faint strains of music coming from inside the house. I rang the doorbell.

Shanda opened the door and greeted me with a big smile. I watched the smile evaporate from her face when she saw that it was me. Who had that big smile been for? Timmy?

"Kendra?" she said, leaning slightly out the door and looking quickly up and down the street. "This is a surprise. How'd you know where I live?" She suddenly looked like a deer caught in the headlights.

I didn't want to get Myra in any trouble so I ignored her question. "You weren't in class today. I was worried when you didn't show up. Can I come in?" I asked, pushing past her into the foyer.

"Well, I had to go talk to my counselor today, and the only appointment I could get was for this morning. I thought I'd be done in time to be at the center but my appointment ran over."

It sounded completely legit but somehow I knew it wasn't true. Maybe it was because she couldn't quite meet my eyes.

I followed Shanda into a living room that looked like it belonged in a turn-of-the-century brothel. Garish red carpet clashed with wallpaper crawling with pink and yellow cabbage roses. Massive mahogany furniture crowded the center of the room while thick, gold, velvet brocade curtains, complete with a fringe, hung in the large front picture window. A crystal chandelier hung from the ceiling and a large gilded mirror adorned with cherubs hung over the brick fireplace, the mantle of which was covered in glass figurines of animals. Every available flat surface was covered in lace doilies. A baby grand piano occupied one whole corner of the room and was draped with what looked like a large royal purple silk scarf. I could easily see lingerie-clad beauties lounging lazily around this room, entertaining flashily dressed men who smoked cigars and sported pinky rings. I glanced in the mirror and caught the glimpse of amusement on Shanda's face as she watched my reaction to the room. This surely didn't look like the living room of a devoutly religious woman.

"This is the only room in the house where my mother let my father have his way. All this stuff belonged to my grandmother, and since none of my aunts or uncles wanted any of it, we ended up with all of it."

I suppressed the urge to ask what her grandmother had done for a living and glanced at a grouping of pictures that crowded the top of a round end table next to the brocade couch. One in particular caught my eye and I walked over and picked it up. It was a group picture of the Holy Cross church choir decked out in green-and-gold choir robes. In it I noticed a much younger Shanda standing next to a beautifully smiling Inez Rollins. I felt tears prick my eyes and quickly put the picture back.

"Have you seen Timmy lately?" I asked, watching her closely.

"I ran into him at Estelle's last night. It was slow so he sat with me while I ate. Why?"

"He didn't show up in class today and I was just wondering if anything had been bothering him lately."

"I only see him in class and I haven't noticed anything different about him."

Only saw him in class? I'd been getting the distinct impression that there was an after-class involvement going on between them. Unless Shanda flirted and acted familiar with all the men she knew. Somehow I didn't think so.

"Oh, I thought you were tutoring him in geometry."

"Yeah, I tutor him. But, mainly I just see him in class. You didn't think he was my man or anything, did you?"

"I did wonder. You two seem kinda close so I naturally assumed—"

"Well, you assumed wrong. I have a man and it's not Timmy Milton. And if there's something wrong with Timmy it's his problem and I don't know anything about it." Her arms were crossed defensively across her chest and her shoulders were drawn up almost to her ears.

Talk about protesting too much. Shanda's little declaration

was long on attitude and short on persuasiveness. No matter what she said about having a man, she sure hadn't acted like she had one whenever I'd seen her with Timmy.

"I'm sorry if I've offended you, Shanda," I said through partially gritted teeth. And I *was* sorry, if I was wrong, but I knew that I wasn't. Diplomacy, which is a fancy word for ass kissing, is not one of my strengths. But I didn't want to offend her further by bringing up example after example of her so-called non-involvement with Timmy.

"It's okay, Kendra. No big deal," she said, relaxing and looking away from me towards the window. She was obviously expecting someone and making no secret of the fact that she wanted me to leave.

"Will I see you in class tomorrow?"

"Sure," she said with a smile, returning to the sweet and friendly Shanda that I knew and liked.

I took the hint, said goodbye, and headed out the front door. As I walked down the driveway, a black Cadillac Escalade pulled up behind my car. I watched as one of the finest black men I'd seen in a long time emerged from the driver's side. His skin was the color of coffee with liberal splashes of cream and his sandy colored hair was cut so short he may as well have been bald. His body was slim and muscular and his belted baggy jeans and tight black T-shirt emphasized a slim waist and well-defined pecs. As he walked past me, I caught a whiff of a spicy lemony-scented cologne that I couldn't place. He must have been about six foot two and anywhere from twenty-five to thirty years old. As we passed each other, he tipped his black Ray Bans down, giving me an appraising glance with eyes as green as emeralds. He must have liked what he saw 'cause he grinned at me with teeth so straight and white that I could almost feel my panties start to disintegrate. Almost. Fine as he was, he was almost a little too pretty for me. But still.

I watched him head up Shanda's driveway. She was waiting at the door and practically leapt on him as he entered the house. Poor Timmy. I wondered if he knew about Shanda and her pretty boy.

I started to head home after the afternoon session at the literacy center. Noreen had spent the entire afternoon in a meeting, which made everyone much more relaxed and happy. It was like old times again. But I couldn't enjoy her absence with the same enthusiasm as my fellow inmates because I was worried about Timmy. The only murder that had occurred recently that Harmon and Mercer could possibly want to talk to Timmy about was Inez Rollins' murder. Timmy's past drug usage, which included at least one arrest that I knew of, didn't necessarily mean that he could be involved in any way with a murder, least of all Inez's. Surely the person who killed Inez was some anonymous psycho. But, then again, I didn't know Timmy as well as I used to when he was a little boy and I'd babysit for him occasionally. Who knew what was going on in his private life?

Instead of heading home, I decided to drive past Timmy's place. He lived with his mother in a condo on Palmer Street. It was in a fairly new development, which had about three dozen small two-story brick units, each one with a different color door. I'd only been there once for a party when the Miltons first moved back to Willow about six months ago. As I turned onto Palmer Street, my heart sank. There were police cars parked in front of the Miltons' unit. I drove past as slowly as I dared, trying to see what was going on. I knew I should stop to see if everything was okay. But I wasn't sure I wanted to know. I spotted Olivia Milton, dressed in her work uniform, standing in front of her front door talking loudly and gesturing wildly at Detective Trish Harmon, who looked like she'd just finished sucking a lemon. Her lips were pressed together and stuck out in what could have been classified as a pout by anyone who didn't know her. More than likely Harmon was just trying to remain calm in the face of the blatant hostility currently being flung in her face. I hoped Olivia was giving her hell.

I saw Mercer standing by a car that was parked in front of the condo. It was Timmy's burgundy Chevy Cavalier. Mercer had on gloves and he and another officer appeared to be searching the car. I didn't see Timmy anywhere, not even in the back seat of either of the two police cars. Things were not looking good. Where in the world was he? A loud blast from a car horn behind me quickly snapped me out of my trance. Not bothering to look back, I sped off down the street.

I wasn't feeling quite ready to go home, so I ended up grabbing dinner at Wendy's and wandering through one of my favorite thrift stores, Déjà Vu. I'm not big on malls and I love a bargain the way old ladies love bingo, though most people I know just think I'm cheap. Practically everything I own is used. Déjà Vu is a tiny hole-in-the-wall connected to a secondhand record shop. I've found most of my favorite articles of clothing while digging through the shop's crowded racks. Ruby Young, the owner of both shops, greeted me when I walked in.

"We got some great new stuff in the back, Kendra. Not too raggedy and don't none of it stink." Ruby was in her seventies and looked like she'd stepped out of a fifties time capsule. She wore gold cat-eye glasses studded with rhine-stones and an unnaturally jet-black beehive hairdo that looked as though something were making a nest in it. She had a raspy voice that sounded like she gargled with rocks. Today she was dressed in a white vintage Chanel suit with black piping and gold buttons.

"Thanks, Ruby. How about evening gowns? Got anything new?"

I was desperately trying to find a blue gown to wear in Lynette's wedding more flattering than the sequined horror she'd picked out for me.

"There might be a couple back there, though I can't make any promises."

I thanked her and headed to the back of the small shop towards the dresses, stopping briefly to admire a fringed silk shawl and breathing in the shop's oddly appealing scent, a mixture of cedar and Ruby's Charlie perfume. I got busy hunting through the jam-packed racks, praying I'd find something fabulous. I found a beautiful powder blue creation with a tea-length skirt right away but was disappointed to discover it had a large stain on the back that looked suspiciously like urine. I quickly put it back. That was the only thing about Déjà Vu that I hated. Ruby's eyesight wasn't what it used to be and she often had more trash than treasure.

Finally, after an hour, I managed to find a very flattering satin halter dress from the seventies in a deep midnight blue, which fell to my ankles and had a daring split up the side. I loved the way it hugged my body in all the right places. I'd recently lost some weight and the dress showed it off well. It looked like something Thelma from *Good Times* could have worn to the prom. Determined to get Lynette to change her mind, I had Ruby hold it for me.

★ ★ ★

I arrived at my duplex on Dorset around eight-thirty. I knew something wasn't quite right when I walked through the door, even before I turned on the lights. But when I heard an exasperated voice exclaim, "It's about time," I almost wet myself. I spun around, almost knocking over a potted plant, and saw a figure sitting in my wicker rocking chair. The last time someone had been waiting for me in my apartment I'd almost died. So, I wasn't feeling very hospitable. I flipped the light switch and saw that my visitor was Timmy Milton. He was looking at me like I shouldn't be surprised to see him.

"Boy, I almost killed you," I said, and meant it. I could have killed him for scaring me.

"Yeah, like what was you gonna do, Kendra? Beat me to death with your purse?"

I looked down and saw that I had my purse clenched in my hand like a weapon. I relaxed my grip and walked over and sat down on the couch opposite Timmy. He had on the same baggy jeans and Dallas Cowboys Jersey he was wearing the last time I saw him.

"How did you get in here?"

"I got my ways," he said with a mysterious smile. It was apparent that he thought I should be impressed.

"Do you know the police are at your place? I saw them searching through your car." I was hoping to wipe the smile off his face and I wasn't disappointed. Timmy buried his face in his hands and groaned.

"This is bullshit, man. I can't believe this is happening to me. I didn't kill that chick! I didn't even know her."

"Do you mean Inez Rollins?" I asked, already knowing the answer.

"Yeah."

"Then why are the police looking for you?" I asked.

Timmy sighed, sat back in the rocker, and gave me an exasperated look. "I was set up, Kendra," he said, like it was the most obvious thing in the world.

I didn't know what I was expecting him to say. But somehow I thought I was going to get a more original answer. Weren't the prisons filled with innocent people who blamed their predicaments on either bad luck or having been set up by the government or persons unknown? I didn't know what to say. Instead, I resorted to the one thing that always gives me comfort during a stressful time: food.

"Are you hungry? Do you want something to eat?" I asked, getting up from the couch and heading into my tiny kitchen. Timmy was hot on my heels.

"Naw. I ain't hungry. I'm serious, Kendra. I was set up and I know who did it!"

I pulled two cans of Pepsi from my fridge and tossed one to him. "Okay," I said, pulling the tab on my can. "Let's hear all about it."

I didn't mean to sound so sarcastic and felt bad when I saw the hurt look that flashed across Timmy's face. I sat down at the kitchen table and gestured for him to sit as well. We sat in awkward silence with Timmy looking like a sulky child for several long minutes during which I realized I was treating Timmy like he was still a crackhead. I was fine with him as long as everything was okay but at the first hint of trouble, I automatically figured he had to be lying. There was only one way to find out.

"I'm listening, Timmy," I said softly. "What's going on?"

"Well, you know I had some problems a while back with drugs?" he said, not quite able to look me in the eye. I nodded.

"Back in Detroit when I was usin', I stole somethin' from a guy who sold drugs and was tight with my dealer."

"What did you steal?" I asked.

"That ain't important," he said, shifting nervously in his seat.

"Well, it must have been pretty damned important if he's setting you up for someone's murder."

"It's not just what I stole that's the problem. It's what happened after I stole it. See, the dude sees me steal it outta his ride, and starts chasin' me. Musta chased me for three blocks. I'm jettin' when all of a sudden I hear somebody holler and then this big thud. I look back and see the dude flyin' through the air. The car that hit him just kept on goin', didn't even stop."

"He's dead?"

"Yeah, he landed on his head. Now, his boy, Vaughn Castle, who I used to buy from, is out to get me 'cause he blames me."

"So why set you up? Why isn't he trying to kill you?"

"'Cause everyone knows he's got a beef with me, and if I turn up dead they gonna be lookin' at him. If he catches another case it'll be his third strike. He'll get sent away for life. Incz was his girl. Hell, I think he smoked her himself. Then he saw an opportunity to get back at me by settin' me up."

I didn't know what shocked me more, what Timmy had just told me about his past, or finding out that Inez Rollins was dating a drug dealer. I hadn't known Inez well. But I knew she was a talented beautician, hard-working and, according to Lynette, full of plans to open her own beauty shop. So, she must have been ambitious as well. She'd always been polite and friendly whenever I'd seen her out in public. And she was a minister's daughter, for crying out loud. She just didn't seem the type to get involved with a drug dealer. But what the hell do I know about the types of women who date drug dealers? Diddly squat, apparently. Suddenly, my boring little life didn't seem so bad.

"How did he set you up? What evidence do the police have against you?"

"Somebody said they saw me runnin' away from the crime scene. Ain't nobody seen me runnin' away from anywhere," he said angrily.

"That's it? That's why the police are after you?" Timmy started shifting around in his seat again and I knew there was more to the story.

"Well, when they came to the crib today, I heard them talking to my mom. I was takin' a nap, and when I figured out what was goin' on, I snuck out my window. I called my mom and she said they found somethin' in my car and towed it away—"

"Please don't tell me you used my phone to call your mother," I said, interrupting him. All I could imagine were the police tracing the call and showing up here, surrounding the house, and dragging Timmy and me off in handcuffs after tear-gassing us. I needed to stop watching so much TV.

"I ain't that stupid, Kendra. Chill. I know they can trace that kinda shit. I used a pay phone. I don't even have my cell. I lost it."

"You said this happened in Detroit. What is this Vaughn guy doing here? Did he follow you?"

"Naw. He lives here. Runs drugs from here to Detroit. Man, I didn't want to come back here, but with no job, a record, and no diploma, I had to go wherever my mom went. I didn't have no place else to go."

"So, now what? Are you going to the police?" It was a

stupid question and I knew it. But hope springs eternal when you're trying to remain uninvolved.

"Are you crazy?" he said, jumping up from the table so quickly his chair fell over with a bang.

"Calm down, Timmy. It was just a question." I was hoping my landlady, Mrs. Carson, hadn't heard the loud noise and gotten scared. Ever since my brush with death four months ago, she'd been keeping a closer eye on me than usual.

"What about your mother? What does she think?"

"My mom knows I didn't kill nobody," he said, picking up the chair and slouching back down into it. "She told me to lay low until she could figure something out. She don't want to see another son locked up." Timmy was referring to his older brother, Dell, who was in prison for armed robbery. I knew Olivia Milton had to be freaking out right now.

"Will you help me? I didn't do it, Kendra. I swear. You believe me, don't you?" He looked so scared, and who could blame him?

I closed my eyes and pressed the cold can of Pepsi against my forehead, trying to relieve the throbbing headache that had suddenly crept up on me. Did I believe Timmy? I really didn't want to because I knew what believing him would mean. The last thing I needed was to get involved in another murder investigation. But the problem was that I did believe Timmy and I knew that with his past drug history and criminal record the police were going to view him as guilty until proven innocent. The deck was stacked against him.

"Yes," I said, opening my eyes, "I believe you. But there's just one thing I need to know." I looked him in the eye.

"What?" he replied warily.

"Are you using drugs again?"

"Hell naw!" he said, sitting up straight in the chair for the first time.

"Then I'll do what I can." *Lord help me.*

Chapter 5

I slept badly that night, which I figured was normal for someone with a fugitive from the law who snored like a freight train sleeping on her couch. Timmy and I had talked for hours about everything from how he got involved with drugs—an ex-girlfriend who died of an overdose—to his love jones for Shanda Kidd. I didn't have the heart to tell him about the other man I'd seen Shanda wrapping herself around the day before. The mere mention of her name seemed to be the only thing that perked him up. Poor guy.

I got up early to get ready for work and tiptoed around quietly so I wouldn't wake Timmy, who slept like he didn't have a care in the world. Before I left, I set out a box of Cap'n Crunch with a note taped to it, warning him not to make too much noise or go anyplace, and for God's sake, not to use my phone. Mrs. Carson may be in her seventies but she can hear a fly fart on the moon. I headed to Perkins to grab some breakfast and kill some time before going to work. While waiting for my blueberry pancakes, I noticed that the half-dozen other people in the restaurant were all engrossed in the newspaper. Even a couple of the servers were huddled together reading a copy. I grabbed an abandoned paper from a nearby empty table and nearly fainted when I saw Timmy Milton's face scowling at me from the front page. It was his mug shot from when he'd been arrested for drug possession a few years ago. He looked horrible. His eyes were blood-shot and vacant, his hair looked like an overgrown hedge, his face was gaunt, and his dry lips looked as flaky as a glazed doughnut. He looked like a complete stranger. No one who didn't know him then would ever recognize him from this picture. Olivia had probably refused to provide an up-to-date photo. Good for her.

Next to Timmy's photo was a picture of Inez Rollins. The story detailed how Timmy was wanted in connection to Inez's brutal murder. The article alluded to evidence found in his car, as well as an anonymous witness who had sup-posedly seen Timmy running away from the crime scene. The police were hoping the witness would come forward and were even offering a five-thousand-dollar reward for any information leading to Timmy's arrest. My mind imme-diately turned to all the things that five thousand dollars could help me buy, like a new car. All I had to do was make a phone call. I quickly pushed the thought out of my mind. I knew if I turned Timmy in, I would not only be betray-ing a trust but his mother would beat my ass. Like most people, I try to avoid ass-beatings at all costs. Besides, I knew Timmy didn't kill anyone. Why would he have killed Inez? The article didn't mention a motive for the murder. But with Timmy's history, I guess a motive wasn't necessary.

Glancing at Timmy's picture in the paper reminded me of the conversation we'd had last night. Timmy felt that his arrest for drug possession had saved his life. Since he was underage and had never been in trouble before, he'd gotten off with probation, was released into the custody of his mother, and was ordered into rehab, where he was able to finally kick his habit. He was doing everything in his power to regain his mother's trust, which had been shattered by his drug addiction and all that it had brought with it. Timmy's lying, stealing, and disappearing for days on end had damaged his relationship with his mother. But Olivia's faith in her son's innocence showed that it hadn't been damaged beyond repair.

I wolfed down my pancakes and headed off to work with all the enthusiasm of a socialite forced to wear Payless shoes. I had been successfully staying out of Noreen's way but I knew by the dirty looks she was always giving me that we were headed for a blowup. It also burned me to know that any confrontation would probably just end up making me look bad. Noreen's sweet-little-old-lady appearance had a way of making her look like she was incapable of doing anything other than baking cookies and reading stories to kids. Mama had suggested that I deal with her by killing her with kindness. I just wanted to kill her.

When I arrived at the center, there was a note taped to the classroom door that said Noreen would be out that day for doctor's appointments. I was so happy I did the Snoopy dance, making some kids heading to the gym for the morning latchkey program laugh like little lunatics. I didn't care. I was going to have a Noreen-free day.

Not having Noreen breathing down my neck gave me an opportunity to think about Timmy's predicament and what in the world I was supposed to do to help him. Everyone seemed a little preoccupied this morning, especially Shanda. We could barely get the students to do any work. All they wanted to do was talk about Timmy and the murder. When Shanda left the classroom to go to the restroom, I decided to find out just how worried she might be about her non-boyfriend and if she might know something that could help him. When I walked into the small, two-stalled restroom Shanda was splashing water on her face. I could see that she'd been crying.

"Hey, it's okay," I said, putting an arm around her. "Timmy didn't kill anybody—" Shanda jerked away from me, giving me a look so hateful it took my breath away.

"You think I'm worried about Timmy's ass?"

"Well, I thought—" I began, not knowing what I was going to say.

"Did you know that Inez was my cousin?" she asked, shocking me.

"Shanda, I had no idea. Why didn't you say something?" I couldn't believe that Inez was murdered a week ago and Shanda never said one word about being related to her. Why?

"Our fathers are half brothers, they have the same mother. We've never really been close. She was older and my mother thought she was too wild for me to hang around with. Then after her mom, my aunt Jeanne, died, and her father, my uncle Morris, remarried, she stopped coming to church and wouldn't have anything to do with the family anymore."

"Didn't she like her stepmother?" I asked.

Shanda smirked. It was a nasty little look that was gone quickly enough but left me feeling like there was an unpleasant side to her that I'd yet to fully see. "Oh, it's just a bunch of family drama, Kendra. I won't bore you with it." In other words, it was none of my business.

"Was there anything weird going on in Inez's life?" Even if they weren't close, Shanda may still know what was going on in Inez's life, especially if it was something scandalous.

"I hadn't talked to Inez in a long time. I don't know what was going on with her. But a couple of weeks ago I did over-hear my parents talking about how Uncle Morris offered to give Inez some money so she could buy her own shop. She told him to go to hell. If I ever talked to my daddy like that, he'd wash my mouth out with soap," she said, flipping a braid over her shoulder.

"You don't really think Timmy killed Inez, do you?"

"I don't know Timmy very well. I don't know what he's capable of. If the police are looking for him, then they must have a good reason."

"What reason would he have to kill her?"

"Who knows? Maybe that stuff he used to smoke damaged his brain," she said angrily as she walked out the door.

I hoped like hell Timmy didn't ask me anything about Shanda when I got home that evening. I didn't want to be the one to tell him his dream girl thought he was a deranged murderer.

By seven o'clock that evening I felt like I'd been put through the wringer. Estelle's was hopping and after three hours of continuously seating people, I could feel my feet throbbing. Not that I was complaining much. Being busy kept me from thinking about anyone else's problems. The rest of my day at the literacy center hadn't yielded anything that could help Timmy. Shanda was in a funky mood for the rest of the morning and wouldn't answer any of my questions, no matter how inconsequential I tried to make them sound. A quick trip home to change clothes for my shift at the restaurant revealed a depressed Timmy who was so bored and restless that he'd cleaned my entire apartment, including my fridge. As much as I'd love to have a full-time cleaner, I had to help the kid before he went stir-crazy and did something stupid.

When business slowed down, I took my break and headed back towards Alex's office. Before I could knock, I heard muffled sobs from behind the closed door. Giving in to my undeniable nosiness, I opened the door a crack and peeked in. Alex was leaned back against his desk supporting a weeping Olivia Milton. Olivia's face was pressed against Alex's chest, in a way that was sure to leave a Shroud-of-Turin-like imprint on his white shirt, and her arms were wrapped around him so tight, I expected him to be blue in the face. But he wasn't. Alex's eyes were half closed and his face was partially buried in Olivia's cloud of curly hair. He looked aroused. Which embarrassed me in much the same way as it did when I once walked in on my parents doing the nasty. Can you say therapy?

Alex and Olivia had been high school sweethearts. When Alex did a stint in the army right after high school, his best friend, Jesse Milton, made his move. By the time Alex came home on his first leave, Jesse and Olivia were married and she was pregnant. Alex was heartbroken and didn't speak to either of them for years. Eventually, time and a new love, Gwen, healed his wounds and he became friendly with the Miltons again. I always wondered what would happen if Olivia decided she wanted Alex back. Looking like a fragile, paler version of Pam Grier, I imagine Olivia could probably get whoever she wanted. I just hoped she didn't want Alex because Gwen would beat her down.

I quickly and quietly closed the door and waited a few minutes before knocking loudly and walking in. They were standing apart now and Olivia was wiping her eyes. I walked over and gave her a hug, which she returned.

"How are you?" I asked. I had decided not to tell her Timmy was hiding in my apartment. That way she wouldn't be telling the police a lie when she told them she didn't know where he was, or lead them to him by calling or coming over. I just hoped I could keep my mouth shut. Crying mothers really got to me.

"I'm hanging in there, Kendra. I'm just praying that they'll catch whoever really killed that girl soon, so they'll leave my baby alone." Alex and I exchanged glances. Neither one of us wanted to be the one to point out to her that the police weren't going to be looking for anyone else since they were sure Timmy killed Inez.

"Do you know where he is, Livvy?" asked Alex, massaging her shoulders.

"No, I haven't heard from him since he called me yesterday. I told him to stay wherever he is until I can find a good lawyer. The police showed up again this morning with a warrant for his arrest. They said they found a tissue with that girl's blood on it in Timmy's car. But that can't be true 'cause I know in my heart he didn't do it. I just hope wherever he is, he's okay."

She looked like she was about to cry again and the urge to tell her where he was gnawed at me. So I quickly asked, "Did they say if they have a time of death? Timmy must have an alibi, right?" Somehow, I'd neglected to ask Timmy this myself.

"They didn't say. But they did ask me where he was between nine and midnight the night that girl was killed. He was at home."

"You sure, Livvy? Weren't you at work?" asked Alex.

"Are you asking me if I'm sure he was at home between nine and midnight? No. I'm not 100 percent sure. But, when I got home the next morning he was on the couch asleep and the TV was still on. He knows I worry so he always lets me know if he's going out. He didn't say anything about going out that night. He doesn't have any friends here." Olivia blew her nose.

Olivia didn't seem to know about Vaughn Castle's vendetta against Timmy. I didn't feel it was my place to enlighten her. I'd just be scaring her even more.

"Kendra, do you think Carl can recommend a good lawyer for Timmy?" Alex asked.

"I'm sure he can. I'll call him as soon as I get home," I promised.

"Thank you, Kendra," Olivia said, hugging me again as a fresh wave of tears overtook her.

I got the hell out of there.

Later that night, after Timmy fell asleep, I called Carl and explained Timmy's predicament, leaving out the part about him hiding out in my apartment.

"He'll need a good lawyer," Carl said. I could tell by how flat his voice sounded that his brother-in-law must have taken a turn for the worse. I'd asked him how John was doing and all he'd done was sigh heavily and change the subject.

"Can you suggest anyone good, someone who might work pro bono? I don't think the Miltons have much money," I whispered, not wanting to wake Timmy.

"Is there something wrong with your phone? I can barely hear you," he said, sounding slightly annoyed.

I took my cordless phone, walked into my closet, closed

the door, and cleared my throat dramatically. "Sorry, I have a sore throat. I think I'm catching a cold. Is this better?" The dust mites in my closet started tickling my nose and I sneezed loudly for good effect.

"Yeah, sorry to be such a grouch. I haven't had a lot of sleep lately. But let me make a few phone calls, okay? I'm sure I can find someone who'd be willing to take his case."

"Thanks, baby. Please give Monica my love and tell her she and John are in my prayers."

"I will, Kendra, but I need you to promise me something."

"What?" I asked innocently, though I already knew what was coming.

"I can tell how much you care about Timmy, but you need to stay out of this mess. I have enough on my plate. I don't want to have to worry about you, too," he said softly. I could hear the genuine concern in his voice and I felt like a loser for lying to him. But it was for a good cause. At least I hoped it was.

"You don't need to worry, Carl. You just concentrate on your family. I'll be just fine. I promise." I gave him Olivia Milton's phone number and quickly said goodbye.

Inez Rollins's funeral was held two days later at Holy Cross Church. I planned on being there for a variety of reasons. Not only would I be paying my respects, I wanted to meet Inez's family, and possibly catch a glimpse of Vaughn Castle, if he even bothered showing up. Even though I had no idea how I was going to prove he set Timmy up, I still needed to see the man to determine what I was up against. I decided to take Mama along with me. She knew Morris Rollins from his early days as a minister. He used to be the associate pastor at her church, St. Luke's, about twenty-five years ago. Mama had been dying to get a look at the inside of what was seen by many to be the most beautiful church in Willow and what she called an eyesore.

Opinions varied in Willow about Holy Cross. There were people, like Mama, who thought the towering steel and glass church was too modern and cold for their tastes. Then there were people like me, who thought Holy Cross was beautiful in its simplicity, and admired the clean lines, and the way the modern look jarred with the quaint, old-fashioned surroundings. Neither Mama nor I had ever been inside Holy Cross. I only attended church on rare occasions and Mama was a loyal member of St. Luke's Baptist Church who prided herself on never having missed one of Reverend Robert Merriman's sermons.

"I hope we can get a seat," said Mama, quickly walking ahead of me towards the front doors. The parking lot was almost filled up and it had taken me five minutes to find a parking place. I hurried after her, trying my best to walk fast in my pencil-slim skirt and high heels. By the time I got to the church entrance and was handed a program by one of the two solemn-looking brothers standing at the front doors, Mama was waiting for me in the atrium looking quite annoyed. But once we were inside it was all I could do to keep my jaw from dropping. The church's open design, high ceilings, and glass walls took my breath away. But, remembering why I was there, I put my admiration in check and followed Mama into the main church hall after we signed the guestbook.

We found places to sit at the back of one of the gleaming, blond oak pews in the center aisle of the church. At last, I was able to look around. It looked as if most of the black community of Willow was crowded into Holy Cross. I waved at Lynette, who was sitting with her family several rows ahead of us. Gwen and Alex were in the row behind them. I noticed that many of the women had braided hair. I figured many of them to be clients of Inez's. Looking towards the front of the church, I saw a large, ornate stained glass window depicting Jesus on the cross, the empty pulpit, and Inez's closed white casket, which was almost obscured by floral arrangements. A large picture of Inez, without her trademark braids, was displayed on an easel next to the casket. The same picture was printed on the front of the program. The picture looked dated, like a high-school graduation picture. I was unable to get a good look at Inez's family, who were presumably seated in the front row.

After about five minutes of listening to muffled sobs, sniffles, nose-blowing, and low whispers, I watched the Holy Cross choir, resplendent in their green-and-gold robes, file into place behind the pulpit. Shanda was among them. Many of the choir members were wiping their eyes with tissues. I noticed that Shanda was stoned-faced and staring straight ahead. She seemed to be purposefully not looking at Inez's casket. The organist, a middle-aged man in a tight brown suit, took his place at the organ and the choir began a soul-stirring rendition of "Precious Lord Take My Hand." I had managed up to that point not to succumb to all of the raw emotion floating around me. But, when the choir started singing "Amazing Grace" with Shanda doing a solo, I started crying and Mama pressed a handkerchief, scented with her rose perfume, into my hand. Shanda had a beautiful, haunting voice and I wasn't the only one moved by it. A few people were overcome and had to be taken out. Boy, do I hate funerals. I was more determined than ever to prove Timmy innocent. He couldn't have caused all of this misery.

Finally, the choir stopped singing and took their seats as the minister took his place behind the pulpit. I looked closely at the man about to give the eulogy and realized he was way too young to be Morris Rollins. I could hear mumbling, whispering, and see the bewildered looks as everyone around me realized it was not Morris Rollins standing behind the pulpit.

"He's probably too broken up," I heard someone behind me whisper.

"Poor man," said another disembodied voice.

I felt a pang of disappointment. I'd heard that Morris Rollins was one hell of a minister. He'd have to be to acquire the funds to build such an impressive church. I flipped through the program and saw that Morris Rollins's name had been inked out and that the assistant minister, George Leach, would be delivering the eulogy. I sat back and listened as Reverend Leach gave Inez Rollins her final tribute.

An hour and a half later, the funeral came to an end. Reverend Leach was an adequate if somewhat passionless minister. But I felt drained just the same after a succession of friends and family members came forth to read scriptures, poems, and to tell funny, poignant stories about Inez. Inez's casket was removed from the front of the church. She would be buried later that afternoon in a private graveside service. A line formed for people to pay their condolences to her family. Mama and I joined the long line and waited for our turn. By the time we reached the front of the church, the crowd had thinned out considerably. I watched one of two women ahead of us embrace an older, attractive black man that I assumed to be Inez' father, Morris Rollins. I used the opportunity to get a good look at him.

Morris Rollins was almost as tall as a basketball player with smooth, unlined, dark chocolate skin. He had a medium build, was bald, sported a goatee, and wore a diamond stud in his left earlobe. I guessed that his charcoal gray suit was custom-made because it was very expensive-looking. He had to be in his early fifties but hardly looked it from where I was standing. He wasn't conventionally handsome but he definitely had a certain something that made you look twice.

The two women he was talking to were trying their best to be comforting, but it looked to me as if Rollins was comforting them. He caught each of them up in a big bear hug before ushering them on their way and turning his attention to us. I noticed one of the women looking back at him wistfully and I couldn't blame her. He was that kind of a man.

"Estelle Mays, it's been too long," said Rollins. He had a low, soothing quality to his voice that made you want to hear more of it.

"Yes, Morris, it has," said Mama, clasping his outstretched hand. "I am so sorry about Inez. You and your family are in my prayers." Rollins hugged her, spotting me over her shoulder in the process. His quick, almost imperceptible assessment left me with the odd feeling that a predator had just picked me as its next meal.

"Thank you, Estelle. It means so much to me that you came today. I thought losing my first wife was hard, but this has been one of the most difficult days of my entire life." He was talking to Mama but he was staring at me. I noticed that his eyes were red-rimmed from crying and I had a strange urge to hug him.

"Morris, this is my granddaughter, Kendra Clayton. Kendra, this is Reverend Rollins."

"Nice meeting you," I said, shaking his hand. His skin felt hot, like he had a fever.

"It's a pleasure to meet you, Kendra. I'm sorry it had to be under these circumstances." He still had my hand in his and it felt like a mild electric current was running up my arm. I felt the blood rush to my face and I giggled like an idiot.

What was with me? I have a man and the last thing I need is to get my panties in a knot over some married, womanizing minister. Mama hadn't missed the vibe that Rollins was throwing my way and didn't look at all pleased, especially since I appeared to be buying what he was selling. She quietly excused herself and went to look for Gwen and Alex. We barely noticed that she'd left.

"I knew your daughter and I'm so sorry for your loss. If there's anything I can do to help, please let me know." I squeezed his hand and gently eased it out of his grasp. He gave me an amused look, which embarrassed me for some reason.

"Thank you. It's been hard trying to see to every detail and to get Inez's affairs in order. But life goes on and things have to be taken care of whether you want to deal with them or not," he said with a weary sigh.

"Well, maybe I can do something? Like pack up some of Inez's things for you? Would that help?" I needed to get into Inez's apartment to look around. This would be the perfect opportunity to do it. Surely there must be something there that could help Timmy.

"That won't be necessary, Kendra. Some of the church sisters will be packing up her apartment. But I appreciate the offer. Perhaps you can stop by my office sometime for a chat. I always enjoy talking to Inez's friends. It makes me feel closer to her," he said in a low whisper, like he didn't want the whole world to hear him.

There was no doubt in my mind where a private visit to his office would lead. The man obviously wasn't too broken up over his daughter's death to try and get him some on the side. But, what was far more disturbing to me was the knowledge that, judging by my reaction to him, he might not have to work too hard to get into my pants.

"Actually, Reverend Rollins, I've recently been watching your talk show and I have to say, I'm very impressed." I hoped the Lord would forgive me for telling such a blatant lie.

"Thank you. We tape new shows every Thursday evening. I would be most honored if you would attend a taping." He was smiling at me and had taken my hand again.

Before I could reply, I heard an anguished moan coming from behind Rollins. I looked and was shocked to see a slim, veiled woman in a hat, dressed in black from head to toe, slumped and almost falling over, in the pew behind him. I hadn't noticed her before. Her braided hair cascaded down around her shoulders. But, the only thing I could see of her face beneath the sheer veil of her wide-brimmed hat were a pair of glassy and dazed-looking eyes that stared straight ahead without blinking.

"Kendra, please excuse me. My wife, Nicole, is having a very hard time with Inez's death. I need to get her home." Rollins immediately went over to help his unsteady wife to her feet. I watched as he slowly escorted her from the church. The difference in their heights made it look like he was walking with a child. Poor woman. I hoped she was too out of it to notice her husband hitting on me practically in her face.

I heard some murmuring behind me and turned to see a group of women looking in disgust at a young couple who were deep in conversation. I recognized the women as stylists from B & S Hair Design and Nail Sculpture. Even if I hadn't recognized them from the shop, I would have noticed their varying hairstyles and colors. With their heads bent together in conversation, they reminded me of a handful of crayons. I looked at the couple they were talking about and realized it was Shanda, no longer in her choir robe, and the same gorgeous young man that I'd seen at her house. Today he was dressed in a dark green suit and cream shirt without a tie. Even though we were inside, he had on the same Ray Ban sunglasses he'd been wearing the last time I'd seen him.

"I can't believe he would have the nerve to show his face here!" exclaimed an outraged sister with a short blond pixie cut.

"I'm surprised he didn't burst into flames when he walked through the church door," remarked a woman with a long red weave.

"If that's what happens when sinners walk into a church then most of the folks in this place would be spontaneously combusting, including all of us," said a woman with an auburn bob, causing her companions to laugh.

I inched my way over towards the group, hoping to hear more. I looked through my program intently while I listened to them vent.

"That little cousin of Inez's needs her butt beat," said a woman with a jet-black updo. The other women nodded in agreement.

"I know you're right. It's bad enough to be creepin' with your cousin's man, but to do it at your cousin's funeral, that's just scandalous," claimed a woman with pink Afro puffs.

"And he's nothin' but a thug. Inez found out the hard way what he was into, poor baby. She's probably dead behind some of *his* mess," said Auburn Bob, bursting into tears and burying her face in her hands. Her companions gathered around to comfort her and the conversation was over.

I was rooted to the spot. Shanda was messing with Inez's

man who was also a thug. That could only be Vaughn Castle. I looked over and saw that the two of them were still deep in conversation.

As I approached to say hello, I heard Vaughn tell Shanda, "Just have your ass over there like I told you, and don't keep me waitin'." He walked off, leaving Shanda looking like she was about to throw up.

"Shanda, girl, you have a beautiful singing voice," I gushed, hoping to put her at ease.

"Oh, Kendra. I'm sorry. What did you say?" She looked back over her shoulder at Castle's retreating form before turning her attention to me.

"Your voice, it's beautiful. I had no idea you could sing like that."

"Her voice is a gift from God almighty," exclaimed a loud voice from behind me. I turned to see the organist in the too-tight brown suit. He was beaming with pride at Shanda, who looked uncomfortable.

"Kendra, this is my daddy, Rondell Kidd. Daddy, this is one of the teachers I work with at the literacy center, Kendra Clayton."

Rondell Kidd was as tall as his half brother, Morris Rollins, and had the same smooth chocolate skin, but that's where the resemblance ended. Rondell was overweight and seriously lacked his brother's fashion sense. His brown suit looked like it had fit him about twenty-five pounds ago. He wore his short, salt-and-pepper hair in an Afro à la Nipsey Russell. I noticed he had on a gold tie tack that said "Jesus Saves." He was smiling at me in such a friendly way that I couldn't help but smile back.

"It's good to meet you, Mr. Kidd. Please accept my condolences on the death of your niece," I said, holding out my hand for him to shake. He grasped my hand firmly, pumping it up and down vigorously like he was jacking up a tire.

"Yes. This is a bad business, very bad. But Inez has gone home to be with her Lord. She's in a better place. God will help us with our loss," he said, looking heavenward like he could see Inez waving to him from the afterlife. For some reason, this made me feel like crying again.

As we stood contemplating Inez in heaven, a petite, middle-aged, brown-skinned woman in a dowdy navy blue dress with a lace collar joined us. She had her hair pulled back into a severe bun and wore thick horn-rimmed glasses and no makeup. The only jewelry she wore was a thin gold wedding band and a cross pendant. Her ears weren't even pierced. She was pretty despite her attempts to look other-wise. She was staring at me and her nose was wrinkled up like she smelled something bad. I had to resist the urge to sniff my pits and check the bottoms of my shoes for dog doo-doo.

"Miss Clayton, this is my wife, Bonita. Bonita, Miss Clayton works with Shanda at Clark Literacy Center." Rondell Kidd grinned at his wife and put a beefy arm around her shoulders, pulling her tightly to his side. He was looking at her like she was the most beautiful woman in the world. Bonita, however, gave her husband a pained look and extri-cated herself from his grasp. Shanda looked like she wished the earth would open up and swallow her.

"So, you're the teacher from that center Shanda's always going on about," said Bonita Kidd. She looked me up and down and, by the dismissive look she gave me, I could tell that I'd been deemed unworthy to breathe her rarified air. I hated people like her.

"Yes. Shanda's been a great help to us at the literacy center, Mrs. Kidd. I'm trying to persuade her to become a teacher. She's a natural with the students."

"You mean she actually interacts with those people?" she asked, looking at Shanda with a horrified expression. "I thought you told me all you did was grade papers."

Shanda looked like she might cry, which was more emotion than she'd shown during her cousin's funeral.

"It isn't God's plan for Shanda to teach, Miss Clayton. After she graduates, Shanda will be in charge of marketing for Holy Cross Ministries. Isn't that right, baby?"

"Yes, Mommy," Shanda said in a small voice.

I really wanted to tell Mommy where to go. But I knew I'd only be burning bridges if I did. I needed to stay on good terms with Shanda in order to get info on Vaughn. If ever there was a time to kill someone with kindness, it was now.

"I'm sorry, Mrs. Kidd, if there's been any misunderstanding about Shanda's duties. But our students at the center are there to better educate themselves and Shanda has been an excellent role model for them," I said, with a big phony grin that made my face ache. Like I've said before, I'm not big on diplomacy.

Bonita Kidd looked at me like I was a lower life-form and declared, "The only thing that will help those people better themselves is if they accept Jesus Christ as their Lord and Savior. By the way, Miss Clayton, what church do *you* belong to?" The three of them were staring at me.

I felt like a contestant on a game show who was about to blow my chance at a new washer and dryer. I haven't attended church regularly since I left high school and I hated when people asked me about it. I knew what was coming next.

Once I said I didn't belong to any church they would make it their personal mission to bring me back into the fold. I decided to beat them to it.

"Ah, well, actually, I was seriously thinking about joining Holy Cross. Reverend Rollins personally invited me to come to a service and I plan to take him up on it." It wasn't exactly true but they didn't know that.

At the mere mention of Rollins's name, Bonita Kidd visibly relaxed. Her husband and daughter, noticing the change in her attitude, relaxed also. This woman must be a joy to live with.

"Well, if the Reverend invited you, then by all means you must come. I'll look forward to seeing you at one of our services. Have a blessed day, Miss Clayton." Bonita Kidd turned on her heel and walked away with Rondell and Shanda trailing behind her.

Since I'd been dismissed, I decided to go to the restroom before going home. I was sitting in a stall when I heard two people walk in.

"Poor Nicole. Did you see the way Reverend Rollins had to practically carry her in and out of the church? She must be just tore up over Inez," said one woman in a nasal voice.

"She must be feelin' real guilty right about now, don't you think? I mean, she and Inez used to be best friends, even closer than sisters. They haven't spoken a word to each other in three years," said the other woman.

"Girl, who could blame Inez? I wouldn't be talking to my best friend either if she married my daddy six months after my mama died. And you know what people were saying, don't you?" asked Nasal Voice.

"Yeah, that Nicole was carrying on with the Reverend while Jeanne was dying. Well, I don't believe it and you should be ashamed to even think it. That poor man has been through enough without having people talking about him behind his back."

"I didn't say I believed it," said Nasal Voice, sounding put out. "I was just asking you if you knew what other people were saying—"

I heard the women's voices trail off as they left the restroom. Morris Rollins sure did have a way with women. I was more curious than ever about a man who could inspire so much loyalty.

Now I knew why Inez had really turned her back on her family and church. I left the restroom and looked for Mama so we could leave. She'd gotten a ride home from Alex, which told me she was pissed.

On my way home, I decided to go check out Inez's apartment. I never knew her very well but I did know that she lived in an old Victorian mansion on Linden Avenue that had been converted into small apartments. She lived in the basement. I'd run into her a couple of months ago when I'd been seriously contemplating moving and had been looking at an attic apartment across the street from her place. I never found a place with rent as cheap as what I was already paying.

I stopped home to change my clothes first and discovered that Timmy was gone. I tore up the apartment looking for him. Hoping that maybe he was trying to trick me, I even looked under my bed. No Timmy, and no note explaining where he'd gone. I sat on my couch to calm myself down and hit redial on my phone to see if he'd made any calls. Mama answered the phone and I quickly hung up. She was the last person I'd called before I left for the funeral. I was not up to listening to her scold me about Reverend Rollins. Timmy hadn't made any calls and there was no note. Where the hell was he? Why did he leave?

It was getting late and I still needed to get over to Inez's before the apartment was packed up. I changed into jeans and a sweatshirt and headed out the door and down the steps. My landlady, Mrs. Carson, was sitting on her porch in her usual striped housedress. Her hair was braided into a crown that sat regally atop her head.

"What have you done now, missy?" she asked me, her eyes narrowed suspiciously. Her Siamese cat, Mahalia, was draped across her lap and looking at me with her usual disdain.

Mrs. Carson is Mama's best friend and I wouldn't have been surprised if Mama had told her all about the interaction between Morris Rollins and me at Inez's funeral. Renting from my grandmother's best friend had its advantage by way of reduced rent. The disadvantage was that Mama always seemed to know my business. I didn't have time to be scolded by my landlady, either, so I hurried down the steps, hoping to get away before she could pull me into a conversation.

"Nothing, Mrs. Carson," I said, starting to walk past her on the way to my car.

"Then why them police officers come by to see you?" I froze and turned to face her.

"What police officers?" I felt my palms get sweaty. Did they know Timmy was hiding out in my place? Did they take him away?

"That hatchet-faced white woman and her fat sidekick. They was knocking on your door a couple a hours ago. I told 'em you was at a funeral. They said they'd come back." She stroked Mahalia, who purred with pleasure.

"I have no idea why they were here," I told her, feeling relieved that they hadn't hauled Timmy away. What did Harmon and Mercer want with me now?

"Well, you be careful wherever it is you rushing off to in such a hurry, you hear me?"

"Yes, ma'am." I got into my car and took off, convinced that Timmy had left because he thought I'd told the police where he was.

Chapter 6

It was after five by the time I got to Inez's place. I got out of my car and looked around. I love Linden Avenue. It's a historic street that used to be one of the places the wealthy citizens of Willow lived. The large mansions of yesteryear have been transformed into apartment buildings and two-family dwellings. Very few of the houses were single-family homes anymore. It was always cool and dark on Linden Avenue due to the massive elm trees that lined the street on either side; their branches met and made a canopy that kept the sun out in the summertime. Now, the trees were beginning to lose their leaves making the street feel naked and exposed.

Inez's apartment was located in the basement of a large Victorian mansion that had been recently restored back to its original lavender, pink, and green exterior. The house reminded me of a fancy wedding cake with colored fondant icing. I was standing by my car trying to figure out how I was going to get into Inez's apartment when the front screen door to the house opened and an elderly white man walked out onto the porch. He spotted me and nodded hello before sitting in a rattan chair. It was now or never. I walked up on the porch.

"Hello, sir. Do you know if the landlord is in?" The man looked up at me with watery blue eyes. He ran a trembling hand over a white tuft of hair that was sticking straight up from the front of his bald, pink head. He must have been in his eighties and looked like an elderly Kewpie doll.

"I'm the landlord. How can I help you?" His voice sounded reedy and high-pitched, like an old phonograph record.

"I'm a member of Holy Cross Church and I'm here to pack up Inez Rollins's apartment." I wondered if Morris Rollins would uninvite me to his office for a *chat* if he knew what I was about to do.

"Oh, yes. That was a real tragedy," said the old man, shaking his head. "She was such a nice young lady. Never had a bit of trouble out of her. It's just a shame."

"Yes, it was. Her funeral was today and her family wants to get her personal effects packed up."

"Where'd you say you were from?" he asked, looking confused.

"Holy Cross Church. Inez's father is the minister. He's too upset to come over here himself." It was mildly disturbing to me how easy lying was getting to be. But just mildly.

"Honey, don't you have any boxes with you? How are you going to pack up anything?" He looked around like he was expecting boxes to jump out of the bushes.

Uh-oh. I felt like a fool. I hadn't thought about boxes when I came up with my brilliant plan. But an excuse quickly popped into my head. "I have a roll of trash bags in my car.

First I'm going to get rid of all of the trash, then bag up what's going to Goodwill." Actually, it wasn't a lie. I did have a roll of trash bags in my trunk from the last time I cleaned it out. I sprinted down the front steps and retrieved the bags, waving them to show the landlord I wasn't lying.

"Oh, okay. Well then, follow me." He slowly raised himself up from his chair and held the screen door open for me. I walked into a small dark foyer that smelled of garlic and fried onions. My mouth watered. Someone must have been cooking their dinner and I was tempted to knock on their door and ask for some.

"This way, miss," said the landlord, walking ahead of me and gesturing for me to follow him down the long hallway. He was walking so slowly I almost stepped on the backs of his shoes. When we reached the end of the hallway, he paused in an archway that led down a set of about a dozen steps ending at a door.

"Here it is. I'd open the door for you, but I have a devil of a time getting up and down these steps."

"No problem, Mr.—"

"Hathaway, Cecil Hathaway. And you'd be?"

"Cleopatra Jones," I replied innocently. I felt bad about deceiving him but I wasn't about to give him my real name.

"Cleopatra. Now that's a nice name. It's got a nice ring to it. Of course, nowadays everyone's named Tiffany, Britney, or Amber. Can you imagine a woman my age named Britney?" We both laughed and then suddenly he became serious.

"Can I tell you something, Cleo?" he asked, looking around like he didn't want anyone to hear him. My heart sank. I didn't really want to hear what he had to tell me, figuring it could be anything from the irregularity of his bowel movements to an abduction by aliens. But I wasn't going to tell him no. He still had the key.

"Sure, Mr. Hathaway. What's on your mind?" I braced myself for the worst.

He leaned in close and looked around again. "I don't think Miss Rollins is resting in peace," he whispered like he'd just sprung some state secret on me.

I figured it would be something weird but was glad it was relatively tame. I could tell by the way he was looking at me that he was expecting me to be shocked. So I played along.

"Really! Wow! Oh my gosh! What makes you say that?" I opened my eyes wide with shock and amazement. I felt like I was faking an orgasm.

"Well, I've been hearing some mighty strange noises coming from down there after she died. I bet her spirit can't move on because of her violent death," he said, leaning even closer. His breath smelled like cinnamon candy.

"What kinds of noises?" I was reluctantly curious.

"Scratching noises, like someone is trying to get out," he whispered.

We both stared down at the door to Inez's apartment. I couldn't hear anything, but I was suddenly spooked. I felt something cold touch my hand and I jumped. But it was just Cecil Hathaway pressing the key into my palm.

"You be careful down there, young lady," he said, and made his way slowly back toward the front door. I heard the screen door creak open and shut as I headed down the steps to Inez's apartment. I paused and pressed my ear to the door. I still didn't hear anything. Feeling more than a little foolish, I unlocked the door and walked in.

I felt around on the wall for a light switch, bumped into something and almost screamed. But once I got the lights on, I could see it was just a wooden coatrack with a denim jacket and an old black sweater hanging on it. The apartment itself was one large room that was divided into two sections: a living room, which probably doubled as a bedroom, and a kitchen area. I ventured farther into the living room. It was hot and stuffy inside the apartment and it smelled like spoiled milk and garbage. If Inez's spirit had come back to her apartment, it was probably to open a window and empty the overflowing trash basket I spotted across the room in the kitchen.

The apartment was sparsely decorated with expensive-looking furniture that didn't match. In fact, it looked like two different people had decorated the place. The floral print chintz sofa clashed with the black lacquer Oriental coffee table. There was a small, round, chrome-and-glass table next to the couch, with a neon purple ceramic lamp perched on it. A small television set sat on a red wooden TV stand with a VCR sitting on top of it and a CD player on the shelf below it. There was a picture of an attractive, middle-aged black woman in a fabric frame sitting in the middle of the coffee table. I guessed it to be her mother. There weren't any other pictures that I could see. The apartment was very neat.

I pulled one of the bags off of the roll of trash bags, tossed the rest on the couch, and headed into the kitchen area. A large square table with a long, flowing, white embroidered tablecloth that could have been an heirloom dominated the space. A look in the sink revealed a bowl filled with mushy cereal and curdled milk. I held my breath and emptied the bowl and rinsed it out. I looked in Inez's refrigerator and found a carton of spoiled milk, which I also poured down the sink, a pack of hamburger, a wilted head of lettuce, half a dozen eggs, a lemon, a bottle of wine, and some Chinese takeout containers from the Red Dragon. There were some frozen dinners and a half gallon of rocky road ice cream in the freezer. I bagged up the reeking garbage to take out when I left so Mr. Hathaway wouldn't get suspicious. I found some canned vegetables, a box of instant rice, several boxes of cereal, and some soup in the cabinets. There was a set of green tin canisters on the kitchen counter by the sink. All of them were empty except the smallest one, which held a small bag of weed and some rolling papers. The lower cabinets held pots and pans.

There was one closet in the apartment that was jam-packed full of clothes and shoes. The tiny bathroom had a tub, a sink, a toilet, and very little room for much else. The bathroom cabinet held birth control pills, aspirin, Band-Aids, toothpaste, mouthwash, and an almost empty tube of KY jelly. A set of wicker shelves on the wall above the toilet held towels and washcloths. A makeup bag sat on the tank behind the toilet and a toothbrush sat in a cup on the sink alongside a bar of dried-out soap.

I was getting frustrated. Inez certainly didn't believe in any kind of clutter. I didn't know what I was looking for, but it didn't appear that anything that could help Timmy would be found in this apartment. So far, the only things I'd found out about Inez were that she loved her mama, liked to get high, had no talent for interior decorating, and experienced vaginal dryness. There was no note on the wall from her ghost, scrawled in blood, declaring, "Timmy didn't kill me." What a waste of time.

I started to leave when I heard voices at the top of the steps. I put my ear to the door and heard Mr. Hathaway telling someone his theory about Inez's spirit and the strange noises. I then heard what sounded like several people walking down the steps towards the apartment. I panicked. It must be the church sisters from Holy Cross. How would I explain what I was doing here? I looked around frantically for a place to hide and dove under the kitchen table just as the door, which I'd forgotten to lock, opened.

"I don't know anyone named Cleopatra Jones from the church, do you guys?" I heard one woman ask. The woman's companions indicated that they didn't, either.

"Hello," someone called out.

I held my breath.

"There ain't nobody in here," declared yet another voice.

"Poor old man. He must be senile," said a third voice. I heard murmurs of agreement.

"Either that or he's been watching too many old movies. He probably thinks Cleopatra Jones is down here having tea with Foxy Brown and Shaft." The woman's companions laughed.

I peeked out from beneath the tablecloth and saw three sets of feet. My heart was beating furiously. My plan was to stay under the table until they left but I had no idea what I would do when they decided to pack the tablecloth.

"Come on, y'all, let's get this over with." I heard the sound of boxes being dropped on the floor and settled myself into a more comfortable position.

After about five minutes of listening to them pack and comment on Inez's effects, I detected movement to my left. I turned and came face-to-face with the source of the scratching noises Mr. Hathaway had been hearing. And it certainly wasn't any spirit. It was a rat. Now, I have no problem with spiders, and I actually think reptiles are cute. But, Kendra don't do rodents of any kind, especially rats. The rat was standing on its hind legs twitching its nose at me. It was probably a standard-sized rat. But at that moment it looked the size of King Kong.

I could feel the scream welling up in me all the way from the tips of my toes. When it finally reached my lungs, I let out a high-pitched shriek that left my chest burning. I tried to stand up at the same time, lifting the heavy kitchen table several inches off the ground, and banging my head hard in the process. I felt myself start to lose consciousness. Before I was completely out, I heard the sound of feet hitting the floor as the church sisters fled the apartment.

I woke up under the table with a throbbing headache. I lay there for a few minutes feeling dizzy, looking around slowly. I was alone under the table. My rat friend was gone. But I wasn't alone in the apartment. I could hear someone walking around. I figured the church sisters must have come back or maybe Cecil Hathaway had decided to brave the stairs. I could only imagine what those poor women must have thought, seeing the table rise up off the ground to the soundtrack of my scream. They must have thought that not only was Inez's spirit in the apartment, but she was pissed as hell. I checked my watch and was surprised that only fifteen minutes had passed.

The dizziness finally subsided and I sat up and peeked out from under the tablecloth again. This time it wasn't the church sisters or Cecil Hathaway. It was Shanda Kidd and Vaughn Castle. Shanda was still in her funeral clothes but Vaughn was dressed in a red-and-black silk tracksuit. I could smell his lemony cologne from across the room. Now that I knew what kind of a person he was, he wasn't nearly as handsome to me as he had been. They were standing together in front of Inez's open closet. Vaughn was rummaging through the closet, looking for something.

"Let's go, V. We've done enough with the phone call and the tissue. The police are already looking for Timmy," whined Shanda. She looked like a sulky child with her arms crossed and her lips poked out.

"I wanna make sure they got enough shit on that mutha-fucka to send him away for life. This might do it," he said, pulling a blue silk scarf out of the closet. I could see the initials I.R. stitched into one corner of the scarf.

"What are you going to do with that?" Shanda asked warily.

"I ain't doin' shit with it. You're gonna go to Milton's crib to console his mom. Then when she ain't lookin', you're gonna plant it somewhere. That way if the cops search the place again they'll find it and connect Milton to Inez." He was looking smug like he was some kind of a criminal mas-termind. What a loser.

Shanda looked doubtful but she took the scarf and quickly stuffed it into her pocket like she didn't want to touch it.

I was stunned. Not because Timmy had been right about being set up, but because Shanda was in on the plot, too. How could she? They finally left and I waited about ten minutes to make sure the coast was clear before emerging from under the table. I looked around, hoping not to see Mr. Rat and quickly locked the apartment and left. When I walked out onto the porch, Mr. Hathaway was sitting in his chair, asleep and snoring softly. I quietly placed the key on the table next to him, hopped in my car, and didn't look back.

Timmy still had not returned by the time I got back home. I popped a couple of aspirin and looked in my refrigerator for something to eat. It was even barer than Inez's. I ordered a pizza and lay down on my couch. When my phone rang I quickly picked it up, hoping it was Timmy. Instead, it was Mama, the last person I wanted to talk to. I love my grandmother dearly. I'm certainly much closer to her than anyone else in the family and she's my only other relative besides Alex that still lives in town. My parents and sister reside in California and Florida, respectively. However, Mama has this knack for making me feel like a misbehaving child. My own mother doesn't even have the power to make me feel as guilty as Mama does.

"I was looking for you at the church. Where'd you disappear to?" I asked, trying to counteract her annoyance by acting annoyed myself.

"You'd have known where I went if you hadn't been smiling and flirting with that married man."

"I wasn't flirting with him, Mama," I exclaimed, sitting up and wincing with pain from my still sore head.

"Yes, you were. I saw you, girl. Blushing and giggling like some fool. You were raised better than that, Kendra."

I could hear her suck her teeth in disgust, and I sighed.

"Don't you sigh at me, girl. That man has no shame. Do you know why he left St. Luke's to start his own church?"

"Why?" I asked casually, already knowing the answer.

"Because in the two years that he was assistant minister he managed to get several women in the congregation pregnant. He was married to Inez's mother, Jeanne, at the time, and Inez was a little girl."

Everyone in town knew Morris Rollins had illegitimate children. No one knew exactly who the children were, since Rollins was rumored to have offered financial support to the mothers only if they kept quiet about paternity. Inez was the only child he publicly claimed as his own.

"Mama, I have a man and I would never mess around

with someone else's husband. It really hurts my feelings that you would think that about me." I tried my best to sound hurt.

"Kendra, I've seen too many good women lose their religion over that man. He's got some kind of power. He knows just what to say to and do to get what he wants."

The power Mama was referring to was called sex appeal. I wondered if she remembered what that was. I wasn't going to ask her, though. I let her vent until my pizza arrived, then politely got off the phone for my date with pepperoni and extra cheese.

The next day I was at work bright and early, lying in wait for Shanda. She showed up looking tired and acting distracted, even snapping at a student who'd asked her a simple question. Framing an innocent person for murder can do that to you. Before I had a chance to pull her aside for a heart-to-heart, Noreen started in on me about some trivial nonsense that only she seemed to care about.

"Kendra, while you were out yesterday, I was looking for the master copies of the grammar and punctuation worksheets. I couldn't find them. Please show me where you keep them," she said primly.

"I keep them here, in my bottom desk drawer." I opened the drawer, quickly located the file, and handed it to her.

"I looked in there yesterday and couldn't find them. Don't you keep your files in alphabetical order so that others may find them when needed?"

"Yes." I could feel myself tensing up. I hated the fact that this annoying old biddy had the power to piss me off so completely.

"Then why aren't they filed under W for worksheets?"

"Because I file them under G for grammar and punctuation," I replied, slamming the drawer shut a little harder than intended.

"I suggest that you type up some instructions so the rest of us can navigate through this mess when you're not here and we need to find something."

She walked off before I could reply. I felt a firm hand holding me down in my seat before I could leap out of it onto Noreen's back. It was Rhonda.

"Steady, girl. She's not worth it. Now, take a deep breath and shake it off."

She was right, of course. I took some deep breaths and chilled.

"See, that's better, isn't it?" she asked. I nodded in half-hearted agreement.

"And for the record, I've always been able to find whatever I needed in that drawer," Rhonda said, and headed off to help a student. I sat fuming and wondering why the hell Rhonda didn't speak up when Noreen was making her snide comments.

Since I already had an attitude, I decided to use it to my advantage and talk to Shanda. I had her meet me on the playground. She didn't seem pleased. I decided not to accuse her outright. I really wanted her to tell me about it on her own.

"Shanda, what's going on? I can tell something is very wrong." We were sitting side by side on the swings. She wouldn't look at me and didn't answer.

"Are you in some kind of trouble?"

"Trouble? What kind of trouble would I be in? I'm not allowed to do anything, Kendra. You met my parents. All I'm allowed to do is go to class, church, and the library. I can't even live on campus. They make all of my decisions. They've planned my entire life out for me." She held her head down and I saw tears running down her face.

I felt sorry for her, but her unhappiness didn't give her the right to ruin someone else's life. "Well, you must be doing something. I saw you with that guy at the funeral. Wasn't he Inez's man?" Her head snapped up and I was again treated to one of her nasty little looks.

"Vaughn is my man now, okay? Whatever he had going on with Inez was over when he met me. He loves me."

I could see that I was getting nowhere fast, but pressed on. "Shanda, I haven't heard good things about him and what he's into. I—"

She held up her hand, cutting me off before I could finish. "You sound just like Inez. She told me lies about Vaughn, too. She was just jealous and wanted him back."

"I thought you told me you hadn't talked to Inez in a long time. Is Vaughn the reason you two weren't close?" I thought about her behavior at the funeral and how she wouldn't even look at Inez's casket. Unless, of course, there was an even more sinister reason for her behavior, like if she killed Inez herself. I knew from past experience what women were capable of doing over the love of a man.

"Look, this is really none of your business." Shanda got up from the swing. "I'm sure Noreen wouldn't be happy to know you're harassing me like this. Maybe I should tell her about it." She started walking back towards the center. Now was my chance.

"And maybe I should tell the police about you and your drug-dealing boyfriend setting up Timmy Milton for a murder he didn't commit." She stopped dead in her tracks. I expected her to break down and confess. Boy, was I wrong.

She turned to stare at me with a strange little smile.

"Prove it," she said, and walked back into the center, leaving me stunned.

Wonderful! Timmy had begged me to help him prove he'd been set up and now Shanda had challenged me to prove that she and her thug boyfriend had been the ones who'd done the setting up. Could my day get any worse? Yes, it could.

"Ah, I don't think so," said Lynette when I showed her the dress I'd put on hold at Déjà Vu. It had taken me a while to convince her to come see the dress. She was holding it up and looking at it like it was a dust rag. I wasn't in the best of moods and didn't bother hiding it.

"What's wrong with it, Lynette? This is a much more flattering style for me and it fits in with your wedding colors."

"Don't get me wrong, girl. It was a nice dress back in the day when some chick wore it to her prom and danced to Donna Summer in it, but not for my wedding. It doesn't even match the style of the bridesmaids' dresses. Now, what's the operative word here, Kendra?"

She was waiting for my reply. I knew it was her wedding. But, we'd promised each other since seventh grade not to make the other look foolish in our weddings. She wasn't living up to her end of the bargain. I didn't answer, so she answered for me.

"The operative word is *my,* as in *my wedding.* Why are you being so difficult? I was thinking about you when I picked out that dress. It's cheap. I thought you'd like it. You like cheap stuff." She was waving the blue dress at me as proof of my apparent cheapness.

I glared at her. "For the millionth time, I'm not cheap. I'm thrifty. There's a difference. And that dress you picked is not cheap. It'll cost me a month's rent."

"The one I had originally picked cost twice that much. I thought I was helping you out by picking something off the clearance rack. That's right up your alley, isn't it?"

"I may not like to pay a lot for stuff but I do believe in quality. What is that dress you picked out for me made out of anyway, steel wool?" I remembered how the dress made me itch around the neckline.

"It's rayon, for your information. You know, my mother said to watch out for jealous females when I was planning my wedding. Don't worry. It'll be your turn one day, Kendra. Maybe."

"Jealous? Oh, so now I'm cheap *and* jealous just because I don't want to wear that ugly dress with the big bow on the ass? *Friends* don't let *friends* look like Smurfs, Lynette."

She busted out laughing, which pissed me off even more.

"So, are you gonna take the damn thing or what? I got someone else interested in it," claimed Ruby Young, who wasn't known for mincing her words. She'd been watching our exchange like a tennis match.

"I'll take it," I told Ruby, tossing my money on the counter and a dirty look at Lynette, who was still giggling. Even if I had to wear the thing out for Halloween, I was going to wear the dress someplace.

"You can buy it if you want to, Disco Queen. Just don't show up to my wedding in it."

"Now, there's an idea," I said, stalking out of the store to the sound of Lynette and Ruby's laughter.

I headed home from Estelle's after my shift later that night feeling like the biggest loser. My grandmother thought I was a potential home-wrecker, Lynette thought I was cheap, Shanda thought I was stupid, and Timmy probably thought

I was a backstabber. So far, I'd accomplished not one thing to help him out. And what in the world did Harmon and Mercer want with me, anyway? I wasn't up for that visit at all.

I was also sick over Shanda. Whether she was willing to admit it or not, she was in for big trouble over Vaughn. I wasn't sure exactly what her role in setting up Timmy had entailed, but surely she'd broken the law.

While I drove, I fingered the blue dress that I'd tossed into my front seat. Every time I remembered Lynette calling me cheap, accusing me of being jealous, and that ugly-ass maid-of-honor dress, it made my blood boil. I put in a Sade tape and tried to mellow out. I started heading to Frisch's drive-thru for some chocolate therapy, or hot fudge cake, as it's listed on the menu, when a thought hit me. I looked over at the blue dress and suddenly remembered the blue scarf Shanda and Vaughn had taken from Inez's apartment. What had Vaughn told Shanda to do with it? Plant it in Olivia Milton's house? I must have cracked my head on that kitchen table harder than I thought to have forgotten about the scarf.

I took a detour to Palmer Street and parked in front of the Miltons' condo. Olivia's car was parked in the driveway and the lights were on. I rang the doorbell.

She looked tired but genuinely happy to see me. I was relieved. "I'm just Miss Popularity this evening," she said, stepping aside to let me in.

The Miltons' condo had a warm and homey feel to it. The furniture was old but well-kept, and a shelving unit with plants and an abundance of family pictures, including some of Olivia and Alex from high school, took up one entire wall.

"How's that?" I asked.

"Timmy's little girlfriend, Shanda, just left about ten minutes ago. She's as worried about him as I am. I didn't even know he had a girlfriend, Kendra. But she seems like a real nice girl. She's a college student."

"I know Shanda. You're right. She's really something." Exactly what she was, I would keep to myself. I tried to look around the condo on the sly, trying to figure out where Shanda could have hidden the scarf.

"You should have seen that little hood rat he was runnin' around with back in Detroit. She's the reason he got strung out on them drugs in the first place. I know God will get me for saying this but I'm glad she's gone. Girl was bad news."

I could tell she wanted to elaborate. But as much as I'd have loved to hear her reasons for being glad Timmy's ex had gone to meet her Maker, I needed to find that scarf.

"I talked to Carl about finding a lawyer for Timmy. Did he call you?" I asked instead.

"Yes. He hooked me up with a friend of his, Howard James. I met with him this morning. He's agreed to take Timmy's case. He said to find Timmy as soon as possible because it will look better if he turns himself in. The only problem is, I still don't know where he is. I got that one call and haven't heard anything since."

"Timmy's innocent and he's got a lot of good people who love him on his side. It'll all work out, you'll see," I told her with an enthusiasm I didn't really feel.

"I really needed to hear that," she said, smiling warmly. "I was just about to make some coffee. Would you like some?"

"That would be nice, thanks." The minute she left the room, I was out of my chair looking around, feeling under cushions on the couch, searching under the table. I couldn't find the scarf. I looked up the stairway off the living room.

"Olivia, can I use your bathroom?" I called out.

"It's up the steps, first door to your left."

I headed upstairs and opened the first door on the right. It was Timmy's room. I went in and shut the door behind me. Timmy's room was a wreck, but I'd seen much worse. I wondered if it was Timmy or the police who had torn up the room. His twin bed was unmade and there were clothes, shoes, and underwear all over the floor. A poster of Janet Jackson graced the wall opposite the door. A small desk with a CD player sat next to the one small window in the room. A large milk crate full of rap CDs sat under the window. I looked through the clothes on the floor and then under the desk. Nothing. I turned my attention to the bed. I looked under it and saw nothing but giant dust bunnies. Then I saw something blue peeking out from between the mattress and box spring. I pulled it out. It was the scarf. I stuffed it in my pocket and I started to leave the room when I heard Olivia Milton's voice in the hallway.

"Kendra? Are you okay in there?" I heard her knock on the bathroom door. Great. Now what was I going to do? I looked frantically around the room—for what, I didn't know. Then I heard a buzzing sound, like a large insect, coming from the direction of the window. I walked over to the window, looked down and saw something metallic glint up at me in the moonlight from down inside the milk crate. It was Timmy's cell phone and it was vibrating. It must have dropped in there when he went out the window. I picked it up and again heard Olivia knock on the bathroom door.

"Kendra?"

I'm not big on cell phones. I barely knew how to work one. I fumbled around with the buttons until I answered it. I heard a female voice. "Timmy? Are you there? Timmy? Where are you?" It was Shanda, and I quickly hung up.

I could hear Olivia jiggling the handle on the bathroom

door and an idea came to me. I quickly dialed the Miltons' main number and prayed it would ring before she opened the bathroom door and discovered I wasn't in there. I was rewarded with the sound of Olivia Milton's phone ringing. I heard her hurry back downstairs to answer it. I quickly turned off the cell phone and slipped out of the room. When I got back to the living room, I saw Olivia hanging up the phone with a puzzled expression.

"Must have been a wrong number. Are you okay?"

"My dinner must not have agreed with me," I said, holding my stomach.

"Well, you probably shouldn't drink any coffee, then. It might make it worse."

"I think you're right. I should be heading home now, anyway. I just stopped by to see how you were doing."

She walked me to my car and we chatted for a few more minutes before I drove off. I imagined the look on Shanda's face when I showed her the scarf. I even had an idea of how I could get her to tell me everything, if confronting her with the scarf didn't work. By the time I got back to my apartment I was feeling much better.

Chapter 7

I put the scarf on Shanda's desk at work the next day, along with a note that said: "We need to talk." When she arrived at work and saw the scarf, she immediately looked at me with an expression of panic. I gestured for her to follow me outside.

"Where'd you get this?" she asked, looking around, clearly afraid—but of whom, I had no idea.

I snatched the scarf out of her hand. "I got it from Timmy's room where you planted it after you went to his house and lied to his mother about being his girlfriend. How could you do this to Timmy? Do you know how much he adores you?"

"How did you know?"

"How I know isn't important. But what I know is. And what I know is that you helped your boyfriend set Timmy up for Inez's murder and I want to know how and why. I really don't want to have to get your parents and your uncle

Morris involved in this, but I will." I was enjoying playing the heavy a little too much.

The mere mention of my telling her family what she was up to had a profound effect on Shanda. She burst into hysterical tears.

"Please don't tell them, Kendra. They'll be so disappointed," she sobbed. I felt myself start to melt. But I resisted the urge to put my arm around her. So much for playing the heavy. I waited for her to calm down.

"I really didn't have a choice, Kendra. I swear. Vaughn made me do it. You don't know what he's like." She was pacing back and forth in front of me, wringing her hands and shaking. The sound of a car backfiring a block away made her jump and look around wildly.

I had a pretty good idea what Vaughn must be like if he was causing her this much distress. She was making me nuts just watching her. I finally grabbed her by the hands, led her over to one of the picnic benches on the other side of the playground, and made her sit down before she started tearing her hair out.

"It's okay, Shanda. Vaughn's not here now. What did he make you do?" I looked back at the building and saw Noreen watching us through one of the classroom windows. I ignored her and turned my attention back to Shanda.

"You know he hates Timmy, right?" she said after looking around one more time. I indicated that I did and for her to continue.

"He's been trying to figure out a way to get at him for a long time. But he doesn't want to go to jail." I didn't blame him. If I looked like Vaughn I wouldn't want to go to jail, either. Talk about a place where being pretty isn't a good thing.

Shanda continued on with her story. "Inez and Vaughn broke up and we started kickin' it. Then Inez finds out about us. She starts telling me all kinds of lies about Vaughn. That he's a drug dealer and he's a bad person. I told Vaughn and he went to talk to her at the shop. But when he got there she was already dead. He touched her and got blood on his hand. He wiped it off with a tissue. Then he got an idea to plant the tissue in Timmy's car. He gave it to me and I did it. Then he had me call the police and tell them I saw Timmy running away from the shop the night Inez was killed." She was looking at me fearfully and she had good reason, because it took everything in me not to knock her off the bench. Stupid, stupid little girl!

"Shanda, honey, listen closely," I said slowly, trying hard to remain calm. "Vaughn *is* a drug dealer. That's how he knows Timmy. Timmy used to buy crack from Vaughn when he lived in Detroit. Didn't Vaughn ever tell you how he knew Timmy?"

"No, he just said Timmy's the reason his boy Ricky is dead."

"Shanda, hasn't it occurred to you that Vaughn is probably the one who killed Inez?"

"No! He's not a murderer," she said, jumping up from the picnic bench and pacing again.

"Shanda, Timmy's no murderer, either. Now, you have to come with me to the police station and tell them everything you just told me." I grabbed her by her wrist and started dragging her towards the parking lot. She went stiff and rigid the way toddlers do when they are about to throw a tantrum, pulled out of my grasp, and started sobbing.

"Nooo, Kendra. You don't understand."

"What, Shanda? What don't I understand?" I felt like tearing *my* hair out at this point.

She slowly lifted up her T-shirt and I gasped when I saw the large, livid, purple bruises on her stomach.

"Oh my God, Shanda. Did Vaughn do this to you?"

"It was my fault. I was asking too many questions. He hates it when I ask too many questions." She pulled her T-shirt down and I handed her the blue scarf to wipe her eyes.

"Shanda, we really need to go to the police. Vaughn needs to be locked up so he can't ever hurt you or anyone else." I reached for her hand again, and she backed away. "I know you're scared. But you can't let him keep doing this to you. He'll kill you one day."

"Scared? I'm not scared of Vaughn. He's my man. I love him! You can't make me tell the police anything."

"If you don't tell them, I will," I said quietly.

"I'll deny everything. You don't have any proof and now I have the scarf, too," she said, waving it in the air. Shit. This just wasn't going to be my day.

I lunged for the scarf and Shanda sprinted off towards the parking lot. I started to chase her, tripped over a tree root, and landed flat on my face.

"What in the world is going on out here?" said a familiar prim voice. I turned and saw a red-faced Noreen walking towards me. "Kendra, please explain yourself." I started to say something sarcastic, when I heard a car start up. I watched help-lessly as Shanda pulled out of the parking lot and sped away.

"I'm waiting," said Noreen, standing over me. I got up and dusted myself off.

"Join the club," I told her miserably, and headed back into the building.

Without Shanda, I was up the creek. She was the only person who could prove Timmy didn't kill Inez. Unless I could somehow prove that Vaughn was the killer, Timmy was headed for a lifetime in prison and a new career making license plates. Telling her parents and uncle had just been a bluff. I knew they wouldn't believe me because it wasn't in God's plan for Shanda to help frame someone for murder.

I was walking around the grocery store in a daze after work. I was so preoccupied that I ran into a woman with my cart, almost sending her flying into a refrigerated display case full of buy-one-get-one-free packs of string cheese.

"You need to watch where the hell you're goin'," exclaimed the outraged sister. She inspected her white capri pants and discovered that my cart had left big black smudges on her behind. She glared at me as I apologized profusely. For one tense moment I thought I was going to get my ass beat right there in the dairy aisle.

She stalked off towards the checkout line, mumbling something about me being a stupid heifer, with her shiny auburn bobbed hair gleaming under the store's florescent lighting. Something tugged at my memory. But it wasn't until I was loading groceries into my car that I remembered who the woman was. She was one of the stylists from B & S Hair Design and Nail Sculpture who'd been at Inez's funeral. The one who had called Vaughn a thug and said Inez had found out the hard way what he was into. I didn't know her name. I only went to the shop every couple of months for a haircut, which usually took about twenty minutes, and was not familiar with many of the newer stylists.

Since I desperately needed to make a case for Vaughn being the one who'd murdered Inez, I had to talk to Auburn Bob about what she knew. But I was dreading it. After ramming her in the rear with a grocery cart and messing up her pristine white capris, girlfriend wasn't quite feeling me at the moment. It would be best if I gave her a day to calm down before approaching her. The next day was Saturday and I had nothing else to do. It would be the perfect day to try and catch Auburn Bob in a better mood. I took my groceries home, ate leftover pizza for dinner, and went to bed early.

I sat in my car across the street from the shop at eleven-thirty the next morning. I had originally planned to go in for a haircut but decided against it. I wanted to talk to Auburn Bob alone. I could see her through the shop's big front window working a relaxer into a teenaged girl's hair. Since it was close to noon, I was hoping she'd leave the shop soon for a lunch break.

It was after one before she finally left. I followed her white mustang convertible, with vanity tags that read "Retha," all the way to Domingo's Cuban Deli on Water Street. I was waiting by her car when she emerged fifteen minutes later with several white Styrofoam containers. She looked happy enough until she saw me. It took a few seconds for her to recognize me from the store. But when she did she looked more wary than mad.

"Can I help you?" she asked, looking around for a potential source of help in case I turned out to be a nut.

"I'm so sorry to bother you but I really need to speak with you. It's about Inez Rollins." She sat the containers on the hood of her car and looked me up and down.

"What about her?"

"I overheard you talking about Inez and Vaughn Castle at the funeral. I need to know about their relationship. Please, it's very important."

"And this is your business because—" She paused, waiting for my response.

"Because an innocent young man has been framed and could end up in prison for the rest of his life."

"You mean that wild-looking boy in the paper the other day?"

"His name is Timmy Milton, and he's not a murderer."

"Well, hell, I know that. When I saw that story I knew that boy didn't kill Inez. I always knew they was lookin' in the wrong direction."

"You think Vaughn killed her, too, don't you?" I was getting excited. Maybe I could help Timmy after all.

"That shady muthafucka had something to do with it, and if it wasn't him, it was something to do with him."

"So you'll tell me about them?"

She looked at her watch. "Yeah, but not now. I gotta get back to the shop. I got a two o'clock appointment. But I could meet you someplace tonight."

"Just name the time and the place and I'm there," I said as I helped her load the containers into her car.

"Okay, eight o'clock at The Spot," she said, getting into her car and starting the ignition. "You can buy me a drink. It's the least you can do for fuckin' up my favorite pants." I watched her pull off then stop abruptly, backing up to where I was standing.

"By the way, I'm Aretha Marshall, and you are—?"

"Oh, sorry. Kendra Clayton."

"See ya later, Kendra."

Spending an evening at The Spot, a hole-in-the-wall bar better known as The Spotlight Bar and Grill, was not my idea of a good time. But I had no choice. I decided to kill time before then by cleaning my apartment. I was scouring out my bathtub when there was a knock at the door. It was detectives Harmon and Mercer. I reluctantly invited them in. Mercer was wearing tan chinos that were wrinkled around the knees, and a blue sports jacket over a red-and-yellow striped golf shirt that hugged his big belly like Lycra on fat thighs. Harmon was dressed in her usual plain drab suit, this one a faded green, and scuffed black flats. I offered them drinks, which they both declined, then asked them what they wanted with little ole me.

"Do you know where Timmy Milton is, Miss Clayton?" Harmon always got straight to the point.

"How would I know where Timmy is?" Boy, was I relieved to actually be telling the truth.

"He was spotted in this area recently," said Mercer.

"And that has what to do with me?" I asked, the picture of innocence.

"Miss Clayton, we'd appreciate your cooperation in this matter. Aiding and abetting a known fugitive is a felony." Harmon always treated me like I was a hardheaded child. I'd been down this road with her before and she still hadn't learned anything about the catching-more-flies-with-honey concept.

"And, again, I ask, what does this have to do with me?"

"We know that your family is friendly with Timmy Milton and his mother Olivia. He was spotted in this area recently and we think he may have come to you for help."

"Detective Harmon, I haven't seen Timmy since before all of this madness started and whether you believe me or not is really no concern of mine."

"So, you don't believe that he killed Inez Rollins?"

"No."

"And why is that?"

"Timmy's no murderer. Why would he have killed Inez?"

"We believe it was a robbery gone wrong. That he approached Inez Rollins in an attempt to rob her for drug money and he shot her in the process," said Mercer, rocking back and forth on the heels of his loafers.

"Timmy's been clean for well over a year now. He has a job at my uncle's restaurant and until all this mess started hadn't missed one day of class at the literacy center. I think I would have noticed if he was using drugs again, Detective." I could hear the emotion creeping into my voice.

"Drug addicts are sneaky about hiding their habits, Miss Clayton. He may not be using heavily again at this point. It's also possible that he only recently started using again."

"And it's just as possible, no, probable, that you're looking for the wrong person. Since you want to talk about drugs, why don't we talk about Vaughn Castle? Does that name ring a bell, Detectives?" They looked at each other in surprise. Bingo.

"What do you know about Vaughn Castle?" Harmon asked, her face turning slightly red.

"I know that he's a drug dealer and he was Inez's boy-friend. I know that he used to be Timmy's supplier and he has it in for Timmy and framed him for Inez's murder."

"You have proof of this?" asked Mercer, looking at Harmon.

"Well," I stuttered, looking nervously from Harmon to Mercer. I couldn't tell them about Shanda. Vaughn would know where the information came from and I didn't want her to end up dead, too.

"Not exactly," I said, watching the light go out of Mercer's eyes. "But it certainly makes more sense than Timmy killing Inez," I concluded weakly.

"Let me tell you what we have," Harmon began, looking a little too smug for my taste. "We have blood evidence found in Milton's car. We also found a crack vial with his prints on it. He has no alibi that we're aware of. We have an eye witness that saw him running away from the crime scene. And the fact that he's hiding from the law doesn't bode well for him. Now I ask you, if he's innocent, why hasn't he turned himself in?" They were both looking at me. I had nothing.

"We know from past experience how loyal you are to your friends, Miss Clayton. But you're not doing Timmy or yourself any favors by helping him. You need to encourage him to turn himself in," said Mercer.

"I'd like you to leave now," I said quietly. I walked over and opened the door.

"One more thing, Miss Clayton," Harmon said before she walked out. "I wouldn't go around talking about your little conspiracy theory. Vaughn Castle is violent and very dangerous. He's the last person you want to mess with, which is why your story about him setting up Timmy Milton just doesn't wash."

"Why is that?" I asked, suddenly uneasy.

"Because he wouldn't go to the trouble of setting anyone up. The last guy he had a beef with ended up hacked to pieces with his body parts spread out over several counties. We still haven't found all of him."

Oh, crap!

After they left, I sat on my couch trying to decide if I should convince Timmy to turn himself in. I desperately needed to talk to him about what the detectives had told me. Shanda hadn't said anything about planting a crack vial in Timmy's car, which meant he'd lied to me about using again. Was helping him worth risking my life? I thought about Shanda's bruises. Somebody had to stop Vaughn Castle. I just hoped I could do it discreetly without him knowing about it. I really like having all of my body parts together as a whole. I tried calling Aretha Marshall at the beauty shop to have her come to my apartment instead. But she'd already left for the day and they wouldn't give me her home phone number.

I finally headed for The Spot after cutting the infamous blue halter dress to knee length and donning a pair of strappy silver sandals. I probably should have dressed less conspicuously but figured skulking around in dowdy clothes would attract even more attention. It was still early so I didn't have any trouble finding an empty table near the bar. After five minutes, my eyes were starting to itch from the mushroom cloud of smoke that always seemed to be hanging in the air.

This was only my third visit to the Spotlight Bar and Grill and I sincerely hoped it would be my last. I could already feel the eyes of several aging players on me, no doubt trying to decide if buying me a drink would be worth their time, money, and skill. The Spot has been an institution in Willow since before I was born. It's a tiny place not much bigger than my apartment and it attracts a very diverse crowd of people looking for everything from a simple drink after work to everlasting love.

I sipped my rum and Coke slowly while I waited for Aretha. Heat Wave's "Always and Forever" played on the ancient jukebox in the corner. I was trying not to make eye contact with anyone when someone asked to buy me a drink. I turned and saw a chubby, vertically-challenged, older black man with processed hair dressed in almost head-to-toe red: red suit, red-and-white dress shoes, white shirt, and a red bowler hat cocked to the side of his fat head. He looked like the end product of someone putting Santa Claus, a leprechaun, and a pimp in a blender. I took a sip of my drink to keep from laughing.

His name was Lewis Watts. I'd met Lewis at The Spot several months before when I'd been here with my friend Bernie, who'd just buried her murdered fiancé. Lewis had bought us numerous drinks and extolled his many imagined virtues in an effort to impress Bernie out of her clothes. However, his efforts were thwarted when I got sick and Bernie rushed me home. Lewis hadn't been pleased. I was very surprised he was giving me the time of day, much less offering to buy me a drink.

"Well, can I get you that drink, or what?" Lewis asked, smiling confidently and waiting for my response. Could it be he didn't recognize me? I hoped not.

"No thanks, I'm cool," I replied, gesturing to my still-full glass.

"It's Kelly, right? Is your friend coming tonight, sweetheart?" he asked, looking around hopefully. He apparently hadn't forgotten his near-conquest of Bernie.

"Actually, it's Kendra. And no, she's out of town," I replied, hoping the finality in my voice would send him elsewhere in his search of a bedmate. No such luck.

"I guess it's just you and me then," he said with a smile. I watched in horror as he plopped down in the seat opposite me. He looked around smugly, like he was Don Juan, and winked at two of his cronies seated at the bar.

"Ah, I'm waiting for a friend," I said. I looked towards the door, hoping to see Aretha walk in. She was already fifteen minutes late.

"Good! 'The more the merrier' is my motto, baby doll. Maybe we can all have a good time together, if you get my meaning." He nudged me and laughed loudly.

I could smell the liquor on his breath. I wanted to crawl under the table. Where the hell was Aretha?

After ten minutes of listening to Lewis brag and make not-so-subtle references to his sexual prowess, and alluding to how his male endowment rivaled that of a horse (a Clydesdale, no less), I'd had enough.

"Do you really think talking to me like this is impressing me?" I asked him.

Lewis looked around like I must have been talking to someone behind him.

"Yeah, I'm talking to you. I didn't ask you to sit down. I told you I'm waiting for someone. Does being hung like a horse cause you to be hard of hearing?" I could hear his friends at the bar cracking up with laughter. Lewis looked from them to me and I knew he had to somehow save face.

"You a snotty little heifer, ain't you? I could tell that the last time you was in here," he said, his eyes narrowing to slits.

"Then why did you come over here?"

"I was just trying to make your day."

"Go make someone else's day," I hissed.

"I ain't going no place. This table don't have your name written on it. I been coming here since before your stuck-up ass was in diapers."

"Then that would make you old enough to be my daddy. You sorry cradle-robbing troll!" Lewis's friends at the bar howled with laughter. I turned away from Lewis, who continued to mumble under his breath about how I should be glad he wasn't my daddy.

Aretha finally arrived a few minutes later. White must be her favorite color, as she was dressed in a tight white satin pantsuit, and white, four-inch sling-back pumps. The Labor Day rule apparently meant nothing to her. She tossed her white clutch purse on the scarred wooden table and sat down, looking amused.

"Sorry I'm late. I had an emergency weave to do. Some sister accidentally caught her hair on fire when she and her man were doing the nasty too close to the campfire when they were camping. The back of that poor woman's head looked like a baboon's ass!" She threw her head back and laughed until tears ran down her face. Then she noticed Lewis and stopped laughing immediately.

"Lewis, what the hell are you doing over here? Is the Don Juan of disability bothering you, Kendra?"

"Yes," I replied, stifling a laugh. I had forgotten that Lewis had told Bernie and me that he was on disability for a supposed bad back when we first met him.

"Goodbye," Aretha said, waving her hand in Lewis's face.

"Well you two hincty broads are missin' out on a good thing. I just cashed my disability check and I was gonna spend it on ya. You can forget about it now," he said, heading off to the bar with his hand tucked inside his suit jacket like a ghetto Napoleon.

"You know, I had a friend who got tore up one night and went home with that fool. She said he's hung low but he fucks like a rabbit." We both laughed.

"How 'bout that drink? I'll have a white Russian," she said, taking off her suit jacket to reveal a white lace bustier. I got up to get us both drinks. Lewis and his friends kept looking at me and laughing.

It was starting to get crowded and I wanted to get this over with so I could leave.

"I don't mean to rush you, but I really need to know about Inez and Vaughn," I said.

"Okay, okay, I can tell this ain't your type of scene. That's a bangin' dress, though, girl," she said with a smile. I thanked her and waited patiently as she drained her drink and lit a cigarette. "So, how much of my conversation did you hear at the funeral?"

"I heard you say something about Inez finding out the hard way about what Vaughn was really into."

"Yeah, that was some ugly shit. I was there when it happened," she said, shaking her head. "We had this stylist at the shop named Renita Franklin, real young chick, probably around nineteen, and just graduated from cosmetology school. Anyway, she was working at the shop for about a month when we all started noticing our supplies were comin' up short. We all order our own stuff, you know, relaxers, shampoo and such. Now, we all borrow stuff from each other but we ask permission and we always replace anything we borrow. We all had to reorder missing supplies, everyone except Renita, that is. She always seemed to have supplies but we were noticing she wasn't ordering shit. Inez was trying to save money to open her own shop but having to constantly reorder supplies was cuttin' into her money big-time." Aretha stopped talking long enough to take a long drag on her cigarette before continuing on.

"We were also noticing that Renita was acting real strange. She would be late for appointments or either show up long enough to do a couple of heads then would leave and not come back until the next day. Some days she wouldn't show up at all and we would all have to take her pissed-off customers and divide them up between us. When she would bother to show up you could tell she hadn't bathed and her breath stank. She looked all spaced out and glassy-eyed—"

"She was on drugs?" I asked, interrupting her.

"Yeah," she said, shaking her head sadly. "Her man got her hooked on that shit. She was stealing our supplies so she could use her money to buy crack for her and her man."

"Vaughn was her dealer, right? Is that how Inez found out?"

Aretha nodded. "One day when me and Inez were closing up, Renita showed up and Inez caught her stealing from her station. Inez went off and started calling Renita names. Called her a crack ho and all sorts of stuff. That's when Renita dropped a bomb on her. She told Inez that yeah, she smoked crack, and she was buying it from Vaughn. Plus, all the times that Vaughn had come to see Inez at the shop while she was working, he was really there to sell Renita drugs. So, not only was her man a drug dealer, he was selling that shit at her job!"

I could feel the hairs on the back of my neck stand up and looked around briefly. I was getting the strangest feeling that we were being watched. I looked around and saw that Lewis was busy bothering some other woman. A young guy in a black do-rag was sitting slouched at the bar nearest to us, staring at Aretha and me intently. I didn't recognize him and figured he was about to try and hit on us, so I looked away.

"Is something wrong?" asked Aretha, looking concerned.

"No," I replied, turning my attention back to her. "How did Inez take the news?"

"Not well. She broke down, poor baby. She really loved that idiot. I could have told her he was into something illegal. But it wasn't any of my business."

"How did you know?"

"Oh, come on, now. The man drives a brand new Escalade, he dresses in expensive clothes—hell, his sunglasses alone cost more than some people's house note. He told Inez he was a car salesman. My uncle sells cars and he's good at it, too. He don't have the kinda money Vaughn's always flashing around."

"Did she confront him?"

"She sure did. He showed up not long after Renita left and they had it out behind the shop. I could hear her screaming and crying. I heard her tell him she never wanted to see him again."

"He didn't take that well, did he?"

"You got that right. I went outside to make sure everything was okay and he had her pinned against the wall by her throat."

"Oh, my God! What did you do?" I was still feeling uneasy but resisted the urge to look around again.

"I didn't have to do anything. When he saw me, he took off. I was going to call the police but Inez wouldn't let me. She was real shook up."

"I bet she was. Did he leave her alone?"

"Nope. He stayed away for about a week, then started sending her flowers and expensive gifts. He thought he could buy his way back into her life. He even offered to give her the money for her shop. But she wasn't having it. I overheard her tellin' him on the phone one day that if he didn't leave her alone, she was gonna tell the cops on him. That did it. He kept his distance after that. Then the dirty bastard started messin' with her cousin, Shanda, just to spite her. Inez tried to tell that stupid girl about Vaughn but she wouldn't listen. Hardheaded. Now, Inez is dead."

"Did you tell the police about this?"

"I would have if they'd asked me. The day they came to the shop to talk to everyone, I was out sick. They never did come back to talk to me. By then they was too busy lookin' for your friend."

"Would you have a problem telling them the same thing you just told me?"

"Sure, but I ain't goin' to the police. If they wanna hear what I got to say, they can come to me."

"And you're not afraid of Vaughn?" I asked in amazement. I wondered if she knew about the poor guy who got hacked up. Probably not.

"If that muthafucka tries anything with me, I got something for his ass," she said angrily. She motioned for me to come closer and opened her purse. I leaned over, looked inside, and saw a black revolver nestled between her wallet and a value pack of Big Red gum. This woman didn't play. I watched as she lit another cigarette.

"What happened to Renita?" I asked, still feeling a little unsettled from seeing the gun.

"Bruce fired her. Last time I saw her was a couple a weeks ago. She was walking downtown looking crazy and strung out. I offered her a ride and she cussed me out. I haven't seen her since." Aretha looked down at her empty glass longingly, then at me. I took the hint.

"Let me get you another drink," I said, wanting to keep her talking.

"Thanks," she said, smiling brightly as I got up and headed to the bar again. By now, the place was really crowded and the smoke and body heat, mingled with the scent of sweat, cologne, and perfume, made it feel stuffy and uncomfortable. I felt a trickle of sweat run down my back. The loud hum of conversation buzzed along to Cameo's "Shake Your Pants." I could barely hear myself think. I looked around again while I waited for Aretha's drink. That's when I spotted him. Sitting at a table in a far corner holding court to an entourage of baby thugs, who barely looked old enough to be in a bar, was Vaughn Castle. I felt my stomach knot up.

He was seated with his back to the wall and was nursing

a Corona. All I could see of his attire was a black T-shirt. He didn't have on his usual Ray Bans and his green eyes glittered in the dimly lit room like a serpent's. He was staring directly at me with a sneer on his face. The young guy with the black do-rag who'd been sitting at the bar was on his left, whispering in his ear, telling him everything that Aretha and I had said about him. Time to get the hell out of Dodge.

How I managed to get Aretha's drink to her without spilling it was a mystery to me because I was shaking so badly. I thanked Aretha and told her we should go. I didn't mention Vaughn's presence in the bar, which would turn out to be a big mistake. After draining her drink and putting out her cigarette, Aretha got up to leave with me. We made our way through the crowd towards the door. I was behind Aretha, about ten feet from the door, when I tripped over someone's outstretched foot. I stumbled and fell onto my hands and knees as Aretha walked out of the bar, oblivious to my catastrophe. I heard loud laughter to my right and turned to see that it was Lewis Watt's foot I'd tripped over, and he'd stuck it out on purpose.

"Oops! Some people just can't hold their liquor," he said, wrapping his arm around the ferret-faced woman he was sitting with. They both laughed like hyenas. My blood was boiling.

I looked around for my purse, which I'd dropped, and felt a rush of panic as I hunted around people's legs on the dirty floor. When I finally found it after a frantic minute, I stood up and swung it back up onto my left shoulder, purposefully hitting Lewis squarely in the back of his head and knocking off his hat.

"Oops! Some people shouldn't have such a big head, asshole," I said, and rushed out of the bar into the night.

I headed towards the parking lot, hoping to catch Aretha before she took off so I could warn her about Vaughn. As I walked towards her white Mustang, I could see a white shoe peeking out from behind the back tire on the driver's side. I ran across the parking lot and around the car. Aretha was lying face down on the ground behind her car. I turned her over and felt her wrist for a pulse. She wasn't breathing and her face was already starting to swell. Her eyes were opened wide and bulging. There was something knotted tightly around her throat and I started screaming as I struggled to untie it. I pulled it off just as a car pulled into the parking lot. A man emerged and, hearing my screams, came running over to help. He shoved me aside and listened to Aretha's chest.

"Call nine-one-one!" he said, tossing me a cell phone from his pocket. He started to administer CPR. He got her breathing again, but she remained unconscious.

Five minutes later, an ambulance rushed Aretha to the hospital. I stood in the parking lot with a crowd of loud and rowdy bar patrons who'd come out to see what all the excitement was about. Two uniformed police officers were trying to restore order and find out what had happened. I just wanted to go home. Even though I'd yet to talk to the police, I had to get out of there. I started to walk across the street to my car when I realized I still had what had been wrapped around Aretha's throat in my hand.

I looked at it closely for the first time and immediately realized it was the blue silk scarf that Shanda and Vaughn had stolen from Inez's apartment. Shanda must have given it back to Vaughn. I dropped it like a hot rock and quickly looked around. I felt hot guilty tears well up in my eyes and did nothing to stop them from running down my face. Why

hadn't I warned Aretha about Vaughn before she left the bar? He must have followed her out when I was looking for my purse. She'd almost been killed and, by using the scarf, Vaughn wanted me to know he'd done it.

Chapter 8

I woke up on my couch early the next morning still dressed in my clothes from the night before. My head hurt and my eyes felt gritty from cigarette smoke and tears. I sat up and the kitchen knife that I'd slept with clattered to the floor. Not that I had counted on the knife for much protection. After all, Aretha had had a gun and it hadn't helped her one bit. I sat on the couch for a few minutes and enjoyed the silence. It was seven o'clock. Not a time I'd normally be up at on a Sunday morning but then again, I wasn't used to being on a crazy drug dealer's shit list, either.

I called the hospital to see if I could find out anything about Aretha. I had gone to the hospital to check on her after leaving The Spot but, not being a family member, I was unable to get them to give me any info. The impatient-sounding hospital operator told me that there was no one by that name admitted to the hospital, which must mean she'd been treated and released. At least, I hoped and prayed that's what it meant. It could also mean she was dead. I felt guilty as hell. I finally got up and headed to the bathroom, peeled off my clothes, and got in the shower. I stood under the hot spray for a long time, hoping it would wash away the mess I was in. I wrapped myself in a towel and headed to the kitchen to make some coffee. Someone was sitting at my kitchen table reading the newspaper with their back to me, and I froze in mid-step. I recognized the Dallas Cowboys jersey.

"Timmy! How the hell did you get in here?" He turned around and grinned, a little too widely, and I remembered that I was wrapped in a towel about as big as a postage stamp.

"You know, you kinda tight, Kendra," he said, still grinning at me. "If I was into older women, I'd hit you up for them digits." I backed out of the kitchen slowly, wondering how *tight* he'd think I was if he saw my naked booty unleashed from its control-top panties. I threw some sweats on and marched back into the kitchen. Timmy had put some coffee on.

"I'm waiting," I said, as I sat down opposite him. "Where the hell have you been?"

"Chill, Kendra. I found a better place to lay low. Safer. I didn't know them cops would be comin' to your crib," he said, leaning back in the chair.

"They said someone spotted you in this neighborhood. You know I didn't call them, don't you?"

"I didn't think that. I know I put you on the spot by comin' here. I left so I wouldn't get you in trouble."

"So, where have you been?" I asked again.

"Can't tell you that. Privileged information. If I told you, I'd have to—"

"Kill me. Okay, I get the hint," I said, relieved to know that he didn't think I'd betrayed him. I already had enough to feel guilty about over Aretha.

"Have you talked to your mother? She found a lawyer to take your case." I got up and poured us both some coffee. I was amused to see that Timmy liked his coffee laden with sugar and cream, just like me.

"Yeah, I talked to her. She and that lawyer want me to turn myself in. I don't know, Kendra. I been locked up before. I thought I was gonna go crazy in there. What if I don't get bail and I have to stay locked up? What if I can't prove I was set up?"

I had no answers for him. I was zero for two. No Shanda, and now I couldn't imagine, after what had happened to her, that Aretha would want to get involved any further, if she was still alive. Timmy had a right to be very scared. I told him everything that I'd found out so far. I could tell by the way he stared moodily into his coffee cup that the news of Shanda's role in Vaughn's plot had hit him hard.

"That explains a lot of shit," he said finally.

"What?"

"Shanda never had jack to say to me unless it was related to school work. I asked her out and she said she had a man. Then all of a sudden, 'bout two weeks ago, she starts flirtin' and smilin'. You know, actin' like she's all into me. I wasn't complainin'. She's hot to death. How was I 'sposed to know she and that muthafucka Vaughn were plottin' to set me up? I even gave her ass a ride home last week. That's when she probably planted that shit in my car." He got up and leaned against the counter.

"Speaking of your car," I said, bracing myself for the worst. "The police told me that they found a crack vial in your car. They think you're using again. Are you?"

"I used to get high in that car, Kendra. Hell, I even lived in that car when my mom kicked me out. Once, I even sold it for a hundred bucks so I could buy crack. My mom found out and bought it back. It was in her name. So, they probably did find a crack vial in it. No tellin' what you'd find in that car if you looked hard enough. But, I'm clean, man. I ain't touched that shit in almost a year and a half, for real," he said proudly. I believed him.

I noticed the front page of the newspaper Timmy had been reading. The headline Woman Attacked in Bar Parking Lot caught my eye and I snatched up the paper. There weren't many details. But I was happy to note that the headline read *attacked*, not killed, and nowhere in the article did it mention that Aretha was dead. I read further and saw that the police were looking for the victim's companion who she'd been seen drinking with in the bar and who she'd left with minutes before the attack. The article went on to say that her name might be Kelly. I groaned and started to say something, but Timmy was gone. He'd snuck out while I was engrossed in the article.

I headed over to Mama's around four for Sunday dinner. I really didn't want to go since she thought I'd been flirting with Reverend Rollins. But, Gwen and Alex usually ate dinner there on Sunday, as well. If anyone would know what was going on with Aretha, it was Gwen. I wanted to ease my mind.

When I arrived at Mama's house on Orchard Street, where she'd lived with my grandfather for almost the entire fifty years of their marriage, she was setting food on the dining room table: roast beef, mashed potatoes and gravy, mustard greens, corn bread, cucumber and tomato salad, and

lemonade. The scent of apple pie wafted out from the kitchen and suddenly my day was looking much brighter. Mama's cooking does that to me. It's better than Prozac.

Alex was reading the Sunday paper in the living room and Gwen was out on the back porch talking on her cell phone. Mama still had on the dress she'd worn to church that morning with a pink-and-white gingham apron on over it. She frowned slightly when I walked in but I knew she was happy to see me.

"Tell your uncle and Gwen dinner is ready, and don't forget to wash your hands," she said, brushing past me to put the salt and pepper shakers on the table. She was apparently still mad.

"Oh, I've been just fine. Thanks for asking," I said sarcastically. She cut me a hard look and I went to do as I was told.

Alex took his seat at the head of the table and said grace. Then we dug in. We ate in silence for a while with only the sound of our forks scraping the plates. Everyone seemed preoccupied. I decided to break the ice.

"You're looking kind of down, Gwen. Is something wrong?" I asked casually between mouthfuls of mashed potatoes.

"Girl, you don't even want to know," she said with a heavy sigh. Gwen was wearing a short, curly red wig that made her look like Little Orphan Annie. I'd lost count of just how many wigs she owned.

"What's wrong?" asked Mama, looking concerned.

"You know, another stylist from the beauty shop almost got killed last night?"

"Who?" I took a sip of lemonade to wet my suddenly dry mouth.

"Aretha Marshall. Somebody almost strangled her to death in the parking lot of The Spot last night. Can you believe that mess?"

"How is she?' Alex asked.

"Oh, she's all right. They kept her overnight for observation and ran a bunch of tests. They cut her loose this morning. She's pretty shook up, though."

I breathed a sigh of relief. "Does she know who did it?"

"If she does, she ain't talkin'. She's gonna go stay with her mama in Dayton for a while," said Gwen, helping herself to another serving of greens.

"That just goes to show you that nothing good comes of runnin' the streets and hangin' out in bars," Mama said. Alex, Gwen, and I looked at each other and smirked.

"I know you all think I'm just an old lady. But young women these days have lost their dignity. They run around in skimpy clothing, sleep with a bunch of different men, have babies out of wedlock, and then complain when men don't want to marry them. I may be old-fashioned, but in my day women had respect for themselves and everybody grew up in the church. Now, nobody thinks they need to go to church anymore." I knew that last part was a dig at me. But I ignored it.

"So, in other words, women these days need to put some clothes on, close their legs, and get back to church," said Gwen, winking at me.

"Amen," said Mama. We all laughed.

"Well now, Mama, sometimes church isn't always the answer. There's a certain minister in town who's led many a woman astray," Alex said teasingly. He loved baiting Mama. But I could have killed him. This was the last thing I wanted to talk about. Mama tensed up and looked at me.

"Yeah, there are some wolves in sheep's clothing runnin' around. Morris Rollins would be one. That man is shameless. You all know my friend Mattie Lyons?"

We all groaned. Mattie Lyons was the source of so many of Mama's stories that we all suspected that she didn't really exist, especially since none of us had ever met her. Mama ignored us.

"Mattie has a niece named Vera, I think her last name is Maynard, who was a school teacher. One summer about twenty-five years ago, Vera came to visit Mattie from Detroit. Vera's husband was on the road a lot for his job so he didn't come with her. Vera started going to church at St. Luke's with Mattie. That was back during Morris Rollins's first year as assistant pastor. Vera was a shy, quiet woman, a good Christian, a loyal wife. She started attending private bible study meetings with Rollins. Next thing you know, Vera's pregnant. It didn't take Einstein to figure out who the father was since she didn't go nowhere but to church. Vera ended up having a minor breakdown when Rollins wouldn't leave his wife, Jeanne. She ended up going back to Detroit. Her husband figured out the baby couldn't be his. He left Vera to raise her son all by herself."

"Now, that don't necessarily make the reverend a bad person," said Gwen, spooning more mashed potatoes onto her plate. "It just sounds like he's got a lot of love to give."

"And, from what I hear, a whole lot of women who want to receive it," said Alex as he and Gwen laughed heartily. I felt my own lips twitching in an effort to keep a straight face. But Mama wasn't laughing. She was staring at me like I was on the express elevator straight to hell.

"And the moral of this little story would be what?" I asked, trying hard not to sound annoyed.

"That even a good woman, who doesn't think she's capable of such behavior, can suffer a fall from grace, Kendra," Mama said quietly.

"Okay, I get the point."

I could tell that Gwen and Alex were confused about what had just transpired. I felt no need to enlighten them.

"Who wants pie?" Mama asked, getting up from the table. We all held our hands up high.

Monday arrived and I was half afraid to wake up for fear of what new and terrible developments were awaiting me. I lay in bed as long as I dared before finally getting ready and heading to work. Shanda was a no-show and I didn't expect to see her at the center at all that week. Midterms at Kingford College were a week away and I knew she'd be busy studying. I also hadn't heard from Timmy again. According to the newspaper, people were spotting him all over the place. The latest sighting had him back in his former neighborhood in Detroit. I was walking around like the devil was stalking me. I carried a can of pepper spray in my pocket everywhere I went and wouldn't leave my apartment after dark. I had been talking to Carl every night on the phone. There was no change in his brother-in-law's condition. He could tell something was wrong with me but I just didn't feel like getting into it with him.

Lynette and I had made up after she came by my place with a peace offering of hot fudge cake, and to remind me I had a fitting at Gracie's Gowns Galore later that week. Needing some kind of normalcy back in my life, and to prove to her that I wasn't cheap or jealous, I agreed to wear the ugly maid-of-honor dress without complaint. I was glad we'd made up because I'd completely forgotten that Lynette's mother was hosting an engagement party for her and Greg on Tuesday night. It was the only time the entire bridal party would get a chance to meet each other before the wedding. I couldn't understand why it was so important to Lynette's mother that we all meet, especially since the wedding was still months away. But, as the maid of honor, there was no way I could get out of going. At least it would be better than sitting around worried that someone was going to strangle me.

I was long overdue for a haircut and headed to B & S Hair Design and Nail Sculpture after work on Tuesday. Everyone in the shop was subdued and quiet. Sheila Robins, the S in B & S and Bruce Robins's wife, was filling in for Aretha as a stylist. Sheila runs the shop's nail salon and doesn't have the flair for doing hair. I watched one older woman leave the shop looking like a pissed-off poodle. Bruce must be desperate for help. I noticed that Inez's empty workstation had been turned into a shrine and was decorated with flowers, cards, and stuffed animals.

"Have you heard anything about Aretha?" I asked Bruce as he massaged almond oil into my dry scalp. The normally fine-as-wine Bruce was looking tired and thinner than usual. I could see the hollows of his cheekbones through the scruff on his face. What had happened to Inez, and now Aretha, was causing his business to suffer. The shop's usually packed waiting room had been uncharacteristically bare when I arrived.

"I'm not sure she's coming back. Whoever attacked her really scared the hell out of her," he said mechanically, like he'd already answered the question a million times that day. I decided not to ask him anything else. He seemed to perk up a little when I gave him a bigger tip than usual.

As I walked to my car, I looked into the Healthy Food Emporium next door to the shop and saw the owner in a clinch with his cashier. A thought came to me and I headed into the store. The wind chime that hung over the door to the shop tinkled pleasantly as I walked in. I'd only been into the store once during their grand opening a year ago. But I knew that the woman the owner was hugged up with was not his wife. By the time I reached the front of the store, the amorous couple had broken apart and the owner had disappeared into the back room. As I got closer I could tell that the cashier was much younger than I first thought; she barely looked out of her teens. She had long, bleached-blond hair that was dark at the roots, and she wore her makeup so heavy she could have graduated *cum laude* from Clown College. Her name tag revealed her name to be Kitten. Since there was nothing feline about her that I could see, I figured it must be a cutesy nickname for Katherine. Kitten smiled when she saw me and I noticed her bright purple lipstick was smeared on her teeth.

"Hi. I'm looking for some multivitamins. Can you tell me what aisle they're in?"

"Sure, they're at the end of the middle aisle on the big display," she replied.

As she spoke, the owner, a runty middle-aged guy with a beer gut and a straggly ponytail, emerged from the back room carrying a box. He walked to the front of the store and started restocking a display of carob candy near where I was headed. I thanked her and headed towards the vitamins.

I pretended to browse through the various brands of vitamins. The owner was behind me, bent over his box. I purposefully backed into him.

"Sorry," I said, looking sheepish.

"Not a problem. You finding what you need?" he asked, standing to face me. I could see traces of Kitten's lipstick in the corners of his mouth. That must have been one hell of a kiss.

"Actually," I said, looking out the store's window dramatically. "There was a strange man following me. So I ducked in here," I whispered.

The owner went outside and looked up and down both sides of the street before coming back inside. "Nobody's out there now. You want me to call the police?"

"No. That's okay. I'm probably being paranoid. You know, since that girl got killed next door. Have you or your wife seen anyone strange lurking around here?" I asked, still whispering and gesturing in Kitten's direction.

"No. But I thought they knew who killed that girl," he said, looking from Kitten to me uneasily. His face was slightly flushed.

"Well, they still haven't caught him. How about your wife? Has she seen anyone?"

"Ah, she's not my wife, and she hasn't seen anyone, either." He turned away from me back to his box. The wind chime above the door tinkled as a woman entered the store. She was dumpy and wore a peasant dress and Birkenstocks with thick black socks. As she passed by the owner, she grabbed his ass. He turned slightly and gave her retreating back a halfhearted smile. I watched her walk past Kitten, who was filing her nails, into the back room.

"Oh, is *that* your wife?" I asked feigning ignorance.

He turned and stared daggers at me but didn't answer.

"You might want to wipe your mouth, lover boy, or your wife's gonna know you've been playing with a certain Kitten."

He straightened up and quickly wiped at his mouth with the back of his hand.

"Did I get it all off?" he asked pleadingly, looking towards the back of the store. His wife had emerged from the back room and was talking to Kitten.

"I'll tell you if you answer my questions."

"What do want from me, lady?"

"Calm down. I just want to know if you saw anybody around the beauty shop the night of the murder next door. It would have been after nine that night."

"What are you, a reporter?" He wiped at his mouth again, still looking at his wife.

"Just answer the question, please."

"The only person I saw that night was some black girl. I saw her go around the back of the shop."

"What time was this?"

He sighed heavily. "I can't remember exactly, maybe around nine-thirty." He kept looking at his wife. For some reason, I was getting the biggest kick out of his discomfort.

"Did you recognize her?"

"I didn't see her face, just her hair. She had long braids."

"Did you see anyone else?"

"No," he said sullenly.

"Did you hear anything after you saw her, like a gun-shot, maybe?"

"No. I left after that."

"Would you be willing to tell the police what you saw that night?"

"Are you crazy, lady?" His voice was high-pitched and panicky.

I glanced at a sign on the wall listing the store's hours. They closed at six every night.

"So, I guess I don't need to ask what you were doing here so late." He glared at me, and started to say something, but his wife walked up behind him and wrapped her arms around his middle. She kissed him on the cheek.

"Is my handsome husband giving you a hard time?"

Handsome? He hardly looked like love's dream to me, but what did I know. Maybe he was packing some major equipment in his pants.

"Not at all, ma'am. He's been very helpful," I replied, scratching the corner of my mouth to indicate where he still had some lipstick. He wiped the corner of his mouth hard before turning to plant a big wet one on his wife. Yuck.

I left the store and headed to my car. The girl he'd seen that night had braids. Could it have been Shanda? I knew there was bad blood between her and Inez because of Vaughn. But could Shanda have killed her own cousin? Maybe that was the real reason she was acting so indifferently at Inez's funeral and why she was so willing to help set Timmy up.

I was running pretty late when I arrived at Lynette's mother's brick tri-level that evening. I had to park around the block and almost fell as I tried rushing down the sidewalk in high-heeled boots. Lynette's mother, Justine, is a stickler for punctuality and I was in no mood to be on the receiving end of one of her my-time-is-precious-how-dare-you-be-late looks. Most of the time I like Justine. But she's moody as hell. You never know if you're going to get hugged or cussed out.

Justine Martin opened the front door before I could ring the bell. I walked straight into an overpowering cloud of her Cinnabar perfume. But I was used to how heavy she wore her fragrance and knew to hold my breath. I could tell she was pissed at me because she tossed her long, black, curly weave, which hung down her back much like a horse's mane, and didn't speak. She was dressed in an emerald green silk pantsuit without a shirt underneath. I could see her lacy, black push-up bra peeking out from beneath her buttoned up jacket. Her feet were crammed into heels that looked two sizes too small for her and were so high I wondered why she didn't have a nosebleed. Her makeup was dramatic and overdone, with eyes ringed with so much eyeliner she looked like an ancient Egyptian queen. Justine's in her fifties but doesn't look it and is determined to retain a tight grasp on her youth, no matter how foolish she may look in the process. She took my coat, looked me up and down, gave my cashmere sweater, long vintage suede skirt and boots a disapproving roll of her eyes, and practically shoved me into the living room where the other guests were congregating. I almost tripped over her terrier, Coco.

"The maid of honor has decided to grace us with her presence," Justine said loudly, making my face burn hot with embarrassment. Apparently, I was the last one to arrive. The three dozen or so people in the room, most of whom I didn't recognize, turned to stare briefly at me before turning their attention back to whatever they'd been doing when I arrived. A jazz instrumental was playing on the CD player and people were helping themselves to an abundance of finger food that had been laid out on the dining room table.

Lynette's fiancé, Greg, looking quite handsome in black slacks and a gray turtleneck, came to my rescue and pressed a drink into my hand. I sipped it and gave him a grateful look.

"As you can see, my future mother-in-law is in rare form," he whispered to me. "I've been trying to avoid her but she keeps grabbing me and introducing me to people as her future son-in-law, the bank president. I wouldn't mind it so much but some of her people keep asking me about why their loans didn't go through." Greg's actually an accountant at Willow Federal Bank, where he met Lynette, who's a personal banker.

We laughed, but I knew how he felt. For the longest time, Justine would introduce me to her friends as Lynette's best friend Kendra, the restaurant owner, when she knows full well I'm just a hostess. I knew her embellishment of my career was to make people think she mixed and mingled with the elite of Willow. The only way I got Justine to stop was by saying I owned and operated the Weenie Hut on Route 40 whenever the folks she introduced me to asked me about my *restaurant*.

"Where's Lynette?" I asked. Greg pointed in the direction of the kitchen and I headed off in search of my best friend.

I heard laughter as I approached the kitchen but when I walked in the laughter stopped and I was immediately met by the silent gaze of several women, three of whom I didn't know. Lynette was sitting at the kitchen table looking un-comfortable. I instantly knew they'd been talking about me and felt my face start to burn again.

"Hey, Kendra," said Lynette, jumping up and giving me a quick hug that I only half returned.

I greeted the other women in the room—Lynette's sister-in-law, Abby, and Greg's sister, Liz, both of whom I actually like a lot, and smiled at the other women, figuring they were bridesmaids, too. Lynette made the introductions.

"Kendra, these are Greg's cousins, Celeste and Cecile Warner from Cincinnati," she said, gesturing to two women who I just realized were identical twins. Celeste and Cecile were both tall and thin, almost to the point of being gaunt. Both twins wore their hair closely cropped and natural but one had her hair dyed a bright orange. The only other dif-ference in their appearances was that one twin was wearing a blue, sequined cocktail dress that looked too big, while the other sported a tight red minidress and thigh-high boots. Both women were guzzling large drinks and, upon further inspection of the way they were propped up against the kitchen counter, appeared to be either drunk off their asses or well on their way to being so. I said hello and held out my hand to the nearest twin. She gave me a moist, limp handshake while her sister belched and rubbed her stomach. I quickly turned my attention to the other woman.

"Kendra, this is a coworker of mine at the bank, Georgette Combs," Lynette said, gesturing towards the pretty, smiling, conservatively dressed young woman seated at the kitchen table. *This is more like it,* I thought as I held out my hand. Georgette reached out to shake my hand and I froze with shock as I saw that her fingernails were at least four inches long. Some of her nails were so long they had actually started to curl into spirals.

"Nice meeting you, Georgette," I said, recovering quickly. I tried not to wince as my hand disappeared into hers and pushed the question of how she wiped without giving herself a hysterectomy firmly out of mind.

"Nice meeting you, too, Kendra," Georgette replied in a high-pitched voice that sounded like she'd inhaled helium. "Come on over here, girl, and sit down next to me," she said, patting the chair beside her. I walked over to her, willing myself not to laugh at that Minnie Mouse voice by filling my head with visions of my pet bunny, Fifi, who got run over when I was eight. I didn't want to hurt this woman's feelings when she seemed so friendly. However, you'd think I'd have learned by now that first impressions aren't always accurate.

"So, Kendra, what's this we hear about you not liking your maid-of-honor dress? I thought it was real pretty," Georgette said, leaning forward in her seat, her friendly smile gone.

"Yeah, what makes you think you're too good to wear what the bride picked out? Ain't none of us complained," piped in the twin wearing the blue sequins, slurring her words slightly.

You could have heard a pin drop as they all waited for my response. I looked over at Lynette, who looked mortified.

"Well, I certainly never meant to come across that way. But this is really between Lynette and me," I said, slowly and deliberately taking deep breaths to keep from working myself up into a full-blown snit. A certain bride-to-be was going to have hell to pay.

"Kendra, you know I didn't mean it like that," said Lynette, looking down at the table.

"Yes, you did. You said Kendra would rather wear a rag from the thrift store than the nice dress you picked out. Didn't she, y'all?" Georgette said, looking around the room for affirmation. Liz and Abby just rolled their eyes and left the kitchen.

"Uh-huh, she did say that," replied the twin in the red dress, loudly, filling the room with her liquor-scented breath.

"You gonna let her talk about you like that, Kim?" asked the blue-sequined twin, shaking a bony finger in my face.

"It's Kendra, and if you want that finger, you better keep it out of my face," I said, getting up from the table, my quest to be diplomatic short-lived. If I'd known I was walking into an ambush, I'd have kept my behind at home.

"Ooh, I'm so scared. Miss Cheap Ass is gonna beat me up, y'all," said the blue twin, lurching around the kitchen, bobbing and weaving like she was ducking imaginary blows. Everyone in the room, except Lynette and me, started laughing hysterically.

"You guys need to quit," said Lynette, sounding like she was about to cry.

"You were the one talking about your so-called best friend. Not us," replied Georgette in a huff.

She and the twins were staring at Lynette and me with glittering eyes and I suddenly realized that these three crazy heifers wanted us to fight. They would like nothing better than to see Lynette and me push back the kitchen table and start brawling and tearing each other's hair out.

I'd had quite enough of Talon Woman and the Double Lush Twins. As far as I was concerned, Lynette and I had settled the dress issue, and even though I was annoyed that she'd been talking about me behind my back, I wasn't about to act a fool for the enjoyment of these crazy women. I pulled Lynette to her feet. "Come on and introduce me to everybody else." I led her out of the kitchen.

"Kendra, I—" began Lynette before I cut her off.

"Not to worry my *friend*. We've already squashed the dress issue, no need to bring it up again," I assured her.

"I swear I had no idea they were like this when I asked them to be in the wedding." Lynette shook her head in dismay.

"Why in the world did you ask them in the first place?"

"I only asked the twins as a favor to Greg's mother. I'd only met them once and had no idea how much they like to get their drink on. I only hope they can stay sober long enough to make it down the aisle. As for Georgette, we both started working at the bank about same time. I thought she was my friend."

Under normal circumstances she probably was Lynette's friend, but there was something about planning a wedding that brought out the worst in everybody involved.

"What was that your mother told you? Watch out for jealous females when planning your wedding. Did she say anything about crazy females? You've got three of them in the kitchen, so watch your back."

We made the rounds and Lynette introduced me to the

groomsmen, who were much nicer than the idiots in the kitchen. One in particular, Greg's best friend and best man, Ken Tucker, took an avid interest in me. Ken was a software engineer in Atlanta and was newly divorced. It was also evident that he was on the prowl, although he was stuttering and sweating so profusely I could tell he was way out of practice.

"K-Kendra, I'm loving th-that skirt you've got on, g-girl," he said, tugging at the tight collar of his shirt. I knew he was flirting with me, or trying to, at any rate. But I couldn't help teasing him.

"Thanks, Ken. You can borrow it anytime you want." I smiled at him to let him know I was kidding, but he looked horrified.

"N-No, I just m-meant that you l-look good, y-you know?"

"I know. I was just messing with you," I said and gave his hand a reassuring squeeze. Just then, someone in an apparent attack of nostalgia put on Zapp's "More Bounce To The Ounce" and Ken lit up like a lantern.

"Th-This is my j-jam," he said, pulling me into the middle of the living room to dance, which would have been fine had there been other people dancing, and would have been even better if Ken knew how to dance.

Now, I'm the first to admit that I'm nobody's idea of a good dancer. I'm not horrible but I long ago gave up my dream of being able to dance so well that people would make a circle around me and clap and cheer. But even I'm better than Ken. Hell, if all my toes were broken and both my arms were in slings, I could still dance better than Ken. And that's not saying much at all. Brotherman's face was tensed up like he was constipated and his spastic, jerky footwork and furious, frenzied fist-pumping made it look like he was mad at the music and trying to pick a fight with it. I, on the other hand, was doing a tired two-step, ducking occasionally to avoid getting punched, not to mention getting drenched from all the sweat that was flying off of Mr. Dancing Machine.

Then Ken suddenly switched gears and leaned forward and started vigorously shaking his behind like it was on fire. I realized he was doing Da Butt, a dance that was popular back in my college days. Everyone was laughing at him, and rightly so. But I had to give Ken cool points because he just didn't seem to care. Realizing I didn't know most of the people at the party well enough to care what they thought, I started doing Da Butt, too. Soon Greg and Lynette joined us and, minutes later, everyone was dancing and laughing. Even Justine was cutting a rug, though I knew her feet had to be killing her in those too small shoes.

Dancing made me hungry. I left the others, who were now doing the Electric Slide, in the living room and headed into the dining room to get some food. With everyone dancing, Justine's dog—Coco, taking full advantage of the unattended grub—had climbed up on the table and was lapping up the spinach dip, standing with her dirty little paws planted right on top of the cocktail bread. I quickly grabbed her and put her in a nearby bedroom, then took the tray with the doggy tainted dip and bread into the kitchen. Georgette and the Sunshine Twins were still talking and again fell silent when I walked in. Georgette got up from the table and put her hand on my shoulder, her claws draped too close to my neck for comfort.

"You're not mad, are you, Kendra? We were just kidding. Weren't we?" she asked the inebriated, semi-comatose twins, who nodded mutely and stared vacantly through red, watery eyes. I remained silent.

"You know, we don't like our dresses, either," Georgette squeaked in a low whisper. "What didn't you like about yours?" Georgette was smiling innocently enough but I knew this two-faced cow was just trying to get me to talk about Lynette so she could run back and tell her what I said in an attempt to get more mess started.

"Let's not talk about those dresses, okay? This is a party. Here, I brought you guys some dip," I said, setting the tray on the table and leaving as they tore into it.

Chapter 9

Wednesday afternoon found me sitting in my car in the parking lot of Floyd Library on the Kingford College campus. I was looking for Shanda and had driven around the campus looking for her car. I'd finally spotted her Honda Civic in the library's parking lot. I parked behind her car and had been waiting for over an hour. I didn't want to miss her. I watched various students emerge from the library. None of them was Shanda. Finally, after another half an hour, I headed into the library to look for her.

Floyd library had been recently renovated and it had been years since I'd been inside. Gone was the orange and pea-green seventies decor with its outdated paper card catalog and mismatched furniture. The library was now completely automated and housed a computer lab full of new Apple computers as well as a coffee shop. The main reading room had hunter-green carpeting, dark tan leather couches and armchairs, and long wooden tables. The reference department and the main stacks were on the second floor.

I wandered around the library, pausing every now and then to glance at studious or sleeping students in my search for Shanda. I found her on the second floor, asleep in a study carrel in the reference department. She was sleeping with her head resting on arms crossed atop an open book. Her long braids hid her face like a curtain. I pulled a chair up next to her and nudged her awake. Since it hadn't exactly been a gentle nudge, she woke up quickly, but looked bleary-eyed and confused for a few minutes before realizing it was me. She groaned softly.

"What do you want?" she asked, rubbing her eyes.

"For starters, I want you to tell the police what you and Vaughn did," I said in low whisper.

"Not this again. Kendra, how do you know that Timmy didn't kill Inez? He probably did, you know. She was already dead when Vaughn went to see her. Vaughn and I are just helping the police to look in the right direction."

"Either you're a fool or your boyfriend has knocked a screw loose in your head, little girl. Do you really think Vaughn Castle has any interest in helping the police do anything? He just wants to screw up Timmy's life, and you know it."

"Timmy's an ex-crackhead with a criminal record who didn't even graduate from high school. Looks to me like his life is already pretty screwed up," she whispered loudly, standing up and tossing her books into her backpack.

"Okay, well, let's explore another theory," I said, blocking her way as she tried to walk past me.

"I'm going to call security," she said, looking panicky.

"Go ahead and call them, Shanda, and they can hear all about how you were spotted at the shop around the time Inez was murdered."

"What? I wasn't at the shop that night!" she exclaimed. A few students poked their heads out from their carrels to see what was going on. I leaned closer to Shanda and lowered my voice.

"I talked to a man who saw a black woman with long braids going around to the back of the shop around nine-thirty the night Inez was killed. Was it you?"

"Hold up. You don't think I killed her, do you? I was at choir practice with twenty-five other people that night. Why would I kill my own cousin?"

"Two words: Vaughn Castle. Everything that has happened in the past couple of weeks leads straight back to him. Maybe you were afraid she was going to tell the police he was dealing drugs."

"You must be smoking crack with your friend Timmy, Kendra," she said, laughing. "I was at choir practice at Holy Cross from seven to almost ten that night. My father was there, too. We went to and from practice together. You can ask him and anyone else who was there that night."

"I will. I think your father would be very interested to know what you've been up to. For instance, that blue scarf you ran off with last week. I know you gave it back to Vaughn because he used it to strangle a woman I was with at The Spot on Saturday night."

"What scarf?" she said, playing dumb. "I don't know what you're talking about. And you better be very careful about what you say about Vaughn."

"Well, maybe I should talk to your father about it," I said confidently.

Shanda looked uncertain for a moment but then a sly gleam appeared in her eyes and I realized my bluff had failed. "If you were going to tell my daddy anything you'd have told him by now. Who do you think he's going to believe, anyway, his own daughter or some heathen who doesn't even go to church?" I heard muffled laughter coming from a few of the carrels.

My face was burning with embarrassment and my hands curled into fists. Shanda noticed and quickly walked away before I could administer the ass-kicking I was dying to give her and that she so richly deserved.

"Miss, are you a student?" asked a voice behind me. I turned and saw a stylishly dressed librarian looking at me like I was loony.

"No. Sorry, I just needed to talk to my little sister," I said, backing away from her.

"Then I'll have to ask you to leave this area. You're disturbing the students who are trying to study."

I've always been a little in awe of librarians. She didn't have to ask me twice. I left. Quietly, of course.

Gracie's Gowns Galore was located in the Kingdom Shopping Center on Grand Street. I've often wondered why the most dilapidated places always had the most ambitious names. The Kingdom Shopping Center had seen better days but, personally, I couldn't remember when. Gracie's was wedged between a liquor store and the Kingdom Flea Market. The original owner, Gracie Parker, died twenty years ago. Her granddaughter, Mona, now operated the shop. I had gotten my prom dress from Gracie's so I knew they had beautiful dresses. However, I couldn't work up much enthusiasm for the one I was being fitted for. Lynette was already there when I arrived. She still hadn't found a wedding gown and flipped through bridal magazines while I was being fitted. Even though we'd put what had happened at the party behind us, there was still a little bit of tension bubbling under the surface. I already had enough to worry about so I played nice. Besides, Lynette was looking completely stressed out. Working full-time, raising two kids basically on her own, living with her well-meaning though exasperating mother, and planning her own wedding, complete with insane brides-maids, had my best friend ready to pull her hair out.

"Now, see, there's nothing wrong with that dress. It looks good on you," claimed Lynette encouragingly as she tossed a magazine into the pile by her chair and picked up another one.

I didn't agree. I looked at myself in the fitting room's long mirror and suppressed a shudder. The dress was fitted in the waist and bodice with a boatneck, three-quarter sleeves, and a flared calf-length skirt that made my legs look stumpy. The lace at the neckline was itching me and I pulled at it irritably. The sash around the middle ended in back with a large bow that, instead of being on my back, was designed to hang down over my behind, making me feel like I had wings on my ass. And if that wasn't enough, the dress was covered in so many sequins that I bet Liberace himself would have drooled with envy. I didn't dare complain. Lynette kept glancing at me with a half-crazed look in her eyes. I didn't want to find out what happens when a stressed-out bride snaps.

"Hold still. I almost pinned my finger to the hem," said Mona. Mona Carter was a tiny black woman in her late forties who, despite the fact that she'd sold thousands of wedding gowns, had never married. She seemed to enjoy living vicariously through the brides she fitted for gowns.

"There," said Mona, standing to survey her work, "all done." Mona and Lynette were watching me, waiting for some kind of positive response. I had to dig deep.

"I guess it's not so bad now that I've had a chance to see

it again." I turned slowly, looking at myself in the mirror, and even managed a halfhearted smile. I was afraid that Georgette and the twins were going to jump out and get me if I didn't make a good show of liking the dress.

"Told you so," said Lynette, looking so happy that I was glad I'd lied. But I still couldn't wait 'til it was my turn and I got to pick out something ugly for her to wear. I had visions of big polka dots to go along with the neon pink tulle and bugle beads.

I headed into the changing room and quickly changed out of the dress. Mona had instructed me to hang it on the rack outside the room along with the other dresses that she was currently altering. There were several dresses on the rack ranging from a simple cotton sundress to evening gowns. One dress in particular caught my eye and I picked it up. It was a gold, silk Oriental-style dress with cap sleeves, a high Mandarin collar, and black frog closures in the front. The dress was actually pretty tame-looking from the front. But the back was another story. The dress was almost completely open in the back from the neck to the waist. I looked inside and saw that it was a size four. I tried hard to remember if there was ever a time in my life when I could wear a size four and concluded that it had possibly been when I was four years old.

"It's sharp, isn't it?" said Mona, who'd walked up on me while I was holding the dress up in front of me.

"Now, this is a dress," I said to Mona. "Whose is it?"

"Nicole Rollins. She's a tiny little thing and it was way too long for her. I had to hem it. It's been finished for a couple of weeks but she hasn't been back to get it. I'm not surprised, though, with what happened to Inez."

"This is a pretty racy dress for a minister's wife, isn't it?"

"To be honest, I don't think she ever planned to actually wear it. Nicole was here shopping one day and saw Inez try on the dress. Inez really wanted this dress but she couldn't afford it. Nicole just bought it to spite her," said Mona, shaking her head.

"That wasn't very nice," I said, hanging the dress back on the rack.

"Yeah, well that's Nicole for you. She always wanted everything Inez had, including her daddy. Now, she's got him and Inez is dead. I tell you, it's just such a shame."

"Didn't they used to be best friends?"

"Yeah, they ran around together all through school. They both got their prom dresses here. But, you know, even when they were friends, Nicole wasn't always very nice to Inez. I was good friends with Inez's mother and she used to tell me some of the mean things Nicole used to do to Inez," Mona said, shaking her head.

"Really. Why did Inez put up with her?"

"Inez was always kinda shy and Nicole was very charming and outgoing. She could be a lot of fun, especially when she was getting her way. Inez just adored her. But that sure changed. When Inez's mother died and Reverend Rollins married Nicole, Inez was heartbroken. Jeanne and Morris were having their huge house built. I think what really got to Inez was that her mother didn't even get to live in that house. She died before it was finished. Inez herself only lived there for a few months. Then, when she found out about her father and Nicole, all hell broke loose and she moved out. Nicole is the lady of the manor now."

"Sounds like Nicole's a real piece of work."

"As long as you were on Nicole's good side, you were okay. If not, look out!"

"What do you mean? Was she violent?"

"Well," Mona said, looking around and lowering her voice. "My nephew Lonnie went to high school with Nicole and made the mistake of lying to his friends about feeling up Nicole behind the bleachers after a football game. She found out and attacked him. Scratched up his face and arms real good. He was a mess. Little Miss Nicole takes her reputation very seriously."

That certainly answered my question. I decided to find out what else Mona knew. "You know, I heard a rumor that Reverend Rollins and Nicole were fooling around before Inez's mom died. That can't be true, can it?"

"It is as far as a lot of people in this town are concerned. But, I'm not so sure. I mean, no, Rollins is no saint. And I know he and Jeanne had problems early in their marriage, but they always managed to work it out. I was at the hospital a lot during those final weeks and he never left her side. If he was cheatin' with Nicole, he sure hid it well. But, I think Inez might have eventually gotten over her father's marriage to Nicole if Nicole had treated her right. She never could resist rubbing Inez's nose in the fact that she was married to her daddy."

I watched as Mona hurried off to help another customer and I thought back to Inez's funeral. Nicole had been in bad shape. Obviously she was regretting her treatment of Inez. Then I remembered something else. Nicole Rollins wore her hair in long braids. Could she have been the woman seen at the shop around the time of Inez's murder? Did she witness something, or was it more sinister than that? There was bad blood between the former best friends. Had it escalated to murder? Was that why Nicole was so distraught? Now that I knew that she also had a violent streak, I intended to find out.

★ ★ ★

It rained all the next day and my mood matched the gloom outside. Not wanting to deal with Noreen, I called in sick from work and slept in. As I lay in bed, I tried to decide how to go about approaching Nicole Rollins. Going to Holy Cross would be the obvious answer but I really didn't want to see Morris Rollins. I found my attraction to him very unsettling. Mama's story about Vera Maynard had me wondering just what would happen if I took Rollins up on his offer to visit him in his office. I didn't want to become the subject of anybody's cautionary tale. It was Thursday and I remembered that Rollins taped his show *The Light and the Way* on Thursday evenings. Surely attending a taping would be safe enough. Nicole was bound to be there. I just had to figure out a way to get her talking about Inez.

Late that afternoon, I worked at Estelle's. Gwen was also working and managed to cheer me up, that is until Timmy's mother arrived looking for Alex. Olivia and Gwen were cordial to each other and Gwen was sympathetic to what Olivia was going through with Timmy. However, Gwen never missed an opportunity to subtly remind Olivia that Alex was her man now and she intended to keep him.

"Olivia, how you holdin' up, girl?" Gwen had emerged from the hostess station to put a comforting arm around Olivia's shoulders.

Gwen was taller than Olivia by several inches. The two women were at the opposite ends of the personality spectrum. Gwen was statuesque, loud, fun-loving, and a flashy dresser. Olivia was quiet, petite, conservative, and—while she was actually better looking than Gwen—didn't have the self-confidence and fashion sense that Gwen did. Olivia had been a stay-at-home mom while her husband Jesse was alive. Gwen had worked since she was sixteen. There were probably things about both women that Alex found very appealing.

"I'm okay, Gwen. Is Alex around?" She sounded slightly annoyed and pulled away from Gwen, who rolled her eyes behind Olivia's back.

"He's in his office," Gwen replied. "You just go on back," she said to Olivia's retreating back as she headed to Alex's office.

I wondered if anything was wrong since Olivia hadn't even acknowledged my presence. Gwen was doing a slow burn.

"You know, I feel for the sister 'cause of what she's goin' through. But if that stuck-up hussy thinks that she's gonna be cryin' on my man's shoulder every damn day, she can think again. I don't play that shit."

"She doesn't have any friends and her family is gone. Alex is the only one she can talk to," I said, trying to put Gwen's mind at ease. Thinking back on that tender moment I'd witnessed between Alex and Olivia, I wasn't so sure that she had nothing to be worried about.

"Yeah, I know. But you know what? That ain't my problem," she said as she pulled a tray out from behind the hostess station and set coffee cups and plates on it.

"What are you doing?"

"I'm going to get some coffee and cookies to take back to Alex and Olivia, of course," she replied, opening her eyes wide with mock innocence.

"You mean, you're going to check up on them?"

"Damn straight," she said, heading to the kitchen for the food. I hoped Olivia didn't end up poisoned.

"Be nice," I called after her. She responded with a devious smile.

It was slow so I folded napkins while I waited for the next customers to come in. I felt the hair on the back of my neck stand up and looked up to see Noreen Reardon's pale, wrinkled face staring at me through the restaurant's large picture window. With her lips pressed together in disapproval and her eyes slightly magnified by the window, she looked like an elderly fish with its face pressed against the side of a fishbowl. I couldn't figure out why she was looking so pissed off until I realized I was supposed to be home sick. My heart sank as she walked into the restaurant and made a beeline straight for the hostess station.

"Kendra, I'm so glad to see you're feeling better." Her words were dripping with so much sarcasm and distaste that you'd have thought she'd just caught me picking my nose.

"Actually, Noreen, I am feeling much better, thank you. I was really in pain this morning."

"Come on now, Kendra. I'm an old lady and I suffer from arthritis and a variety of other ailments. I find that aspirin works wonders for pain. You'll have to come up with a better excuse than that."

If she wanted a better excuse, then far be it from me to deprive her of one. "You caught me, Noreen. I just didn't want to say what was really wrong with me. It's kind of embarrassing." I leaned forward, looked around dramatically, and gestured for her to come closer. She leaned in, eyes gleaming in anticipation.

"Actually, Noreen," I whispered, placing my hand on hers and looking her straight in the eye, "I've been having a terrible bout of ringworm. I just can't seem to get rid of it. You understand, don't you?" I squeezed her hand. She quickly pulled away from me in horror, tossed me a venomous look, and hurried out the door without looking back. I knew I was going to pay for my moment of fun at Noreen's expense, but at the moment I could not have cared less.

After about a half an hour, Alex emerged from his office with Olivia. I could tell that she'd been crying. She gave me a weak smile as Alex guided her past the hostess station and out the door. Gwen was right behind them and stood at the door watching as Alex walked Olivia to her car. She looked at me and shook her head.

"What's wrong?" I asked.

"Boy, when it rains, it pours," Gwen replied, still shaking her head.

"What?" I demanded.

"Olivia has breast cancer. She found out this morning."

"You have got to be kidding me!" I couldn't believe it. Talk about bad luck.

Alex came back into the restaurant. He could tell by my expression that Gwen had told me the news.

"It's just a small lump and she probably won't even have to undergo chemo if it hasn't spread to her lymph nodes," Alex said. I could tell he was upset all the same. I instantly thought about Timmy. When had he last talked to his mother? Did he know?

"Well, that's good news, right?" I asked them, confused by the grim looks on their faces.

"Yeah, it is," said Gwen. "Her doctor wants her to have the surgery right away. But Olivia is refusing to be treated until Timmy turns himself in. She hasn't heard from him and doesn't know where he is. And she's also startin' to have doubts about his innocence. She can't understand why he won't turn himself in. She's worried that he may have skipped town."

"I've been wondering about that myself," said Alex, running a hand over his bald head.

I wanted to tell them the truth so badly, and I might have

if I knew where Timmy was. But until I had some kind of solid proof of his innocence, the fewer people who knew what was going on, the better. After what had happened to Aretha, I didn't want anything else to happen, especially to anyone I loved. I kept my mouth shut and continued to fold napkins.

The parking lot of Holy Cross Church was almost as crowded on that Thursday evening as it had been for Inez's funeral. I parked and, not knowing where the taping was being held, followed a group of people I assumed were there for the same reason. I had chosen my outfit very carefully and was dressed in a conservative lavender cowl neck sweater, black slacks, leather boots and coat. I didn't want to give Reverend Rollins any ideas about why I was there by dressing provocatively. I wasn't even wearing perfume. I just hoped his wife Nicole was around so I could talk to her and leave.

I pulled my coat around me as I walked across the lot. The unseasonably warm weather that had hung on through September and into October had finally left and the cold fall air had me digging into the back of my closet for warmer clothes, namely my prized black leather trench coat. I considered the coat, which I'd stumbled upon at Déjà Vu a few years ago, to be a tribute to my tenacity and extreme thrift. I got in the only fight I'd ever been in when I spotted the coat at the same time as another bargain-loving shopper. We got into a tug-of-war right in the middle of the store. The other woman, a skinny white chick who looked like she needed a good meal more than a coat, head-butted me and busted my lip. I grabbed a handful of her hair and almost ripped it out of her head but I still managed to hang on to my prize. Once blood from my split lip dripped on the coat, the other woman abruptly let go and I went flying into a rack of shoes. It was an undignified display and not one of my proudest moments. I didn't care. Where else was I going to find a black leather trench coat in pristine condition for seventy-five dollars?

Once inside, I followed the others down into the church's cavernous basement, which had been turned into a television studio. There was a stage set up talk-show style with a desk for the host and an uncomfortable-looking couch for guests. The backdrop on the wall behind the desk and couch was painted to look like clouds with rays of sun shining through. There were about a hundred folding chairs set up for the audience. Each seat had a white gift bag sitting on it. Two television cameras were set up in front of the stage at opposite ends and a large microphone dangled from above. To the right of the stage was a piano and about two dozen more folding chairs. Another microphone hung down over this area, as well.

The seats in the audience were filling up fast and I grabbed one in the back. The gift bag contained a CD made by the Holy Cross Choir called *Divine Intervention;* a novel entitled *I Will Follow Him,* depicting a young black woman in a dress with a plunging neckline stretched out in a grassy field with her face and one arm stretched heavenward; a small bible; and an ink pen with Holy Cross Ministries spelled out in gold letters. The choir filed in and sat in the seats to the right of the stage. Shanda wasn't with them but her father, Rondell Kidd, dressed in a too-tight argyle sweater tucked into equally tight navy blue dress pants, sat down at the piano. I sure hoped he didn't have gas or it would be the end of his pants. Rondell's wife, Bonita, was rushing around with a clipboard, making sure everybody was in the right place and generally bossing everyone around. I noticed more than a few people giving her very unchristian-like looks behind her back. She was dressed just as dowdily as she had been when I met her. Her plaid skirt and twin set looked straight out of the fifties, and not in the stylish, retro kind of way, either.

Morris Rollins emerged from behind the curtains on the stage and started talking to the camera crew. One of the cameramen must have made a joke because Rollins laughed and when he did, his smile lit up the entire room. I felt my stomach do a little flip-flop. I've always been a sucker for a man with a killer smile. I suddenly missed Carl even more. Rollins was dressed casually in tan slacks, a red crewneck sweater, and loafers. I could see the diamond stud sparkling in his ear from all the way in the back row. After getting his wireless microphone attached to his sweater, Rollins started greeting the audience members in the first row, stopping to speak to each one, hugging some, and slapping five to others. You certainly couldn't say the man was unfriendly. Though one could argue that being friendly was part of his whole problem. Some of the women in the audience whom he greeted had pressed themselves against him in such a familiar way that I wondered just how well they knew the reverend.

I noticed Bonita Kidd watching from the stage as Rollins made his rounds. She was staring at him with so much naked love and admiration that she didn't even notice her husband had walked up and asked her a question. Rondell looked from his wife to his brother and I saw a momentary flash of fury on his usually placid face. Rondell waved his hand in Bonita's face to get her attention and she glared at her husband so fiercely he took a step backwards. I couldn't hear what Bonita said to Rondell, but whatever it was sent him back to his piano with a hurt look on his face. I wondered if it was in God's plan for Bonita to be in love with her brother-in-law.

By the time Rollins reached the third row, which was two rows ahead of where I was sitting, Bonita whispered something to him and he headed back towards the stage to take his place behind the desk. I felt strangely disappointed. Remembering why I was there, I looked around for Nicole Rollins but didn't see her or anyone else with braids. The lights in the studio dimmed, indicating that it was showtime. The show opened with the Holy Cross choir singing a rousing rendition of "This Little Light of Mine," which was apparently the show's theme song, and was included on their CD. I wondered where Shanda was. Probably off somewhere being a punching bag for her psycho-thug boyfriend.

Rollins's soothing voice brought me out of my thoughts as he greeted the viewing audience and introduced the show's guests. The first guest was Ermaline Pierce, a minister from Trinity Baptist Church in Cleveland, who would be discussing the role of female ministers in the modern church. Joining Ermaline were the Trinity Baptist Church Faith Dancers, who would be performing. Also on the show was Melvina Carmichael, a local author of Christian romance novels, who would be discussing her latest release, *I Will Follow Him*. I flipped over the book that had been included in our gift bags and saw a picture of a solemn-looking woman in glasses.

Rollins stood and the audience applauded as the Reverend Pierce made her way onstage to the sound of Rondell Kidd's organ intro. Reverend Pierce was a big, light-skinned woman, almost as tall as Rollins, dressed in a flowing yellow caftan. Her hair was hidden in a multicolored turban, and she wore a large cross on a strand of wooden beads. Her voice was loud and booming and she constantly sounded like she was delivering a sermon. But she was also very funny and a great storyteller. She regaled the audience with stories of how hard it was to be taken seriously as a female minister at the start of her twenty-year career and her struggle to get more women to "heed the call," as she put it, to become ministers.

Rollins proved to be a good host and knew just how to graciously move the conversation forward when Reverend Pierce got a little too long-winded. After her interview, and a ten-minute question-and-answer session with the audience, the Trinity Faith Dancers—eight girls ranging in age from six to eighteen—performed to "Stomp" by God's Property. The girls were dressed in black leotards and multicolored tunics in the same material as Reverend Pierce's turban. Their energetic synchronized movements mirrored the lyrics of the song perfectly. They received very enthusiastic applause.

Next up was Melvina Carmichael, who approached the couch like she was afraid it would bite her. Melvina was brown-skinned, rail-thin, and slightly bucktoothed, wearing a shapeless sweater dress and black pumps. I could tell by the way she tipped across the stage that she wasn't used to wearing heels. She took a seat on the couch next to Reverend Pierce, quickly shook hands with Rollins, and squinted blindly into the audience. She must have left her glasses at home. I heard some scattered giggling and instantly felt sorry for the woman, who clearly was out of her element and didn't look any happier in person than she did in her picture. Once again, Rollins proved to be a smooth and gracious host.

"Ms. Carmichael, you've written ten Christian romance novels in the past twelve years. Where do you get your ideas?" He leaned forward in his seat in anticipation, like he truly cared about what she had to say.

Melvina swallowed hard and nervously looked at the audience. "Well, Reverend Rollins," she began timidly, "I get my ideas from real life situations. Things that I see going on in society. Then I take those situations and I add a God-centered theme."

"Amen, sister," declared Reverend Pierce so loudly that Melvina jumped and almost fell off the couch.

"Tell us about your new book, *I Will Follow Him*," said Rollins, quickly squelching the dirty look Melvina was shooting Reverend Pierce.

"It's the story of a young woman who must decide whether to stay at home and marry her college sweetheart or go to Africa to work as a missionary."

I wondered what in the world that had to do with the scantily clad woman on the cover crawling across an open field. Maybe the answer was in the book.

"Ah, yes, I remember my own missionary work quite well," said Reverend Pierce. It appeared the reverend was re-luctant to give up the spotlight. Her comment was met by a smattering of applause, which Reverend Pierce took as her cue to continue. But Rollins pressed forward before she could say anything more.

"So, does the 'Him' in the title refer to God?"

"Now Reverend, I don't want to give away too much of the plot," said Melvina, giggling. "Let's just say that my heroine has a hard time deciding which 'Him' to follow, her sweetheart or her Lord."

"Yes. Yes. The eternal struggle between matters of faith and matters of the heart, I understand it all too well," said Reverend Pierce, shaking her head. "I've counseled many women who are going through the same situation. Ah, the stories I could tell." She turned to face the audience like she was going to tell one of her stories. I could almost hear the anticipation in the room.

Rollins attempted to steer the conversation back to the topic at hand. But Melvina, realizing her interview was rapidly going down the tubes, decided to take matters into her own hands. She jumped up from the couch and teetered perilously close to the edge of the stage.

"Are there any writers in the audience?"

The audience, disappointed at being denied the chance to hear Reverend Pierce's story, was silent. And the silence was brutal.

Why I raised my hand I do not know. Maybe it was because I was having a flashback to my senior year of college, when I gave a grammar workshop while doing my student teaching. A roomful of bored and semi-comatose high school students, who would rather have had their eyelashes pulled out one by one than answer any of my questions, did not make for a good time. I knew how the shy author was probably feeling. Or maybe I was just trying to impress Rollins, who was staring at me with a mixture of surprise and relief. Either way, I was the only one who raised a hand and Melvina smiled at me so gratefully that it was too late to turn back.

"What's your name, miss?" asked Melvina, flashing a triumphant glance at Reverend Pierce, who was looking sulky.

"Yes, please stand up and tell us about your writing," said Rollins, who was smiling mischievously. "I'm sure Ms. Carmichael has some helpful tips and advice for you."

Wonderful. I wasn't expecting this. I stood slowly, my mind desperately trying to figure out what I was going to say. I'd never written creatively in my life unless you counted a few horrific poems written in college that my poetry professor deemed twaddle. I didn't even know what twaddle meant but I knew it wasn't anything good. Everyone was staring at me as I stood with my mouth hanging open and my hands twisting nervously. My composure wasn't helped at all by the knowledge that this was being taped for television.

"Don't be shy," said Melvina encouragingly. I noticed how much more relaxed she seemed now that the spotlight had shifted to me. Why in the world did I raise my hand? A thumbtack enema couldn't be worse than this.

"Uh, my name is Kendra Clayton," I began. My mouth was dry and my voice came out sounding strangled. "And I…um…am writing a science fiction novel," I declared. Melvina looked a little taken aback. Apparently she wasn't expecting my answer. Neither was I.

"How fascinating," she gushed.

I wished Reverend Pierce would interrupt again as I was now dying to hear her story, but she just rolled her eyes and sat back in defeat.

"We'd love to hear all about it, wouldn't we folks?" asked Rollins, who had come out from behind his desk and was now leaning against it. The audience clapped enthusiastically. He was getting a big kick out of this and I wanted to punch him.

They were all waiting to hear about my masterpiece in progress. I quickly thought about all the episodes of *Star Trek* that I'd seen. I thought about the *Star Wars* movies and even *E.T. the Extra-Terrestrial*.

"It, um, takes place on the planet Zircon. And involves a forbidden romance between Zirconian Princess Zippy and Prince Qumquat of the planet Ooom." I looked around, daring anyone to laugh. Rollins looked like it was taking everything in him not to bust a gut, Melvina looked like she was wondering what kind of an idiot I was, and Reverend Pierce was laughing and trying to disguise it as a cough, or maybe she was choking. I couldn't tell, but figured she was laughing when no one rushed over to administer the Heimlich maneuver. The audience looked confused.

"What's the title of your book?" asked Melvina.

"The Princess and the Planet Oom," I replied like it should be obvious.

"How original. And is this a stand-alone novel or will there be other books about the planet of Doom?" Melvina asked, standing so close to the edge of the stage I was afraid she'd fall off.

"Oom, not doom. It's the planet Oom," said Reverend Pierce, who was now laughing and not bothering to hide it. I was starting to get a little mad. How dare she laugh at my imaginary book!

"Did you have something to ask me about writing, dear?" That was a good question. What advice could I ask her about a book I wasn't really writing?

"Yes," I said. "How do I get published?" I figured it was a safe enough question. But Melvina's face turned hard and she crossed her arms and shook her head in disgust. You'd have thought I'd just asked her the color of her bloomers.

"All you aspiring writers are the same," she spat out, still shaking her head. "You all seem to think that there's some big secret to getting published that we published authors are keeping from you. Well, I'm here to tell you that there isn't. Getting published takes a lot of hard work and persistence. I studied the publishing business and I mastered my craft. It took me almost twenty years of rejection before I signed my first book contract. And I know what you're going to ask next," she said, putting her hands on her hips. "The answer is no. I won't show my publisher your book about the planet of Doom or Zoom or whatever it's called."

"It's Oom," I said weakly, but she didn't hear me.

"You have to put forth some blood, sweat, and tears. You have to pay your dues like I did. There are no free lunches in this life."

You could have heard a pin drop as I sank back down in my seat. I was mortified. I couldn't believe I'd felt sorry for this woman. Even Reverend Pierce had stopped laughing in the face of Melvina's tirade. Rollins's look was unreadable.

"Thank you, Ms. Carmichael. That was *very* helpful," he said with just enough sarcasm to make the audience giggle and Melvina slink back to the couch and take her seat.

Rollins quickly thanked his guests for being on the show and reintroduced the Trinity Faith Dancers, who performed to a song by the Holy Cross Choir. Rollins ended the show with a passionate plea for donations to Holy Cross Ministries. His pitch was so slick and his demeanor so humble it almost had me digging deep into my own purse. But I was ready to leave, having accomplished nothing more than getting myself embarrassed on television. Nicole never did turn up. I got up from my seat and headed towards the basement steps when I felt a firm hand on my shoulder. I turned to see Rollins smiling down at me. He smelled like Lagerfeld, one of my all-time favorite colognes.

"I hope you'll accept my apologies, Ms. Clayton. I've known Melvina Carmichael for many years and she's always been wound a little tight. She's really quite a lovely lady when you get to know her." He had taken my hand and was squeezing it lightly. I felt a warm, tingly sensation running up my arm and I had an overwhelming urge to climb the man like a tree.

"No harm done, Reverend," I said, looking away from him. His intense gaze was making me nervous. "I guess that's what I get for lying," I said, laughing to show I wasn't mad, at least not at him. I tried to pull my hand away but he held on.

"There's no fault in trying to be helpful. You were very amusing. I haven't had much to be amused about recently. Everyone's been telling me I should postpone the tapings for a while. But being here at Holy Cross gives me so much comfort. Keeping busy keeps me from thinking about my loss. I'm so happy you decided to come tonight."

"Well, I found myself with some free time this evening and decided to take you up on your offer."

"I'm glad you did."

He finally let go of my hand, but I could still feel the warm imprint of his fingers. "I was hoping to meet your wife this evening. I didn't get a chance to meet her at the funeral. Is she okay?"

Rollins looked uncomfortable. "Actually, she's not doing very well. She's grieved herself sick. She's got a bad case of the flu and is at home under a nurse's care. She can't have any visitors."

"I'm sorry to hear that," I said, but somehow knew he'd told me a lie. Why didn't he want me to talk to her?

"If you'll excuse me, Ms. Clayton, I have some details I need to attend to." He started to walk away and I realized my chance to get more info on Nicole was walking away with him.

"Reverend Rollins," I called out. He turned and gave me a quizzical look. "I have a confession to make. I'm having a personal problem and I really need to talk to somebody about it. I was hoping you'd have some time for me this evening. I mean, if you're not too busy, that is?"

That predatory look, the one that had said "fresh meat" when I'd first met him at Inez's funeral, appeared again briefly before he gave me a kind smile. "Of course, I have time for you. You're more than welcome to wait for me in my office. I promise I won't be long." He gave me directions and I headed up the basement steps wondering what I'd just gotten myself into.

Chapter 10

Rollins's office was located just off the large atrium at the church entrance. The door was unlocked and I let myself in. I was expecting a large, lavishly decorated office and that's just what I found. Lush, pale gold carpeting covered the floor and a large circular oak desk sat in the center of the room like an island. The wall behind the desk was made of multicolored glass blocks and gave a distorted view of the street below. Instead of chairs in front of the desk there was a dark gold love seat with red silk accent pillows. The shelves built into the cream-colored wall to the right of the desk were filled with books, glass vases, and several small woodcarvings. A sliding panel in the wall to the left of Rollins's desk was open and revealed a large-screen television, CD/DVD player, and an aquarium of tropical fish. I looked up and saw that a mural depicting Rollins in the pulpit delivering a sermon had been painted fresco-style on the ceiling. Good grief. Somebody needed to get over himself.

I sat on the love seat for a few minutes but, being the supremely nosy person that I am, was soon up looking around. Rollins's huge desk held dozens of pictures and I took the time to look at each one. Many were of him in his ministerial robes with members of his congregation. Several were family pictures of him and his brother Rondell when they were young men. I was surprised to notice that Rollins's looks had gotten better as he'd aged. The pictures showed him to have been a lanky young man who looked uncomfortable with his height. I almost didn't recognize Rondell. He was much slimmer and his clothes fit. There were many pictures of Inez as a little girl and even one of Inez as a teenager with a protective arm around her younger cousin Shanda. Shanda was looking up at Inez with an expression that can only be described as worshipful. Whatever their relationship had become at the time of her death, there'd been a time when Shanda had adored her cousin.

I noticed a more recent picture of Inez, her father, and another pretty young woman that I didn't recognize. Rollins was in between the two young women with his arms around both of them. They were all smiling widely. Both Inez and the other woman wore braids but Inez's hair was done in a much more intricate design, pulled away from her face, while the other woman wore her braids hanging loosely to her shoulders from a center part. This must be Nicole Rollins. While Rollins barely looked like he was in his fifties, he still looked old enough to be Nicole's father. I didn't blame Inez at all for being angry with her father. I tried to imagine my father marrying Lynette if something happened to my mother. I couldn't do it. But I did get a sudden idea of what

I would say to him about my so-called problem when he arrived for our talk. I sat the picture back in its place and noticed a stack of papers in the middle of the desk.

I picked up the stack and flipped through it. It was mostly bills, invoices, and estimates for work that had either been done or was going to be done at the church. I glanced at a letter towards the bottom of the stack, and realizing what it was, pulled it out. It was a letter from Rollins's insurance company denying his life insurance claim on Inez pending the outcome of the police investigation into her death. The letter went on to point out that this was standard procedure when the cause of death was listed as homicide. I looked at the date and saw that it was sent less than a week after Inez's death. Rollins apparently hadn't wasted any time trying to cash the policy. As lavishly as the man lived, it wouldn't surprise me if he were having money problems.

I heard voices in the hallway and quickly stuck the letter back in the stack and returned it to its place on the desk. The door to the office opened while I was still standing at Rollins's desk. Rollins stood outside the door with Melvina Carmichael. It was clear she wanted an invitation into the office and equally clear he didn't want to extend one. She stood staring up at him with a wistful expression. Boy, what was it about ministers that made women swoon? Was it the power, the glory, the closeness to God? Maybe they were trying to get closer to heaven.

"Thank you so much, sister Carmichael. I'll let Nicole know she's in your prayers." Melvina Carmichael looked past Rollins into the office and spotted me before I could move out of her line of sight. I knew what she was thinking by the contemptuous look she flashed me before walking away, slowly shaking her head. I had apparently gone from being a lazy writer looking for a free ride to a home-wrecking ho as far as Melvina was concerned.

I sat back down on the love seat just as Rollins turned and walked through the door. I gave him a big smile.

"Well, now, Miss Clayton," he said, giving me a devilish smile and taking his place behind his desk. I caught another whiff of Lagerfeld. "What can I do for you?"

The question was innocent enough but I got the distinct impression from the look in his eyes and the way he leaned forward in anticipation that he was hoping I had a problem he could solve with something other than his ministerial skills.

And, given my attraction to the Reverend, I was just hoping he'd keep his distance and stay seated behind his desk.

"I'm actually a little embarrassed," I said, laughing and looking down at my lap. "I think maybe I'm just overreacting."

"Please don't be embarrassed, Kendra. Can I call you Kendra?" His voice had such a soothing hypnotic quality to it that I found myself instantly relaxing. I was also impressed that he remembered my first name. This man was dangerous.

"Of course," I said, stopping short of asking him if I could call him Morris.

"You just take your time, Kendra," he said with a look of genuine concern.

"It's my boyfriend," I said.

Rollins leaned back in his chair looking a tad disappointed. "He's not abusive, is he?"

"Oh, no. It's nothing like that. He's, well, a lot older than me and we're having problems." This was the only thing I could think to tell him that might loosen his tongue about Nicole. Surely, being married to a woman young enough to be his daughter would make him empathetic to someone in a similar situation. At least I hoped it would.

"How much older is he?" Rollins asked, the gleam returning to his eyes.

"In his fifties, probably around your age. Not that you look like you're in your fifties," I added quickly.

He threw back his head and laughed. "Well, that's good to know."

"He's a good man. We get along very well. But, lately we don't seem to have much to talk about."

"And you think this has to do with your age difference?" he said, leaning back in his chair and lacing his fingers together behind his head.

"Yes, don't you? I mean, he used to call me all the time. Now I'm lucky if I hear from him once a day."

"Kendra, all relationships go through phases. How long have you been seeing each other?"

"Almost a year."

"Well, now, there you have it. Having been in a relationship for a year, things are naturally going to cool off. That's not necessarily a sign of trouble or an indication that your age difference is the problem. You said you still get along well, right?" He was looking at me like I was a silly, paranoid woman panicking because my man didn't call me every five minutes. Clearly I needed to come up with something more serious.

I leaned in closer to the desk and Rollins unlaced his fingers and leaned forward to hear my revelation. "That's not the only problem we're having." I whispered. "There are some, um, sexual issues as well." I tried my best to add some anguish to my voice but probably only succeeded in sounding like I had a feather up my butt. Nevertheless, Rollins looked sufficiently curious.

"Is it something you feel comfortable discussing?" he asked. I realized I was treading on dangerous ground bringing up the subject of sex with a married man I had no business being attracted to, but I'd already brought it up and he looked very interested in hearing what I had to say.

"Well," I began, looking more than a little embarrassed. "I won't bore you with the details. Let's just say that our age difference has been a big factor in our intimate relationship. The desire is there, but he's not always able to do anything about it, if you know what I mean. You do, don't you?"

"Don't worry, Kendra. You don't have to spell it out. I know what you're talking about. Not from personal experience, mind you." We both laughed. Although, I wondered why men always felt obligated to assure women of their potency. Whether he could get it up or not was no concern of mine…really.

"You know, Kendra. As a minister I should probably be counseling you on abstinence." He paused when he noticed my mortified expression then quickly added, "Don't worry, it's not my place or intention to judge you. Only God can judge."

I wasn't looking mortified on my own behalf. I was looking mortified because I couldn't believe a man who was known to be one of the biggest players in town had just brought up abstinence. Wasn't he afraid the heavens would open up and zap him with a lightning bolt? I glanced up at the ceiling, half expecting a crack to appear. I heard Rollins laugh again.

"I know what you're thinking," he said, leaning forward again.

"You do?" I rubbed my suddenly sweaty palms on my pants.

"Yeah, it is kind of hideous, isn't it?"

"I beg your pardon?" I asked, suddenly confused. Rollins gestured towards the painting on the ceiling.

"It was a wedding present from the congregation. They had it commissioned when Nicole and I were on our honeymoon. I can't stand it, but I didn't have the heart to tell them."

"Oh, the painting," I said, relieved. "No, I don't think it's hideous at all. It's just a bit overwhelming." That was a serious understatement.

"It was my sister-in-law Bonita's idea. She hired a local student artist to paint it. Do you know Joy Owens?"

"Joy painted this?" I was incredulous. Joy's work was usually quite bizarre. I was amazed that she hadn't painted Rollins with horns and a tail.

"Yeah, I guess Bonita really had to stay on top of her. Some of my parishioners told me that one day she came in to check on the progress of the painting and Ms. Owens had painted me with bloody fangs standing in a field surrounded by a flock of dead, dried-up sheep," he said, grimacing.

So, Joy had depicted Rollins as a bloodsucker who'd drained his flock dry. This was too much, even for Joy, and I laughed until tears rolled down my face and my sides ached. I was afraid I'd offended him but when I looked up he was not only smiling but had come out from behind his desk and was standing in front of the love seat, offering me a box of tissues. There were only a few inches separating us and my face was eye-level to his crotch. I couldn't help but notice that he was quite well-endowed and I was supremely embarrassed about having such unholy thoughts in a church. I took a tissue but he still stood in front of me like he was waiting for something. Feeling flustered and not quite knowing what else to do, I quickly scooted over. He sat down next to me. It was a tight fit and our thighs were touching. This man was slicker than snot on a wet floor. I was torn between leaving before I ended up like Mattie

Lyons's niece and staying just to see what kind of moves the reverend had up his sleeve. I still hadn't found out anything about Nicole, so my decision was made.

"Joy's work is very unconventional. This is probably the tamest thing she's ever painted. I haven't offended you, have I?" I asked, wiping my eyes and pressing my legs together to put some space between us.

"Of course not. I'm very well aware that there are folks who think that I shake my congregation down for everything but their gold fillings so I can live high on the hog. But most would be surprised to know that my first wife, Jeanne, came from a wealthy family in New York. Her parents made sure their daughter lived in the manner to which she was accustomed even after we were married. They were very generous to me, as well. As for my congregation, I do ask a lot of them but I don't ask them for more than they can give, and every dime collected from donations and the collection plate goes straight back into this church," he said, looking sad and misunderstood.

"You don't have to explain anything to me, Reverend Rollins," I said, giving him a smile. I wondered what shape his finances were in now that his first wife was dead. Why was he so hot to cash in the insurance claim on Inez?

"You have a beautiful smile, Kendra. You should smile more often."

Oh, boy. Here we go. "Thank you, Reverend." He took my hand and squeezed it gently and that familiar warm tingly sensation started tap dancing on my common sense, which was telling me that it was time to go. But I couldn't move. My limbs felt like jelly.

"You know, I've lived in this town all my life and I've never run into you before. Where have you been hiding?"

"Nowhere. I've been right here all the time." He was still holding my hand and looking into my eyes. He leaned towards me and I closed my eyes and almost puckered up. But instead of laying a big juicy wet one on my lips, he gave me a soft quick peck on the forehead before getting up from the love seat and sitting behind his desk. I felt like a kid whose ice cream fell off the cone before I could get a lick. I was obviously no more immune to Rollins's charms than any of his other conquests. What would I have done if he'd given me a real kiss? I already knew the answer and it didn't make me feel too good about my morals.

"So, you don't think I should be having sex, huh?" I asked with just a touch of sarcasm.

He looked at me with a startled expression before laughing heartily. "I'm sorry, Kendra. We kind of got sidetracked from your problem, didn't we?"

"Just a little."

"You'll have to decide what's best for you with regard to your intimate relationship. A doctor would be better suited to answer your questions. Maybe it would be a good idea to focus on the things that first brought the two of you together. I know it's hard. I can understand how age differences can affect a relationship. My wife Nicole and I had the same kinds of problems when we first got together."

Now we're getting to it. "How so?"

"Oh, the usual stuff. I constantly have to explain things to her that she's too young to know about. I remember our first date when I took her to a Sidney Poitier film festival. She'd never even heard of him. Her favorite actor is Will Smith. I'm a jazz lover and she likes hip-hop. She spends a lot of time surfing and shopping online. I barely know how to turn our computer on. It was hard for us to find some common ground but we managed to do it."

"Sounds like Nicole and I have a lot in common. Maybe I could get together with her for coffee and girl talk sometime?"

"I'm sure Nicole would love to meet you, Kendra. But now's just not a good time."

He sounded a little exasperated and I was afraid I'd blown it. "Oh, I understand. Whenever it's best for her. I couldn't help but notice the pictures on your desk. Is that your wife in the picture with you and Inez?" I asked, gesturing to the picture of him and the two young women with braids.

"Yes, this is Nicole," he said, picking up the picture. "This was a happier time," he said softly.

"I heard that Nicole and Inez used to be best friends. This must be very hard for her."

"It's hard for both of us. Inez never understood about Nicole and me. I couldn't blame her. I had hoped she'd come around but she never did. She couldn't understand how I could get married again so soon after her mother died. But Jeanne had been sick for so long and was in such pain that it was a blessing when she passed. She wasn't herself during the final year of her life. She was gone long before she actually died. I really needed someone and it turned out to be Nicole." He placed the picture facedown on the desk and stared moodily at his desktop.

"Did Nicole and Inez ever make up?"

"No, they avoided each other like the plague. I think she blamed Nicole even more than me. She thought Nicole purposefully went after me when her mother got sick. But it's not true. There was no big seduction staged by either of us. It just happened."

"Sometimes people have a hard time seeing their parents as human beings with needs of their own," I said.

"You're very insightful, Kendra," he said.

Our eyes met again and I decided it was time to go. "Well, it's getting late and I have work tomorrow. I appreciate you talking to me. It really helped a lot." I stood up and started to put on my coat when Rollins came up behind me and eased the coat up onto my shoulders. He put his arms around me, embracing me from behind.

"Anytime you want to talk to me about anything, you feel free to stop by, you hear?" I felt the warm feather-light touch of his lips against my neck before he let me go.

"I will," was all I could manage to get out before I quickly left.

I was in a strange mood as I drove home. I could still smell Morris Rollins's cologne and feel his lips against my neck. Damn him! Thoughts of Carl popped into my head, making me feel guilty and confused. But there was one thing that was crystal clear: Morris Rollins didn't want me to talk to Nicole. Why? I was positive it wasn't because she was sick and overcome with grief and I was also sure it wasn't because he was sizing me up as a potential lover and didn't want me to be friends with his wife. I bet his first wife must have known and interacted with the female church members he had fooled around with. And, if Nicole had something to do with Inez's death, I couldn't imagine him shielding her, either. If I were Morris Rollins, and my wife had been involved in my daughter's death, I'd serve her up to the police on a silver platter. No, there was something else at work.

I was fairly certain it was Nicole the health food store owner had seen going around the back of the shop the night

Inez was murdered. I couldn't imagine why she would go to see Inez since, as Rollins put it, they avoided each other like the plague, but she must have been there and seen something that put her life in jeopardy. Maybe Nicole witnessed Vaughn kill Inez. Or even worse, maybe Nicole saw Shanda kill Inez and Rollins was trying to protect his family from scandal. Either way, I had to talk to Nicole. Whatever she had seen, she had to tell the police so Timmy could be cleared and Olivia could have her surgery.

B & S Hair Design and Nail Sculpture was on my way home and I happened to glance in the window as I drove by. There was a light on in the shop. It was after ten o'clock and I was surprised that someone was in the shop so late. I stopped and parked my car. I peered through the window and was surprised to see Aretha Marshall's auburn-bobbed head bent over a box. I knocked on the window and she jumped and looked around wildly, like an animal that was being hunted. I waved and gestured for her to let me in. I could tell she didn't want to and I really couldn't blame her. She unlocked the door and let me in. She looked awful. She was dressed in a dingy white turtleneck sweater and faded jeans. She wasn't wearing any makeup and the dark circles under her eyes made it look like she had two black eyes. She kept tugging at the neck of her sweater and I saw a flash of the vivid bruise the scarf had left around her neck.

"Girl, I am so sorry about what happened. Are you okay?"

"Yeah, I'll live," she said sarcastically. I followed her back to her station. She was apparently packing up.

"Did you quit?" I asked, gesturing towards the boxes.

"I was leaving, anyway. I got hired as a stylist at a day spa in Dayton. That's where I'm from originally. I wasn't 'sposed to start 'til next month but I'm leaving before I get my ass killed."

"I feel so bad about what happened. I had no idea he'd be there that night. I—"

"Don't worry," she said, cutting me off. "It ain't your fault. I been known to run my mouth when I get a coupla drinks in me. I shoulda known better," she said, shaking her head sadly.

"Do you remember what happened?"

"Unfortunately. I remember going out to my car. I had my keys in my hand and someone grabbed me from behind. He kept pulling whatever he had 'round my neck tighter and tighter. I couldn't breathe. Kept telling me I had a big mouth and I needed to learn how to keep it shut. Next thing I remember is being in the ambulance. I never even saw the muthafucka. I didn't even have time to grab my gun. It happened that fast."

"So you couldn't even tell the police for certain who it was who attacked you?"

"Nope, and even if I could, I wouldn't. I'm sorry, girl-friend, I loved Inez to pieces but I can't help you with this. I'm not trying to end up dead behind someone else's shit."

I wasn't about to ask her to risk her life again. So I thanked her and left.

I arrived at my duplex barely remembering the drive home. I wasn't paying attention to my surroundings or I might have heard the person who rushed up behind me, grabbed me by my hair, and slammed me onto the hood of my car. I felt all the air go out of my lungs and couldn't catch my breath to scream. My head was being pulled back so hard my neck felt like it would snap. I felt hot breath in my ear and smelled familiar, lemony-scented cologne. I tried to twist around to see him but he had me pinned on top of my car and his handful of my hair made me wince with pain when I tried to turn my head.

"You wanna end up like your friend did the other night don't you, bitch?" I finally found my voice and opened my mouth to scream but only managed a loud whimper before he let go of my hair and clamped his hand over my mouth.

"See, I can't stand bitches who can't mind their business and run their mouths about shit that don't concern them. 'Cause that's the kinda shit that gets you killed, understand?" He pulled me up by the back of my coat and spun me around to face him. I was still pinned between him and my car. I couldn't even knee him in the balls. His face was so close to mine that I could see the pores in his nose and smell the liquor on his breath. He was drunk and his green eyes looked wild and crazy under the streetlights. He definitely looked capable of hacking someone to pieces. I was about to wet my pants. For a split second, I thought about trying to reason with him. But I decided it would be the equivalent of trying to talk a hungry lion out of eating me.

When I didn't answer, he shook me like a rag doll. "I said, do you understand?" My head snapped backward and, re-membering back to my tussle over my leather coat, I pur-posefully threw my head forward, causing my forehead to butt him hard in the mouth. He grunted and his hands flew to his mouth. I shoved him away from me and he overbal-anced and fell. I turned to run but he grabbed at my leg. I pulled free, stumbled, and almost fell.

"Bitch! I'm gonna kill you! Look what you did!" he shrieked at me. I turned and saw that his mouth was bloody and he spit out what looked like teeth. Uh-oh. I messed up pretty boy's grill and he wasn't taking it well at all. He lunged at me and I closed my eyes. That's when a sound similar to the blast of a cannon sounded from behind us, stopping Vaughn in his tracks. I turned to see my seventy-two-year-old landlady Mrs. Carson standing on her porch, dressed in her striped housedress and faded terry-cloth slippers, with a shotgun cradled against her shoulder and aimed straight at Vaughn Castle.

"That first bullet was a warning, boy. The second one is for you. I already done called the police so get yo ass outta here before I put a bullet in it!"

Vaughn looked like he wasn't about to be punked by a little old lady but when the neighbors started coming out on their porches to see what the commotion was, he turned and ran down the street to where his Escalade was parked and we all watched as he drove off, tires squealing.

"You okay?" asked Mrs. Carson, who had come down off the porch to where I was standing by my car. She'd left her shotgun on the porch. I'd heard her say on numerous occasions that she had one but had never really believed her. I was glad to be wrong.

I nodded my head, still not able to speak, and let her lead me into her house where she fixed us both a glass of homemade peach wine.

"Did you really call the police?" I asked after a few sips of the sickeningly sweet wine. We were sitting at Mrs. Carson's kitchen table and her cat Mahalia stared down haughtily at us from her perch on top of the refrigerator.

"Nope. Just said it to scare him. You gonna have one hell of a hickey on your forehead, missy."

I felt the tender spot where my head had connected with Vaughn's mouth. It was sore and a little swollen. I was happy the skin wasn't broken or I'd probably have to be treated for rabies.

Mrs. Carson was strangely silent. I was expecting her to grill me about what was going on and then follow up with a lecture but instead we sipped our wine silently. She seemed to be avoiding eye contact with me.

"Please don't tell Mama," I pleaded. Dealing with my grandmother on top of everything else wasn't something I needed.

"Don't worry. My lips are sealed," she assured me. Now I knew something wasn't right. Even though I begged her not to tell, I never expected her to agree. Mama and Mrs. Carson are best friends and tell each other everything. Keeping something from Mama, especially if it was about me, went against the natural order of things.

"Okay, what's up? You haven't asked me what's going on. I didn't get a lecture. Now, you aren't even going to tell Mama I was attacked? Why are you acting so strange? You're not sick, are you?"

"Nope. Just tired and ready to go to bed." She got up from the table and started rooting through a drawer by the sink. When she found what she was looking for she slid it across the table at me and I had to catch it quickly before it fell on the floor.

It was a Swiss Army knife that looked like it had never been used. The blade was still quite sharp and very shiny.

"What's this for?" I turned it over in my palm

"Well, what do you think it's for, Kendra? It's for protection. I'd give you my shotgun but I might need it. 'Specially if that fool comes back here to start some mess with me." She drained her wineglass and took my half-empty one and put them in the sink. "And you need to go to the police first thing in the morning and report what happened tonight. I'll back you up but I can't deal with no police tonight. Stevie's here."

That explained everything. Stevie is Mrs. Carson's son and the Carson family fuckup. He's almost fifty, has never had a job, and is in and out of jail due to his nasty little habit of taking things that don't belong to him. He's well-known to the Willow police department and if they found out he was staying with his mother, they'd probably search her house and find a multitude of stolen property. Mrs. Carson has four other hardworking and law-abiding children, but sticky-fingered Stevie is the apple of her eye and she won't hear a word against him. I listened closely and could hear the television on in her basement accompanied by loud snoring. Poor guy. Stealing must be very tiring.

I looked down at the knife she'd just given me and looked at her questioningly. She visibly puffed up. "It ain't stolen, Kendra. Now go on home before somethin' else happens. And you better go down to that police station tomorrow or I *will* tell Estelle."

I wasn't planning on going to the police until after I talked to Nicole Rollins. Then I would go to Harmon and Mercer and tell them everything. But I wasn't about to tell Mrs. Carson this. Instead, I hugged her, thanked her for the knife and for saving my hide, and headed for my own apartment. I had a late dinner of a peanut butter and jelly sandwich and was in my nightshirt, all ready for bed, when I heard movement outside my door. I figured it was probably Mahalia lurking around looking for mice but I grabbed the Swiss Army knife just in case it was Vaughn Castle, back to seek revenge for his jack-o'-lantern smile. I pressed my ear to the door and listened. I didn't hear anything so I flung the door open, startling the tall dark figure standing on my landing and causing me to drop the knife on my visitor's foot, making a small hole in the toe of his expensive cross trainers.

"Kendra, what the hell?" It was Carl, and he was a sight for sore eyes in a black nylon warm-up suit, smelling of Obsession for men. Instead of answering him, I leapt on him, wrapping my legs around his waist and kissing him passionately. He responded enthusiastically, kicked the door shut, and carried me into the bedroom where we made up for lost time several times and in numerous positions throughout the night.

"If I knew I'd get that kind of welcome I'd go away more often," Carl said early the next morning as we lay in my bed wrapped around each other. I was pleasantly sore and sleepy, with my head resting against Carl's chest and my thigh between his legs, nestled against his soon-to-be-erect-again penis. He was massaging my backside. I was warm and happy and, much like Mahalia after a mouse dinner, felt like purring. I looked at Carl with an expression that I hoped would let him know that I was ready for another go 'round. He looked at me with a sleepy smile that quickly turned to horror.

"What happened to your head?" he asked, rubbing the tender spot on my forehead that had now become a large knot. I felt my forehead and was alarmed to find that the spot had swelled up even more overnight. I leaped out of bed and rushed over to the mirror and almost screamed. The knot had puffed and swelled so that it now extended outward almost an inch, making me look like a unicorn.

"Damn, Kendra, I didn't do that last night, did I?" Carl had gotten up and was standing by me in the mirror. I didn't want to tell him about being attacked, so if he wanted to believe that the knot was caused by him knocking my forehead into the headboard during our bootyfest marathon last night, then so be it. The ridiculousness of the situation—complete with us both standing butt-naked and goggle-eyed in the mirror—suddenly hit me, and I started laughing hysterically.

"Think of it this way," Carl said, grinning like a fool, "you can always use it to hang stuff on." I punched him in the stomach and he chased me back into bed.

Later that morning, I sat in the kitchen with a compress full of ice pressed against my forehead while Carl cooked us breakfast. As I watched him cook bacon I realized I could get used to having him around all the time. A hot guy who knows how to cook bacon without burning it is definitely an asset in my book. I idly wondered if Morris Rollins knew how to cook.

So far, Carl and I have managed to keep our relationship casual, since we live in different cities, and basically only see each other on weekends. I was worried that things would fizzle out if we were together more often. I didn't want to push for more face time too fast since Carl is newly divorced from a white woman who left him because her disapproving daddy gave her an incentive by dangling a lot of money in her face. Even though he's a pretty stoic guy and never mentions his ex, I know Carl still has to be smarting over the betrayal.

"So, what's going on with Timmy? Did he turn himself in yet?" I almost dropped my bag of ice. It was wishful thinking to imagine that the subject of Timmy wouldn't rear its ugly head.

"No, and we're all getting really worried. Especially now."

"Why?" he asked, placing a plate of bacon, eggs, and toast in front of me. I filled him in on Olivia's condition.

"You know this doesn't look good for him, don't you? If he didn't do it he really needs to turn himself in. My man Howard James is a hell of a lawyer. Timmy couldn't ask for better representation. He's even going to do it pro bono."

"You're not telling me anything I don't already know. I feel really bad about this whole situation. Can we change the subject, please?"

"Kendra, you haven't gotten mixed up in Timmy's mess, have you?" he asked between bites of scrambled egg. I could tell by his intense stare that it wasn't a casual question.

Damn! I really didn't want to lie to him. I got up and emptied the melting ice from my compress into the sink without answering him.

"Kendra, please tell me you're not involved in this. You don't know where he is, do you?" His cell phone rang before I could form my lips around a believable lie. He answered it but didn't take his eyes off of me. Whatever the caller told him, I could tell it wasn't good news. I watched as Carl ran a shaky hand over his face.

"Damn. Okay, I'm on my way back now," he said in a flat voice. He slowly put the phone down.

"What's wrong?"

"John died a half an hour ago. I need to get back to Cleveland."

"Oh, my God! I'm so sorry," I said, coming over to him and putting my arms around him. He hugged me back hard. I felt bad that in my excitement to see him I'd forgotten to ask how his brother-in-law was doing. Sadly, there was no need to ask anymore.

Chapter 11

After Carl left, I got ready for work. The swelling on my forehead had gone down some but the knot was still there in all its glory. I put a black headband on, leftover from my teenaged fascination with the movie *Flashdance,* and pulled it down low over my forehead. Okay, I looked like a fool but there was nothing else I could do to hide it except possibly use a Band-Aid, and that would look even more foolish. I headed off to work happy that Fridays are half days at the center. That left me with the whole afternoon to try and figure out a way to see Nicole Rollins without her husband being around. I thought hard, trying to figure out if anyone had ever mentioned Nicole having a job—maybe I could drop in on her at work—but nothing came to mind. I honestly couldn't envision Nicole having a job other than spending her husband's money, which meant I was going to have to do something that I really didn't want to do: pay a visit to the Rollins home. I'd worry about that later.

When I arrived at work, Rhonda handed me a message after commenting on my headband and telling me she had a torn sweatshirt and leg warmers I could borrow to complete my look. The message was from Leah Johnson, the volunteer coordinator at Kingford College, informing me that Shanda would no longer be volunteering at the center and would fulfill the remainder of her hours at another agency. I had a bad feeling about this. While I wasn't surprised that Shanda didn't want to be around me—and, to be honest, the feeling was mutual—I knew how much she loved working at the center and was shocked that she hadn't called herself to tell Rhonda or Noreen she was quitting. I tried to get hold of Leah Johnson for more info but she was in a meeting. An hour later she returned my call and told me that Shanda's mother, not Shanda, had called her the day before to get her daughter's volunteer assignment changed to Holy Cross Ministries. Even though I was pissed at Shanda, I was also worried. I decided to head over to her house to see if I could catch her before she left for her classes. I told Rhonda I had an emergency and left.

Upon turning onto Shanda's street, I saw an ambulance parked in her driveway and someone being loaded into the back. A near hysterical Bonita Kidd jumped in as well. I watched it pull out of the driveway and race off in the opposite direction. I felt my stomach start to churn. I pulled up in front of the house just as Rondell Kidd came flying out the front door wearing a tight, yellow, terry cloth sweat suit and black dress shoes. I really wanted to believe that he'd thrown that outfit on in a rush but I knew better. I watched him jump into his car and back down the driveway. I ran up to the car.

"What happened?" I yelled through the open driver's-side window. I could see tears running down Rondell's cheeks.

"Shanda slit her wrist. I can't talk now. I gotta get to the hospital." I quickly jumped away from the car as Rondell pulled out of the driveway and tore off down the street. He didn't even stop at the stop sign and almost hit another car.

I got in my car and headed to the hospital. Shanda had tried to kill herself. Why? She had complained about her parents running her life, but slitting her wrists seemed like an extreme reaction to overbearing parents. More than likely this had something to do with Vaughn Castle. Did he threaten her? Did he beat her up again? How many women were going to suffer because of Vaughn? I arrived at the hospital and was heading into the emergency room when I heard someone calling my name. It was Morris Rollins.

"My brother Rondell called and said they were bringing my niece to the hospital. I couldn't get much sense out of him. You haven't seen him, have you?" Rollins looked past me into the emergency room.

"No. I just got here. He told me the same thing when I stopped by their house this morning." I wasn't about to tell Morris Rollins that his niece had tried to kill herself. That was his brother's job.

Rollins looked taken aback. "I didn't realize you knew my niece."

"Shanda volunteers at the literacy center where I work. I got worried when she didn't show up for work today, so I stopped by her house."

Rondell and Bonita emerged from behind a set of swinging doors and spotted Rollins. Bonita ran across the room into his arms and collapsed. Rollins and Rondell had to practically carry her over to a lumpy-looking plaid couch in the waiting area, where she buried her face against her brother-in-law's shoulder and sobbed. The way she was carrying on I was sure Shanda must be dead. I heard Rollins ask his brother what was going on.

"We found her in the bathtub this morning," said a distraught Rondell. "Her wrist was cut but the paramedics said that the cut was too shallow and she missed a major artery. She musta been in the tub all night, bleedin' slowly. She lost a lot of blood but she'll be okay. They're giving her a transfusion."

"But why? Why, Lord, why?" screamed Bonita. "Why would she hurt herself? What reason could she have?" Then Bonita looked across the room and found a name for her pain, and it was spelled K-E-N-D-R-A. Her face contorted in rage and she pointed an accusing finger in my direction.

"You! You had something to do with this. I know you did. What did you do to my baby, you heathen? She was fine 'til she started working at that center with you and those losers." She pushed away from Rollins in an effort to get at me, no doubt intending to tear me limb from limb. I could have probably taken her, but brawling with someone's distraught mother wasn't going to solve anything or win me any popularity contests. Rollins managed to restrain her. Both he and Rondell Kidd were looking at me curiously, like they couldn't quite figure out what planet I was from. I should have left but I was rooted to the spot by Bonita's melodrama. I felt like a deer blinded by headlights.

Rollins gently shifted Bonita into her husband's arms and came over to me. I expected him to demand an explanation and in that instant I decided to tell him about Shanda's involvement with Vaughn. I was quite sick of carrying the whole load around on my back and would have been more than happy to let Shanda's family deal with her. But, to my surprise, he didn't ask.

"Kendra, my sister-in-law is upset. It might be best if you left so we can get her calmed down." His voice was kind enough. But his eyes were hard and his hands were clenched into fists. Surely he didn't think I had something to do with what Shanda had tried to do? I could feel tears of self-pity start to well up in my eyes.

"I'm sorry, Reverend Rollins. Please tell the Kidds that Shanda is in my prayers," I said, my voice cracking a little, and left quickly before I made a fool of myself by blubbering like a baby.

He caught up with me in the parking lot. I felt a hand on my shoulder as I opened my car door. I turned and was pulled into a warm Lagerfield-scented embrace. The stress of the last couple of weeks finally caught up with me and I buried my face in his black cashmere sweater and bawled.

"No one is blaming you, Kendra," he said, gently stroking my hair. It dawned on me that this was the second tragedy to happen to a member of Rollins's family in as many weeks and here I was crying on *his* shoulder. I was mortified and quickly pulled out of his arms.

"I know. I feel stupid. Thanks for the hug but I really need to get back to work." I got into my car and started to close the door, but Rollins grabbed the handle and leaned down to whisper in my ear.

"Anytime you want to talk or just need a hug, let me know." He closed my door and I watched as he headed back into the hospital.

When I arrived back at work, Noreen was standing in the hallway outside the classroom. Not realizing she was waiting for me, I started to walk right past her but she blocked my way.

"Kendra, I was looking for you earlier and you weren't here. Please explain where you've been."

I told her about Shanda and, figuring that I'd explained myself to her satisfaction, attempted once more to enter the classroom. But Noreen wasn't finished flexing her muscles.

"May I ask why you think you have the right to just come and go as you please without even telling anyone where you're going?"

"What are you talking about? I told Rhonda where I was going. Didn't she tell you?"

"Yes, she did. But, Rhonda's not the one in charge around here, is she?"

"No, she isn't, but you weren't around and I had an emergency." I was trying hard to be calm but I could feel the blood rushing to my face.

"You mean Shanda had an emergency. What did it have to do with you? Are you a relative of hers?"

"No. But I didn't realize I had to be a relative to show concern for one of our volunteers who's going through a crisis."

"You seem to be under the delusion that you're more than just a teacher, Kendra. But that's all you are, a teacher, nothing more. I'm the one in charge and your only job is to help these students prepare for their GED examination, and you haven't even been doing that very well, in my opinion. You're disorganized, unprofessional, uncooperative, and dishonest. I've been documenting every single instance of your insubordination and I expect you in my office after class this morning so we can talk about your future with this program."

I could feel myself getting hot and my face felt like it

would burst. Noreen had picked the wrong time to mess with me and it was high time I let her know that her tiny reign of terror was over, at least as far as I was concerned.

"Excuse me, but who in the hell do you think you're talking to? You nosy, hypercritical control freak! *You* seem to be under the delusion that you're running things around here. *You* don't have an office. That's *Dorothy's* office and you're nothing but a glorified babysitter until she gets back. Now, I know you taught kindergarten for thirty years, so I can understand if interaction with adults might be a bit difficult for you. I've worked in this program for almost five years and I've never had any complaints about my professionalism. You, on the other hand, have some serious issues, lady. Your micro-management is driving everyone around here crazy. We don't need you breathing down our necks every minute of every day with your nitpicking comments. You're so busy spying on us it's a wonder you get any of your own work done. This program was running just fine before you got here and it will continue to do so when Dorothy gets back, which won't be soon enough for me."

"I'm afraid that's wishful thinking, because I got a phone call from Dorothy last night and her mother isn't healing as fast as they'd hoped. She doesn't know when, or even if she'll be back. I had a long talk with her about you and she told me that I was in charge in her absence and could handle things any way I see fit." Noreen was staring at me with her arms crossed and an expression so smug and condescending that my hand actually started to itch from wanting to slap her so badly.

"I cannot believe that you would burden Dorothy with this bullshit of yours when her mother is ill and she has much more important things on her mind. You're pathetic," I said in disgust.

"I may be a lot of things, Kendra, but I'm still your boss until further notice and since you want to be so difficult and don't want to live up to my high standards for teaching in this program, I have no choice but to pursue formal disciplinary action against you."

"Well, you know what, Noreen?" I said, having heard quite enough. "Since you know so much about my job and how I should be doing it, you can do it for me. I'll be back either when Dorothy or when someone with good sense is in charge." I turned and walked away with Noreen's loud voice echoing in the empty hall behind me.

"Where do you think you're going? Kendra! Kendra, I asked you a question!"

"I'm going home and *you* can go straight to hell!" I yelled over my shoulder.

"Don't bother coming back, Kendra! You're finished! Do you hear me? I'll make sure you never work as a teacher again!" Noreen's voice was a high-pitched shriek.

In an impulsive bit of immaturity, which I felt was fully warranted, I spun around to face her. I wondered if she could see the steam pouring out of my ears. "Since you're so fond of documenting things, document this, and then you can kiss it!" I yelled and quickly mooned her before walking out the door. I was feeling quite proud of myself, but I could hear Mama's voice in my head saying, "Fool, what have you done?" I ignored it.

I drove around for a while and finally, predictably, ended up at Frischs' Big Boy, nursing a double portion of hot fudge cake. My feeling of triumph had deflated a bit when I'd gotten to the center's parking lot and looked up at the windows of the classroom to see all the students hanging out the windows. Some had been applauding and cheering, while others just looked sad. Rhonda looked like she'd just swallowed a bug. I didn't blame her. Now she'd have to deal with Noreen alone. Poor baby. I had a bit of money in the bank so I'd be okay for a little while. I didn't think beyond a little while, opting instead to savor the thick, hot-fudge-covered chocolate cake with cold vanilla ice cream sandwiched in between. With what had just happened at work and Shanda's suicide attempt occupying my mind, I didn't notice the person who sat down at the counter next to me until I heard a familiar voice doing what it did best—complaining.

"What's a sister gotta do to get some service up in here?" Joy Owens asked aloud to no one in particular. A few seconds later a waitress handed her a menu and set a glass of water and some silverware in front of her.

I glanced over and watched her examine her silverware for cleanliness and couldn't believe that a chick known all over town for her bad attitude and poor customer service skills was looking for reasons not to leave a tip. Unbelievable. So far she either hadn't noticed me sitting at the counter or she just wasn't speaking. My bet was on the latter. I couldn't help but laugh, thinking about the painting on Rollins's ceiling. Joy looked over and glared at me.

"What are you doin' here? You get fired?" she asked, not realizing how right she was. I didn't feel like talking about work, especially not with Joy, of all people.

"I'm eating, Joy. What are you doing here?" I said sarcastically.

"Mighta been looking for a job after what happened at your uncle's restaurant," she said with a sly smile.

"What happened?" I asked, my head jerking up out of my cake plate.

"The health department showed up today for a surprise inspection. Said they got an anonymous call about an employee with an infectious skin disease working at the restaurant."

Great, as if I didn't already feel horrible. Now I'd caused trouble for Alex because of my prank on Noreen. But I didn't feel bad enough to confess that it was me and my fictional case of ringworm that had prompted the visit from the health department. Apparently, Noreen wasn't taking my abrupt departure, or my mooning her, very well.

"That's insane. Who in the world would tell a lie like that?" Personally, I think I missed my calling as an actress.

Joy shrugged and lit up a cigarette. A waitress walking past us to serve another customer set an ashtray in front of her, and Joy shot her a dirty look. "It was probably that pissed-off ole biddy from last month. Remember the one who got all shitty with Alex when he told her she couldn't make any substitutions on the side items for the special? Nasty bitch ranted and raved that she'd make sure nobody ever ate there again. Guess she was serious about that shit. But that man from the health department was only there a few minutes. Seemed kinda pissed that he had to come out at all."

Thank God, I thought, breathing a sigh of relief. Against my better judgment, I decided to ask Joy about the painting she'd done for Rollins's office.

"I saw the picture you did of Morris Rollins for Holy Cross, Joy. It was a lot tamer than your usual work. I was impressed."

She rolled her eyes but I could tell despite her usual funky attitude that she was pleased by the compliment.

"I guess I'm 'sposed to be flattered that you like that piece-of-shit painting? I only did it 'cause I needed the money."

"I'm curious. How'd you even get a gig like that?"

"One a the secretaries in the art department at Kingford

goes to that church. She told me they were lookin' for an artist. I gave 'em the cheapest estimate and got the job."

"So, what was it like working there?"

"Why are you all up in my business? How'd you even see the painting, anyway? I know you don't go to church. So, you musta been either on your knees or on your back *prayin'* with the good reverend, right? Wonder what that man a yours would think if I told him?"

"Why do you always have to be so nasty? All I did was ask you a question. You make me sorry I even tried to talk to you." I started to get up from my stool when she stopped me.

"Damn! You can't even take a joke. You need to chill, for real, Kendra," she said, laughing spitefully.

She and I both knew she hadn't been kidding. I sat back down only because I really wanted to know about her experience working for Holy Cross.

"It wasn't too bad workin' there," she said, shrugging her shoulders. "They mainly left me alone to do my thing. But the reverend's sister-in-law was a trip. Always breathin' down my neck and tellin' me to repaint shit. Like I didn't know how to paint. So, I got even with her ass. I painted the painting I wanted to paint. You shoulda seen the look on that heifer's face when she saw *my* interpretation of her precious brother-in-law. She went off. That was some seriously funny shit." She laughed and, imagining Bonita's shock at seeing what Joy had done, I laughed with her.

"Yeah, I've met Bonita Kidd. She's definitely uptight all right."

"You'd a thought she was the wife instead of the sister-in-law. Her husband was cool, though, with his too-tight-clothes-wearin' ass."

"You get to meet Rollins or his wife?"

"Nope. After she threatened not to pay me, I redid the painting, and got straight the fuck outta there. That's the last time I'm doin' some shit like that. I'm an artist. I can't have anybody fuckin' with my artistic vision like that. Where the hell is that waitress?" she asked, looking around fiercely.

Since my chocolate therapy session was over, I paid my bill and headed to my car. Then I remembered something that seemed a little strange to me from when I was at the hospital. Rollins had shown up. But Nicole wasn't with him. Was she at home? Did I dare go to their house to see her? I figured I had nothing to lose and, filled with chocolate-induced courage, headed over to the reverend's home.

Morris Rollins lived on the north side of Willow. I found this out by making a quick call to Gracie's Gowns Galore and talking to Mona Carter. One good thing about living in a small town is that, if you didn't know something about someone, you were usually only a phone call away from someone who did. According to Mona, Rollins had shunned living in the ritzy, exclusive area known as Pine Knoll in favor of the next most expensive area in Willow called Briar Creek. It was much newer than Pine Knoll and severely underdeveloped. Only four streets made up Briar Creek. The development had been abandoned when the builder went bankrupt, and only twenty of the planned fifty-plus luxury homes slated for construction had been built. The area behind the development was densely wooded and rumored to be home to packs of vicious stray dogs and homeless people.

The Rollins home sat majestically at the end of a cul-de-sac on a street called Rose Lane. It was a huge brick two-story that looked like a miniature castle and even had a small tower. Living modestly apparently isn't something that appeals to Reverend Rollins. There were four other equally large homes on the street, all with expensive cars in the driveways, except Rollins's, whose driveway was empty. The yards were immaculate with beautiful landscaping but it all looked a little too neat, a bit too artificial to me. I parked on the street and put on a pair of sunglasses before walking up the winding driveway to the front door. I rang the doorbell and heard it echo through the house. After about a minute, a short, middle-aged white woman in a nurse's uniform and a bulky blue sweater answered the door. She looked annoyed, like answering the door wasn't her job and she didn't appreciate having to do it.

"Hello, I'm here to see Nicole Rollins. Is she in?" The nurse rolled her eyes. What was wrong with everybody today? Was there something in the water that was giving everyone a shitty attitude?

"Mrs. Rollins is sleeping right now. She's ill and I have strict instructions from her husband that she not be disturbed for any reason," she said and started to close the door. I wondered why a nurse was answering the door. I was surprised the Rollinses didn't have a maid. Or did they?

"Is Florence here?" I asked, dredging up the first name that came to mind. I sure hoped this woman had never seen *The Jeffersons.*

"Who's that?" she asked, looking confused.

"You know, Florence, their maid," I said impatiently, giving off some attitude of my own.

"Reverend Rollins told me their maid is on vacation. I never knew her name."

"How long have you been Mrs. Rollins's nurse?"

"A week, and who did you say you were?" She was looking

at me suspiciously, probably trying to figure out what in the world a woman wearing dark sunglasses and a headband, looking like a reject from Prince's entourage, wanted with Nicole Rollins.

"I'm Mona Carter. I own Gracie's Gowns Galore and Mrs. Rollins had scheduled a fitting today for a new dress. She asked me if I wouldn't mind coming out here to do it. I'm sure she told me to come today."

The nurse looked like she wasn't quite sure what to do. I looked past her into the large, brightly lit foyer. From the little bit I could see it looked like a very beautiful house. But I hadn't really expected anything less. I even thought I detected a hint of Morris Rollins's cologne.

"I'm sorry, Miss—"

"Carter, Mona Carter." I could see by the look on her face that this wasn't going to work.

"Right. I'm sorry, Miss Carter, but Reverend Rollins was very adamant about not disturbing his wife. And to be honest, I really need this job and don't want to mess it up. You understand, don't you?"

The only thing I understood was that I desperately needed to talk to Nicole Rollins and this woman was in my way. I didn't know when I'd get another chance to see her with her husband out of the house. I wanted to get this over with so I could tell Harmon and Mercer everything and go on with my life, which now involved looking for a new job.

"I had no idea Nicole was even sick. What's wrong with her, anyway?" I whispered, hoping maybe she'd throw me a crumb about what was going on with Nicole. No such luck.

"I'm not at liberty to discuss that. Now, if you have any more questions, I'll have to ask you to consult Reverend

Rollins." She closed the door in my face before I could say another word. Shit! What was I going to do now?

I started to walk back to my car when a large truck bearing the name Lehman's Used Furniture turned into the driveway. The truck stopped next to me.

"Are you Mrs. Rollins?" asked the muscular brother driving the truck.

"No. I don't live here. But Mrs. Rollins is home."

"Thanks, ma'am," he said, and continued up the driveway.

I stopped and watched him park in front of the house. The driver jumped out and opened up the back of the truck while his partner, a short, squat, older black man in a baseball cap, rang the doorbell. I crept back up the driveway and hid behind a clump of bushes near the truck. I was hoping there would be a chance to sneak into the house while the door was open for the deliverymen. But from the conversation I could hear the driver's partner having with the nurse, it sounded like she might not let them into the house, either.

"Look, sweetheart, all I know is that we're scheduled for a delivery today at this address. Now, we can bring it into the house or leave it right here in the driveway, makes no nevermind to us. Either way, it's not stayin' in our truck. We got pickups to make and there ain't no room with that thing back there. So, what's it gonna be?" There was something distinctly familiar about the man's voice. But I couldn't place it. The truck was shielding my view of the front door so I couldn't tell who he was.

"Reverend Rollins never told me about any delivery. Go ahead and unload it and I'll call the reverend to see where he wants you to put it."

I ducked down low as the deliveryman went around to the back of the truck to help the driver. Minutes later the two men unloaded a large pine armoire, the kind people use as a second closet. Dang. Did Nicole have that many clothes? Or maybe it was for the reverend himself. The nurse still hadn't come back to the door to tell them where to put it, so it sat in the driveway behind the truck. The drivers waited by the front door, smoking cigarettes. Finally, the nurse came back to the door.

"Okay, guys, the reverend said you could bring it on in. It goes in the maid's room here on the first floor, just off the foyer. I'll hold the door."

I had to think of something quick 'cause it didn't look as if I'd get a chance to sneak in with the nurse standing at the door and I couldn't take any chances. I looked at the unattended armoire and made a hasty decision I hoped and prayed wouldn't land me in jail. While the deliverymen were stubbing out their cigarettes with their backs turned, I ran over and jumped inside the armoire. I had plenty of room to stand up and turn around. I was able to close one side of the armoire's double doors. There were no handles on the inside allowing me to close the other door and I knew I'd be found immediately. I started to panic. I heard one of the deliverymen talking.

"Hey, man, grab that tape measure from the truck. I don't think the door's wide enough. We gotta measure."

I got an idea and rooted around in my purse until I found some dental floss and quickly pulled off a long piece. I wrapped it around the screws on the inside of the door that attached the handle and pulled it shut. I then wrapped the dental floss around the screws holding both handles in place until the doors were tightly closed from the inside. It was dark and airless inside the armoire, just what I imagined being in a pine coffin would feel like, and I was starting to feel claustrophobic. Just when I thought I wouldn't be able to stand it, I felt the armoire tip backwards as it was being lifted. I braced myself and remained as motionless as possible.

"Damn, this thing is heavy!" exclaimed a strained voice I recognized as the driver's. "I must be tired 'cause I sure don't remember it being this heavy when we unloaded it."

"I just hope we can get this big bitch through the door. We already runnin' behind schedule," replied the other familiar-sounding man breathlessly.

"Just be happy we don't have to take it upstairs." I heard the other man murmur in agreement.

Technically speaking, I couldn't feel too insulted since they didn't know I was inside. But I was still embarrassed, and vowed to cut back on the pizza and hot fudge cake. I held my breath, foolishly thinking it might make me lighter. A few minutes later, after successfully navigating the front door, I felt the armoire being set down and tilted forward to an upright position. But in the process my sunglasses, which I'd stuffed in my pocket, fell out and hit the bottom of the armoire with a clatter.

"What was that?" I heard the driver ask.

"I don't know," said his partner. I thought I would wet myself as one of the men started trying to pull the doors open. But, I held on tight to my dental floss, wincing in pain as it bit into my fingers. The tug of war lasted about a minute before they finally stopped. I wasn't out of the woods yet.

"Ain't there a key to this thing?"

I looked down and saw a small keyhole under the handle of the door on the left-hand side.

"It must still be in the truck. I'll go look for it. Why don't you get that nurse to sign for the delivery?"

I listened closely to the footsteps as they left the room. I needed to get out quickly before they came back and discovered the key didn't work. I didn't hear any movement in the room so I unwrapped the dental floss, opened the doors and got out. I looked quickly around the small, minimally decorated bedroom. But, I soon found out I wasn't alone. As I headed towards the door of the bedroom, I heard a gasp of shock and whirled around. One of the deliverymen, the short older man with the baseball cap, was still in the room, sitting against the headboard of the bed. He was staring at me like he'd seen a ghost. I finally found out why his voice was so familiar.

"What in the hell? Kelly? What the fuck were you doin' in there?" exclaimed Lewis Watts. It was no wonder that I hadn't recognized him at first because he wasn't dressed in the Santa Super Fly gear that I'd seen him in at the Spotlight Bar & Grill. Today he looked like an everyday working man. "I'm waitin' for an answer, Miss Snotty," he said, lounging against the decorative pillows on the bed and, having taken off his baseball cap, no doubt smudging them with his hair pomade.

I glared at him. This was the last thing I expected and the last thing I needed. What could I say? I was busted big-time and for once didn't have an excuse. But Lewis didn't hesitate to come up with one for me.

"You been followin' me, ain't you? Wanna make up for bein' so mean to ole Lewis, huh?"

I couldn't have heard him right. Did he really think I was hiding inside furniture to get next to him? His ego was bigger than he was. I shifted nervously from foot to foot. I could tell he was enjoying my discomfort immensely. I decided to try and appeal to his sense of justice, knowing full well he probably didn't have one.

"Look, I'm here for a very important reason that has

nothing to do with you. An innocent young man could go to jail for the rest of his life for a crime he didn't commit. I need to talk to Nicole Rollins and this is the only way I could get in here to do it. Please, it's very important that you don't tell anyone I'm here," I pleaded. Lewis put his hands behind his head and leaned back farther.

"Is that right? So, you on some kinda secret mission, huh? You must think you James Bond or somethin'. Well, how much is keepin' me quiet worth to ya, baby doll?" he asked, leaning forward and patting the space next to him on the bed. "Why don't you set yo fine self on down over here next to me so we can get to know each other better?" He was grinning at me like a rat that just won the cheese lotto.

"Have you lost your damn mind?" I asked in amazement. While I was determined to talk to Nicole Rollins and try to help Timmy out of his situation, I was going to have to draw the line at being felt up by a repulsive little man who barely came up to my armpit.

"Then I think I'll tell that nurse she got an intruder so she can call the cops," he said angrily, getting up from the bed and heading towards the door. I could hear the driver talking to the nurse at the front door. I watched helplessly as Lewis started to walk out of the room with his back straight and head held high, the picture of righteous indignation. Then all of the sudden I remembered something he mentioned to me both times I'd seen him at The Spot.

"Hold up, player," I said before he got out the door.

He turned, smiling at me in triumph, and walked back over to where I was standing and started to put his arms around me. *Eww!*

"Aren't you on disability?" I asked casually. His arms froze in midair. "Yeah, that's what I thought. So, I guess Social Security won't be too happy if they find out you're delivering furniture when your back is supposed to be bad? I bet they're paying you under the table, right?"

"I don't know how they 'spect a man to live on them little checks," he said, bending over and clutching his lower back dramatically with both hands. I rolled my eyes. I could hear the voices of the driver and the nurse getting closer.

"Sounds like a personal problem to me. All I know is you've got about two seconds to forget you saw me here or I'm going to get on my phone to that hotline they're always advertising on TV. You know, the one about reporting disability fraud." Actually, the only hotline I knew about was to report cable theft but I could tell by the way Lewis's eyes were popping out of his head that he believed there was such a hotline.

"Damn, girl! You don't have to be like that. I thought we was friends." To demonstrate our so-called friendship, and to keep me from busting him, Lewis grabbed me and shoved me back inside the armoire just as his partner and the nurse walked through the door.

"Who you in here talking to?" I heard his partner ask.

"I was on my cell phone to my lady. You know how high maintenance she is, man. She can't get enough a ole Lewis." Both men laughed and I almost gagged.

"I found the key. Let's see if this works," said the driver. *Uh-oh,* I thought.

"Oh, I got it open, man, no problem. It was just stuck," said Lewis. "Now, if you'll just sign this, ma'am, we'll be goin'."

"Good, I'd really like to get back to my soaps. I didn't realize when I took this job I'd have to be the housekeeper, too," said the nurse, sounding highly pissed off.

"I hear that, sweetheart. Fine lookin' lady like you shouldn't be treated like no servant. So, what's wrong with Miz Rollins, anyway?" Lewis asked. I could hear their voices starting to get fainter and figured they had left the room and were headed towards the front door. I wanted to hear if the nurse told Lewis about Nicole so I got out of the armoire and hid behind the still open door to the bedroom. I heard the nurse saying something about a nervous breakdown. Did Nicole have a nervous breakdown? Lewis's charms apparently worked on some women, since the nurse had given him info she refused to give me.

From my hiding place behind the door, I watched the nurse close the door behind the deliverymen and head back to wherever in the house she had been watching her soap operas. With the day-to-day drama of real life, I wondered why anyone needed to watch soap operas. Most of us were living one every day, especially me. I quietly crept out of the room, finding myself back in the foyer. There was a double staircase leading up to the second floor. I sprinted quickly up the nearest staircase, severely overestimating my physical fitness, and had to lean against the railing overlooking the foyer to catch my breath.

Hanging on the wall behind me was a large formal family portrait of Reverend Rollins, Nicole, Rondell, Bonita, and Shanda. Inez wasn't in the picture. They were all smiling, but upon closer inspection, the smiles seemed a bit strained. Rollins, wearing the hell out of a gray pinstriped suit, was seated in a chair with his family standing around him. Nicole, beautifully dressed in a burgundy silk wrap dress, was standing behind Rollins with her hand on his shoulder and her long braids cascading down her back. In contrast, Rondell, Bonita, and Shanda looked like poor relations. Rondell's ill-fitting blue suit looked thirty years out of date. Bonita's striped dress was not only dowdy but made her hips look huge. Shanda, wearing a flowered dress with a lace collar, looked like she was twelve years old. I bet her mother had picked out the dress.

Both sides of the staircase led to separate hallways that met in the middle of a shared landing. I turned down the hallway on the side I'd come up on. At the end of the hall was a set of elaborate double doors that I hoped signified the master suite. I tried to pull the doors open but they were locked. I jiggled the handles in vain. Nicole must have really been in a bad way to have to be locked in her room. I looked in the decorative brass boxes on the marble-topped hall table just outside the room, thinking maybe the key might in one of them. No such luck. I had a sinking feeling I knew where the key was: in the pocket of the nurse's sweater.

I crept back down to the first floor and followed the path the nurse had taken after she'd shown the deliverymen out. I found myself in a formal dining room which led into a large black and gold gourmet kitchen. I tiptoed into the kitchen and saw the nurse with her back to me, sitting in a chair in the family room that opened up off the kitchen. She was watching *The Young and the Restless.* She was also still wearing the sweater. Wasn't she hot in that thing? I ducked down behind the large island that dominated the center of the kitchen to think. I needed that key. How in the world was I going to get it? I could turn up the heat on the thermostat, but it would take too long for it to get hot enough for her to take the sweater off. I needed to get into Nicole's room before her husband returned.

I peeked out from my hiding place and watched as the nurse took periodic sips from a large plastic tumbler of orange juice sitting on the long low table next to her. The table sat between the nurse's chair and a love seat. On the opposite end of the table, closest to the love seat, I spied a small key on a large plastic key ring. This had to be the key to Nicole's room. I was thrilled that it wasn't in her sweater pocket after all. But how was I going to get it? I didn't dare reach for it—she'd see me. I frantically looked around the kitchen for something I could use to distract the nurse. I finally found a nice big dead fly in the corner of the kitchen underneath a brass plant stand. I carefully picked up the fly by its wings and crawled up behind the nurse's chair. Just as I was ready to drop the fly in her juice, she picked up the tumbler. I was afraid she'd drain it but when she set it down again, I was happy to see there was still more than enough to achieve the desired effect. I dropped the fly in for its orange juice embalming and scurried back behind the island. There was always the chance that she wouldn't react the way I hoped. If not, I'd be screwed. If I found a fly floating belly up in my juice, considering where flies spend most of their time, I know I'd be seriously grossed out. I waited and a minute later, I was rewarded by the sound of a strangled gasp. I poked my head out in time to see the tumbler tossed into the air and it, along with the contents, landing on the gagging nurse. She jumped out of the chair cussing and spitting and covered in orange juice.

"Fuck, fuck, fuck," she growled. I watched her rub her tongue so hard it looked like she might rub off her taste buds. I truly hoped she hadn't swallowed the fly. In spite of my situation, I couldn't help but laugh.

"Is someone there?" I clamped my hand over my mouth before any more sound could escape. "Mrs. Rollins, is that you?" I was frozen to the spot as the nurse walked through the kitchen right past me into the dining room. All she had to do was turn around and I'd be toast. I held my breath and watched as she headed out of the dining room without looking back. I ran into the family room, grabbed the key off the table, and dove behind a leather couch as the nurse returned to the room. Lewis was right. This was some James Bond shit and I couldn't wait for it to be over. Timmy owed me big-time.

I looked to my right and saw another staircase. A quick peek revealed the nurse on all fours scrubbing orange juice from the carpet. I headed up the back staircase as quietly as possible, since the stairs weren't carpeted. I had no idea where I was but kept moving until I found myself once again on the landing overlooking the foyer. With key in hand, I approached the double doors to the master suite and let myself into the room, closing the doors behind me. The room was large, with a high ceiling and a hardwood floor covered with oriental rugs. Blue and gold curtains, embroidered with flowers, and cream sheers hung in the windows. Heavy mahogany furniture made the room look a little crowded. Vases filled with fresh flowers and family photos covered the tops of the dressers. A large stuffed bear reclined in a rocking chair by the bed. There was something a little odd about the room that I couldn't put my finger on.

I detected faint rustling sounds coming from the direction of the ornately carved four-poster bed. The bed's sheer curtains were drawn but I could hear Nicole tossing, turning, and thrashing around. She must be having quite a nightmare, and I wondered for the first time about the wisdom of trying to talk to her. If she had really had a nervous breakdown would I be able to get any sense out of her? And, more importantly, if she knew anything that could help Timmy, would the police believe her, given her current mental state? I approached the bed and Nicole cried out loudly, making me jump.

"She's dead! No, sweet Jesus," Nicole moaned and continued thrashing around.

Realizing that she must be talking about Inez, I felt the hair stand up on the back of my neck. I slowly parted the curtains and saw Nicole lying on her side facing me. She was tangled up in the bedsheets, with her long braids hanging in her face.

"Mrs. Rollins? Nicole, are you awake?" I gently touched her shoulder and she sighed and rolled onto her back. As she did, her braids fell away from her face and I gasped. I felt like I'd been kicked in the stomach. I looked wildly around the room at the family pictures, noticing they were of Inez as a cheerleader, Inez at the prom, Inez on Santa's knee, and realizing why the room seemed so odd. This wasn't Morris and Nicole's bedroom. It must be Inez's old room, and the sleeping woman I was looking down at was not Nicole Rollins but Inez Rollins.

Chapter 12

Before I could fully grasp that I was looking at a woman everybody in town, including the police, thought was dead, Inez sat straight up and screamed at the top of her lungs.

"Daddy, don't!" Inez began flailing and swinging her arms like a psychotic windmill looking for a fight. I tried to calm her down and caught a forearm to the forehead, smashing me right in my swollen knot and sending me flying backwards off the bed onto the floor with a loud thud. I was paralyzed for a few minutes until I heard rapidly approaching footsteps. I rolled under the bed. I heard the door to the bedroom swing open, and saw a pair of chubby legs encased in white stockings ending in orthopedic loafers run across the room.

"Mrs. Rollins, are you all right?" I heard the panicked nurse ask. Inez's only response was a loud snore. "You scared me half to death. I thought you fell out of bed," the nurse whispered to Inez's sleeping form.

The nurse had called Inez Mrs. Rollins, not Ms. Rollins. She thought the woman she was taking care of was Nicole and that could only mean that Morris Rollins was passing Inez off as Nicole. It also meant that Nicole must be dead. I needed to get out of the house and take my newfound revelation to Harmon and Mercer. I felt like a huge weight had been lifted from my shoulders. Timmy couldn't be held responsible for the death of a woman who wasn't dead, which meant he'd have to be cleared of all suspicion. He could come out of hiding, and Olivia could have her surgery. I was happier than anyone hiding under someone else's bed had a right to be. I watched as the nurse headed towards the bedroom door. Once she left, I could make my escape. However, I should have known it wasn't going to be that easy. I saw the nurse's legs stop, pausing at the bedroom door. I poked my head out a bit farther and saw her looking at the keyhole. Damn. She must have realized the door should have been locked. I hadn't thought to lock it behind me when I came in.

"I could have sworn I locked this door. What in the world is going on around here?" she said aloud. My heart sank as I watched the nurse walk back towards the bed and stop.

"Are you really asleep, or are you faking?" I heard her ask Inez. Of course, there was no response, as Inez was really sleeping. But the nurse was undeterred. "You can pretend all you want, Mrs. Rollins. I don't know how you're doing it but I know you've been sneaking out of this room. I'm going to sit right here next to this bed until your husband gets home." The nurse then removed the large stuffed teddy bear from the rocking chair by the bed and proceeded to sit down.

I felt like crying. Plus, I was starting to feel a bit claustrophobic. I waited, hoping she would realize Inez was really asleep and leave the room. No such luck. The nurse sat rocking back and forth, humming Broadway show tunes to herself. I was treated to a tuneless medley that included "Hello Dolly," "If I Were A Rich Man," "There's A Place For Us," and "Oklahoma!" It was hot under the bed and I was getting cramped from lying in the same position for so long. Sweat started trickling down my face, making the knot on my forehead itch. Heat makes me sleepy and that, combined with the nurse's humming and Inez's soft snoring, was lulling me into a stupor. With no place to go and nothing to do but wait, I drifted off to sleep, hoping like hell I didn't start snoring myself.

I woke in a panic after a bizarre dream about marrying Lewis Watts while wearing the ugly blue maid-of-honor dress, not remembering where I was, and unable to move. When I finally remembered my predicament, I looked out from under the bed to see that the nurse was no longer sitting in the rocker. Her chubby gams had been replaced by a man's long legs clad in brown slacks with a pair of enormous feet shod in expensive leather loafers. The lord of the manor had returned. As much as I wanted to roll out from under the bed and demand he tell me what the hell was going on, I had to get out of the house, quickly. Somehow I didn't think Rollins would remember his offers of hugs and conversation if he found me hiding in his house. As nice as he'd been to me, I didn't want to incur the man's wrath, especially since he appeared to have faked his daughter's death. Who knew what else he was capable of?

I thought back to the funeral and the heavily veiled, dazed-looking woman Rollins had told me was Nicole. Had Rollins actually had the balls to pass off his doped-up, very-much-alive daughter as his wife at her own funeral? If

Inez was being drugged and locked in her room, was it for her own safety or to keep her from telling who'd really killed Nicole? Then I remembered Inez calling out the words, "Daddy, don't," in her sleep. Don't what? What didn't Inez want her father to do? If I had to guess, with my choices being "Don't kill Nicole," "don't kill me," or "don't run with scissors," I'm sure I'd be closer to the truth in choosing one of the first two. Was Morris Rollins a murderer? My heart sank.

I heard the shrill chirp of a cell phone ringing. Rollins answered it with a terse hello.

"Slow down, Bonita, I can't understand a word you're saying." He sounded like his patience was evaporating like water drops on a hot griddle. "What? He knows? He knows what?" Rollins paused to listen to whatever his sister-in-law was telling him. Then I heard him groan. I took a chance, peeked out, and saw him leaning forward in the rocker with his forehead resting in the palm of his hand. The cell phone was still in his other hand, pressed against his ear. Bonita was talking so loudly that I could hear her under the bed. But I couldn't hear what she was saying, just a loud buzzing chatter emanating from the phone.

"Oh, my God," I heard Rollins whisper softly. It didn't sound like good news.

"Where is he now? Okay, Bonita. Now, calm down and tell me where you are." Rollins stood up and I heard him walking slowly towards the bedroom door. "I want you to meet me at the church in an hour, you hear me? Good." Rollins was headed out the door when a voice stopped him.

"Daddy?" Rollins was back across the room and by his daughter's bedside in two strides.

"Hey, baby girl. What are you doing awake? You're

supposed to be getting your rest." I felt Inez shifting in the bed above me.

"Where you going, Daddy?" Inez sounded groggy and weak.

"I'll be right back, baby. You just lie back down and get some sleep. Here, it's about time for another pill."

"Don't want no more pills. Daddy, we gotta tell 'em. We gotta tell 'em." I heard Inez's voice trail off into a sigh then heard her breathing heavily; she must have fallen back to sleep. Rollins stood by the bed for another minute to make sure she was asleep and then quickly left the room.

I rolled out from under the bed. A quick peek at the clock on the bedside table told me it was almost three o'clock. I'd been under the bed for two hours and my limbs felt numb. My stomach had an imprint of my purse on it, which I'd been laying on top of the whole time. I looked down at Inez, who had indeed fallen back into a deep slumber. I wondered what she wanted to tell and to whom she wanted to tell it. I resisted an urge to try and wake her. I had to tell Harmon and Mercer she was still alive. Whatever secret Inez was keeping, Harmon and Mercer could deal with it. Being trapped under a bed for two hours gives a person amazing perspective. I left the room and crept down the steps.

I heard Rollins talking to someone, probably the nurse, in another room and decided to make a break for it. I quietly unlocked the front door, stepped out into the afternoon sunshine, gently pulled the door shut behind me, and hurried down the driveway to my car. I jumped into the driver's seat and started to put the key in the ignition when I felt fingers twisting into the hair on the back of my head. I yelped and tried to get out of the car and was pulled back against the driver's seat by the collar of my jacket. I looked into the rearview mirror and was greeted by the sight of Vaughn Castle. I felt something sharp poking me in my neck and realized with horror that it was the Swiss Army knife Mrs. Carson had given me. I had dropped it on my porch in my excitement over seeing Carl and had completely forgotten about it until now. Vaughn must have been at my apartment.

"Your granny ain't here to save your ass this time, bitch," he said in a hissing lisp, like his tongue was having a hard time adjusting to the extra spaces left by his missing teeth. I seriously doubted drug dealing provided any kind of a dental plan and sincerely hoped he'd be snaggle-toothed for the rest of his life.

"What do you want?" I asked. I kept my eyes on him in the mirror.

"Just start this raggedy muthafucka and drive. I'll tell you where to go."

I did as I was told and Vaughn told me to drive towards the wooded area at the back of the Briar Creek development. Once I stopped the car, he reached between the seats and took my keys from the ignition. I looked around desperately for someone whose eye I could catch who could run for help. But all I could see were trees, dirt, and litter. There was nobody around who could help me. Vaughn kept the knife's tip pressed against my neck with one hand while he had a firm grip on my jacket collar with the other. I had rolled out from under Inez's bed and landed right in a pile of shit.

"Where's Milton?" he asked. I could feel and smell his hot foul breath against my cheek and wondered how I had failed to notice his odor of stale beer, cologne, and funk when I'd gotten in the car. I felt like throwing up.

"I don't know where he is," I replied truthfully, trying hard not to move my head.

"Liar," he said, poking me in the back of the head. "I know you tight with him and his mom. Shanda told me. So I know you know where his ass is."

"Why do you hate him so much?" I wanted to keep him talking, mainly to buy time, but also to see if his story matched Timmy's.

"That's none a your fuckin' business, bitch." I felt a spray of spittle on my neck. Yuck! Telling him to "say it, don't spray it" would probably earn me a fist in the face, or worse, a knife in my jugular, so I gritted my teeth and kept silent as visions of him cutting me into tiny pieces flooded my brain. I looked at him again in the rearview mirror and realized by his red, glassy eyes that he was high as a kite.

"He was hiding out at my place but he told me he was going back to Detroit. I haven't seen him in a week," I offered, hoping to appease him.

"I don't believe that shit. Shanda told me—"

"Did you know Shanda tried to kill herself?" I asked, quickly cutting him off in the hope he would let down his guard. Instead, he just tightened his grip on my collar and laughed like I'd just told him a big joke.

"Well, I guess it's a good thing I cut that silly ho loose. She was gettin' way too clingy, anyway. She wasn't a bad lay. Matter a fact, I used to bring her out here to this very spot to fuck her. But she couldn't give good head to save her life. Made her practice on bananas and she still couldn't get the shit right."

Now *there* was a mental image I really didn't need. "You broke up with Shanda?" I knew her suicide attempt had something to do with this loser. Shanda loved Vaughn so much she'd helped him frame an innocent man for her cousin's murder only to have him dump her. She must have been devastated. "She loved you. She slit her wrist, probably over you. Don't you even care that she almost died?"

"Shanda don't love me any more than I love her. She's just a sad little girl lookin' for attention. She don't care where she get it from. If she really wanted to kill herself, she'd a done it. Let me guess, her mom or her pops found her in time, right?"

"She loved you enough to help you frame Timmy, didn't she? Why did you kill Inez, anyway?"

"I didn't kill that ho! I went to see that bitch to tell her to stop runnin' me down behind my back and when I got there her ass was already dead with half her face splattered against the wall," he said, clutching my collar tighter.

Which would have made it easy for Rollins to lie and identify Nicole as Inez. But, why? Did Vaughn mistake Nicole for Inez because of their braids, and kill her? Did Inez witness the murder and Rollins was trying to protect her?

"And then you decided to frame Timmy. He must have really screwed you over pretty bad. You don't strike me as the kind of man who would let himself be played." That hit a nerve, and I saw Vaughn's jaw clench.

"Not me, my boy Ricky Maynard. Milton's the reason Ricky's dead and I'm gonna make that muthafucka pay. Ricky got run down like a damn dog in the street chasing Milton's ass. That nigga thinks he can bring me down like he did Ricky. But he 'bout to find out who he messin' wit. I'm bulletproof. Can't nobody get wit me," he said, breathing down my neck. From the little bit he'd told me, his story seemed to match Timmy's, except for that last part, which just sounded plain crazy.

"Timmy didn't know Inez or have any reason to kill her. It shouldn't take long for the police to figure out that the one person who had a reason to hurt her was you." He let go of my collar and grabbed a handful of my hair, pulling my head back against the seat. If I got out of this alive, I was going to have one hell of a headache.

"I told you I didn't kill her. But, since you think you so smart, bitch, answer me this: If I killed Inez, why would I bother putting a bloody tissue in Milton's car when I could have just planted the piece on him?"

The gun. It had completely slipped my mind. No one had ever mentioned the gun. It wasn't in any of the articles I'd read about the murder. I'd figured the police were withholding information on the murder weapon.

"You mean it wasn't there at the scene?" I asked in a whisper.

"I'm tired of answering questions. It's time you answered mine. Where is Milton? I need to know so the police can get another anonymous call about his location." I felt the knife press against my neck breaking the skin. A small warm trickle of blood ran down inside my collar.

I realized that, no matter what I did or didn't tell him, he was going to kill me, anyway. There was no way he could let me go. I knew too much. I thought about my family and how devastated they'd be when Harmon and Mercer broke the news of finding my body in the deserted, wooded area that Vaughn was sure to drag it into. I wondered if they'd be able to find all of me. I started to cry, which pissed him off.

"Did you hear me? Where's Milton?" he asked again, louder this time. I cried even harder, lapsing into hiccupping, heaving sobs.

"Here I am, bitch!" came a familiar voice from outside the car. The passenger door on the driver's side flew open and I watched in the rearview mirror as Timmy Milton dragged Vaughn Castle ass-backwards out of the car and proceeded to administer a beat-down worthy of Mike Tyson in his prime.

Timmy had caught Vaughn off guard and had him on the ground so quickly that all he could do, in the face of all the kicks and blows Timmy was raining down on him, was to flail pitifully at Timmy's legs with the Swiss Army knife, which he'd somehow managed to hold on to. I jumped out of the car and stomped on his wrist, causing him to let go of the knife, and kicked it underneath my car. Timmy aimed a punch at Vaughn's face. Vaughn managed to move his head, but still caught the brunt of the blow on his temple. He was out cold.

Timmy and I stood staring at each other. I was still sniveling. Timmy was panting hard like he'd just run a marathon. He came over and put his arm around me.

"You okay, Kendra?"

"I'll be all right," I said, wiping my face with the back of my hand. "How in the world did you know where to find me?"

"I been followin' this fool. Saw him sneak into the back a your ride. I didn't want to cause no scene in that ritzy neighborhood and have them callin' the police so I followed y'all out here. Woulda been here sooner but that brokedown whip I was drivin' stalled out at the stop sign back there. I had to leave it parked in the street. I ran all the way down here."

"Why were you following Vaughn?" I asked, looking down at the man in question and suppressing an urge to kick him.

"Better to be the hunter than the hunted. Know what I'm sayin'?" he asked, then, sensing my confusion, explained himself. "I figured if I was followin' him, I'd know what his ass was up to. I was goin' crazy sittin' around waitin' for his punk ass to find me. I wasn't feelin' that at all. So, after he attacked you, I started tailin' him—"

"Wait a minute," I said, holding up my hand to stop him. "How did you know he attacked me?" Timmy stared at me with an annoying smirk but didn't answer. Vaughn started moaning and we both stared at him, panic-stricken.

"We need to tie his ass up before he comes to. You wait here," Timmy said, searching Vaughn's pockets and pulling out a set of car keys. "I'll be right back," he said, after seeing the look of fear on my face.

Timmy ran off in the direction he'd come from, leaving me alone with the unconscious Vaughn. I got on my hands and knees and retrieved the knife from under my car, just in case, and picked up my car keys, which Vaughn had dropped when he was pulled from the car. I spotted an orange plastic jump rope in the weeds by my car and grabbed it. I started to tie Vaughn's hands with it but was too afraid to touch him. I waited for Timmy. Minutes later he returned, driving Vaughn's Escalade.

"Where'd you get his car?"

"He parked it a block over from where you was parked. Help me turn this mutha over." We turned Vaughn over and Timmy pressed his knee in Vaughn's back, in case he woke up, while I used the jump rope to tie his hands tightly behind his back. My hands were shaking and sweating badly, which was a good thing, since I hoped it would keep my prints from sticking to the plastic rope. I then helped Timmy lift Vaughn into the back of his Escalade. No easy feat since he was dead weight. I spied something blue on the floor in the back seat. It was the blue scarf that he'd used to strangle Aretha Marshall. I got a chill as I realized he must have been watching me that night and seen me drop it in the street. I could feel myself getting angry just thinking about Aretha's blue lips and swollen face. I balled up the scarf and stuffed it in Vaughn's mouth.

Timmy locked the car and wiped off the keys and everything else we'd touched with his shirtsleeve. He wrapped the keys up in a dirty discarded diaper found lying not far from the spot where I'd found the jump rope. He lobbed the diaper like a grenade deep into the woods. He took the Swiss Army knife and sunk it to the hilt several times in each one of the Escalade's tires. When Vaughn woke up, he'd be in for one hell of a surprise. Timmy and I got into my car and drove away, leaving a still unconscious Vaughn locked in his undriveable car. It would probably be a while before anyone would find him, giving me plenty of time to report both of his attacks on me to the police.

I drove Timmy back to the car he'd been driving, a rusted-out orange Chevy pickup truck that I'd never seen before, which was indeed parked right in the middle of the street with a couple of angry motorists gathered around it. One had pulled out a cell phone and was no doubt about to call the police. Timmy jumped out to assure them that the car would be moved quickly. I had to give him a jump to get it started, after which Timmy proceeded to drive off without even looking back. I called out after him but he didn't stop, and left me standing in the middle of the street in a cloud of exhaust. Damn! I didn't even get a chance to tell him about Inez being alive. Feeling pissed off, frustrated, and quite dirty, I quickly hopped into my own car and took off.

I headed for the police station, which took me straight past Holy Cross Church. The parking lot was empty of cars except for a gold Mercedes Benz and a brown Lincoln Town Car. I looked at my watch and realized Morris Rollins was probably at Holy Cross meeting with Bonita at that very moment. I wondered what was going on and if it had anything to do with the fact that Rollins was hiding Inez.

I'd overheard Rollins saying something about someone knowing something. I wondered whom he and Bonita had been talking about and what this person might know. My curiosity got the best of me—again. Vowing that this would be my last act of snooping before going to Harmon and Mercer, I parked my car across the street from the church and got out. I pulled my coat tightly around me, crossed the street, and headed across the parking lot. I hoped no one would notice me and get suspicious, but since I was dirty, wearing wrinkled clothes, had matted hair, and a knotted up forehead, I figured anyone who did see me would just think I was in need of Jesus and therefore in the right place.

The door to the church was unlocked, but the atrium was dark and empty. Upon entering, I saw a glow of light underneath Rollins's closed office door and crept up to it. I pressed my ear to the door but heard nothing. I heard voices coming from behind me in the direction of the church's basement steps. It was Rollins and Bonita, and they were arguing. Their voices were getting closer. I quickly ducked inside Rollins's office.

"Well, how much does he know, Bonita?" I heard an exasperated Rollins ask his sister-in-law.

"He knows Shanda might not be his daughter," I heard Bonita say in a trembling, tear-filled voice. "It's like I told you. The hospital didn't have enough of Shanda's blood type on hand. So they were going to have me, or Rondell, donate blood for her transfusion. I wasn't a match so Rondell said he'd donate his blood and…and…" Bonita was unable to finish her sentence and dissolved into a fit of loud, snot-filled sobbing.

"I understand, Bonita. It's okay. I know you had to tell him. We should have told him the truth years ago. Does he know I might be Shanda's father?" Rollins asked gently.

"Yes, I tried to explain but he...he called me a...a...whore and just took off. I haven't seen him since. Oh, Morris, what are we gonna do?"

"What we aren't going to do is get hysterical. I'll try and find Rondell. Don't you need to get back to the hospital to check on Shanda?"

"Yes," Bonita said, then blew her nose loudly before continuing. "They said I could take her home this evening if she was feeling better. Oh, my God! What am I gonna tell her? She'll be asking for her daddy. What do I tell her?"

"Just tell her he'll be home soon. You can do this, Bonita. Now, can I count on you to pull yourself together?"

I peeked through the doorjamb and saw Bonita nod mutely.

"Promise me you'll find him, Morris. We have to make him understand."

"I will, sweetheart. Now, you go and take care of Shanda." I watched as Rollins ushered Bonita out the door before turning and walking towards his office.

Crap! *Here I go again,* I thought as I flattened myself against the wall behind the door. But, to my great relief, Rollins just stuck his hand inside the door, flipped off the light, and pulled the office door shut, locking it. I heard his retreating footsteps as he left the church. I breathed out a sigh of relief. Then I realized that while I probably wasn't locked in Rollins's office, I was most likely locked inside the church. I waited a few minutes, then left the office to check the church's front doors to find that they were indeed locked. I frantically fumbled around the dark church hoping to find a way out, with no luck. All the doors and windows were locked tight. Resigned to my fate, I reluctantly returned to Rollins's office.

I sat at his desk, resisting the urge to turn the lights on as they might attract unwanted attention. It was only then that

I was able to give some thought to what I'd overheard. Morris Rollins might be Shanda's real father. I thought hard about Shanda. Did she resemble Rollins in any way? As far as I could tell, Shanda looked more like Bonita than either Rollins or Rondell. I wondered how she'd take the news. Would it matter at all to her that Inez might not be her cousin but her half sister? And, how would Inez feel knowing that her father had cheated on her mother with her uncle's wife? Boy, Rollins sure had a mess on his hands. But somehow I knew he'd come out unscathed, smelling like a rose, and possibly with a new daughter to boot. And Bonita? I tried hard to imagine prim and proper Bonita Kidd and Morris Rollins in the throes of passion. I could feel an attack of the giggles welling up in me as an image of a naked Bonita popped into my head—hair loose and flowing, mouth open, head flung back—straddling Rollins and riding him hard, like he was the odds-on favorite at the Kentucky Derby who'd fallen into last place.

Then an image of a heartbroken Rondell Kidd popped into my head. Horrible fashion sense aside, he seemed like such a nice man. I remembered the pride in his face when he talked about Shanda's beautiful singing voice and how terrified he'd been when she'd been rushed to the hospital. How could he possibly handle the fact that his only child might not be his and—to make matters even worse—she might have been fathered by his own brother, a brother who was rumored to already have more children than he was supposed to? If Shanda hadn't tried to commit suicide, the truth may never have come out. Would Morris and Bonita ever have confessed? My guess was no. I was happy this wasn't my problem. I had my own problems, the most pressing one being how I was going to get out of the locked church. I supposed if I wanted out badly enough I could call someone. But there was no excuse that I could come up with that would explain my being here in the first place. How in the world could I explain being locked inside Holy Cross Church to Mama? She'd immediately think I'd been involved in some kind of tryst with the reverend. Although, technically speaking, he was now a widower twice over.

I rooted through Rollins's desk in hopes of finding a set of keys to the front door or any door, for that matter. No such luck. But I did, however, find a big bag of miniature Hershey bars in his bottom drawer. I hungrily tore open the bag and began eating. I hadn't had anything to eat since my hot fudge cake earlier in the day. Could a woman live on chocolate alone? I was about to find out. Since I had time to kill, I snooped through the rest of the desk drawers.

I didn't find anything of much interest at first, just several boxes of Kleenex, a bottle of antacids, an assortment of pens, pencils, and pads of notebook paper, telephone books, a nail clipper, a multitude of file folders, and a bottle of cologne. I was half expecting to find condoms and porn magazines, but not at all surprised when I didn't. I halfheartedly flipped through the folders but most of them just contained receipts, order forms, applications and lots of bills for work done or about to be done on Holy Cross. The pile of bills I'd flipped through on his desk before was nothing compared to what was filed in the desk drawer. Bills for work done on the roof, plumbing bills, repairs on the building's foundation, landscaping bills, and so forth and so on. It appeared that Holy Cross's upkeep was costing a small fortune. No wonder Rollins asked so much of his congregation. He'd told me every dime went back into the church, but apparently donations didn't cover everything. How could the reverend live so lavishly, and support a much younger wife with expensive tastes, when Holy Cross was such a money pit? Unless Reverend Rollins was dipping into the donations to support his lush lifestyle and leaving Holy Cross's upkeep to suffer. Was that the reason he had been so hot to cash in on an insurance policy on someone who wasn't even dead? Did he need the money to live on? Whatever his reason, he was risking jail time for fraud if I was right.

I refiled the folders in the correct order and tried closing the drawer. But it wouldn't close all the way. Something was stuck in back of the drawer, preventing it from closing all the way. I had to remove the entire drawer to reach it. It was another unmarked file folder. In the folder I found copies of three huge life insurance checks. All the checks were made out to Morris Rollins. Each check was attached to a copy of a death certificate. I could feel my stomach start to knot up as I flipped through the file. The names on the death certificates were Richard Charles Maynard, Gina Camille Parks, and Joseph Robert Porter. For some reason, Richard Maynard's name was familiar to me. Morris Rollins was listed as the father on all three death certificates. Wasn't Vaughn Castle's dead friend named Ricky Maynard? But something else about that name tugged at my memory. I saw that the mother's name on the certificate was listed as Vera Maynard. Then it hit me: Vera Maynard was Mattie Lyons's unfortunate niece who'd had an affair with Rollins years ago. She was the girl Mama always talked about. Richard must have been the result of that affair and he was also apparently Vaughn Castle's dead friend Ricky. I looked at his death certificate and saw the cause of death was listed as vehicular homicide. Morris Rollins had been awarded a life insurance check for one hundred thousand dollars when Ricky met his unfortunate demise at the tender age of twenty-five. I looked at the other certificates.

Gina Parks had been the daughter of Morris Rollins and Melvina Carmichael Parks. Good gravy! The reverend and the Christian romance writer? No wonder Melvina had given me such a contemptuous look when she'd seen me waiting in this office for Rollins. They had a bond because of their child. And even if the child was dead, Melvina still must have deep feelings for the reverend. Why was I so shocked? Hadn't I, and the entire town of Willow, been hearing rumors about his illegitimate children for years? It was like finding out that a mythical race of humans actually existed. I read on and saw that Gina's death was attributed to anaphylactic shock at the age of sixteen almost three years ago. I vaguely remembered reading something in the paper a few years ago about a teenaged girl dying from a bee sting. Could this have been the same girl? Rollins had received a mere twenty-five thousand dollars in life insurance upon Gina's death.

Lastly there was Joseph Porter. His mother was listed as Carla Porter. Her name wasn't familiar to me. Joseph's death had been an accidental drowning at the age of eighteen, almost five years ago. Rollins received a check for seventy-five thousand dollars when Joseph died.

I sat in Rollins's empty office and stared at the love seat I'd sat on only a week before. I couldn't believe I'd been ready to succumb to the charms of a man who obviously took the love, affection, and admiration of the women around him as his due. Hadn't the man ever heard of condoms? How many other children did he have? Were they dead, too? Either Morris Rollins had the worst luck of anyone I'd ever seen when it came to personal tragedy or there was something

much more sinister at work here. And just how did
Inez figure in to all of this? I took the file with the info on
Rollins's deceased children and put it in my purse. I knew
Harmon and Mercer would be very interested in seeing it
when I finally got a chance to get to the police station. Until
then, I settled myself in for the long night ahead.

Chapter 13

The sound of voices outside the office door woke me up. Bright sunlight streamed into the office through the colored block glass windows that overlooked the parking lot. Remembering where I was, I quickly jumped up off of the love seat that I'd slept on. My neck was stiff from sleeping in a cramped position and my mouth tasted like stale chocolate. But I put that out of my mind as I frantically looked around for a hiding place. The voices outside the office were female, and judging from their conversation, they were there to clean the church. I could hear every word of what they were saying but they didn't seem about to enter the office, at least not yet. I waited, and ten minutes later they'd moved to another part of the church. I opened the door a crack and, seeing no one in sight, ran like my tail was on fire straight out the front doors. I didn't stop until I got to my car.

It was a little after seven when I got home. Not wanting

to waste any time in getting to the police station to tell Harmon and Mercer what I'd found out, I took a quick shower, and scarfed down a bowl of Cap'n Crunch. I turned on my TV as I dressed and was about to turn it off when the morning news came on and a familiar face flashed onto the screen, stopping me cold. It was Vaughn Castle. I turned up the TV and sat down heavily on the edge of my bed. According to Tracey Ripkey, Channel Four's star news reporter—whose hair seemed to get bigger and blonder with each newscast—Vaughn Castle's body had been found tied up in the back seat of his vandalized car. He'd been beaten and shot in the head. The camera cut to a shot of Vaughn's Escalade being towed away. I noticed that the back window on the driver's side was shattered. Ripkey then started interviewing people in the crowd that had gathered at the scene behind the police barrier.

"I was telling my husband just the other day that something bad was going to happen out here," sniffed a prim white woman in a red pantsuit who looked like a poster child for the upwardly mobile. "We live down the street and when we bought our house we were told this entire area was going to be developed. That was two years ago and it still looks like a jungle back here. We moved here to get away from this sort of thing. If we knew there would be this kind of trouble out here we'd have never come." There was a murmur of agreement among the others in the crowd.

The camera switched back to Ripkey. "Police have several witnesses who reported seeing two suspicious vehicles in this area yesterday afternoon. One was an orange Chevy pickup truck and the other was a small blue car that may have been either a Nova or an Escort. The victim, Vaughn Castle, was a known drug dealer with prior convictions for drug trafficking. Police believe his death may be the result of a drug deal gone wrong. Whatever the reason, the residents of Briar Creek will have a hard time regaining their peace of mind. I'm Tracey Ripkey, reporting live from Willow. Back to you, John."

I stood up shakily, feeling as if the room was spinning out of control. I barely made it to the bathroom in time before throwing up my cereal. I finally pulled my head out of the toilet, brushed my teeth, and splashed water on my face. The first thing that popped into my head was the last thing I wanted to think about. If the police found out it had been Timmy and me with Vaughn, and that we'd tied him up and put him in his car, they'd arrest us on the spot for his murder, no questions asked. I was already in trouble for helping a fugitive. The fact that Vaughn had set up Timmy would just be our motive for Vaughn's murder. I remembered back to Timmy wiping everything down before we left and managed to convince myself that, despite our cars having been spotted, nothing that had happened the day before could be traced back to us. Vaughn had probably been killed by another drug dealer, possibly one of the thuglets I'd seen with him at The Spot who was trying to make a name for himself. Either way, it wasn't my problem.

I'd just go to Harmon and Mercer as planned, show them the folder, and tell them that Inez was still alive. They could talk to Inez and find out what really happened that night. Timmy would be cleared. Olivia could have her surgery. I could go on with my life. All would be right with the world. I was feeling so much better. I'd feel even better if Shanda had a change of heart and was willing to come clean. But I knew I couldn't count on Shanda. Even though Vaughn had dumped her like yesterday's trash, people had a way of elevating the dead to sainthood, purging themselves of every bad memory of the deceased. Shanda was probably still very much in love with Vaughn and still unwilling to say a word against him. I wondered if she even knew he was dead. The police could deal with her, too.

I got up, put my coat on, flung my purse over my shoulder, and headed for the front door feeling quite pleased with myself. Funny, how things can change in an instant. I opened the door and saw two police cars pull up in front of my duplex. I stood frozen in my doorway. Were they there for me? I decided I didn't want to find out. I slammed my door shut, ran to my bedroom, and climbed out the window. I jumped down into the backyard from the roof of Mrs. Carson's back porch. I almost twisted my ankle but managed to run down the alley behind the house just as I heard the police pounding on the door demanding to be let in. I found myself on a side street. Panting, I looked up the block and saw, to my relief, a city bus coming down the street towards me. It stopped at the corner and I hurried to catch it before it pulled off. I bought a daily pass and headed to an empty seat in the back to think. What in the world was I going to do? Did the police find out what happened with Vaughn? I knew I shouldn't worry. I was innocent, after all. Well, innocent of murder, at any rate. But visions of prison and a cellmate named Big Bertha loomed in my mind. I'd never even gotten so much as a parking ticket. Now this.

I rode around on the bus for two hours, too afraid to get off for fear the police would be waiting for me. Bus fumes and being wedged between two cleanliness-challenged people were making me sick to my stomach. I finally decided to get off at the library after a wild-eyed woman started hissing at me. She was wearing a matted, full-length fur coat buttoned up to her chin, high-topped tennis shoes, and smelled strongly of cough syrup and cat piss. When I asked her what her problem was, she accused me of fucking her boyfriend Woody. No amount of denials on my part convinced her that Woody and I weren't getting it on regularly behind her back. When I tried to tell her I didn't even know anyone named Woody, she pulled a ragged stuffed Woody Woodpecker doll out of her enormous handbag, threw it at me, then proceeded to laugh maniacally just like the cartoon woodpecker. As I hurriedly stepped off the bus into the cold fresh air, I could hear her accusing some other poor innocent soul of fucking Woody.

The library was fairly crowded for that time of the morning, but I was able to find a comfortable leather chair near the magazines and newspapers. I grabbed a copy of the newspaper from the stand. Vaughn Castle's murder was front-page news. The article didn't tell me anything that I hadn't already heard on the news. My stomach growled loudly and I rummaged around in my purse for the remainder of the miniature Hershey bars I'd stolen from Rollins's office. Disappointed at not being able to find any more chocolate, I pulled out the file I'd also stolen from the office. Realizing I had nothing but time and was in the perfect place to get more info on Rollins's deceased children, I headed over to the periodicals desk.

"May I help you?" asked the bored-looking male librarian sporting a mullet and a shaggy mustache with crumbs from his breakfast nesting in it.

"I need to look up some info on three accidental deaths. How would I go about doing that?"

"First off, do you know the names of the deceased, and the dates and places where the deaths occurred?" he asked, looking quite reenergized, like he'd been waiting all morning for someone to ask him a question.

"Yes, I have the names. One of the deaths occurred here in town, one in Springfield, and the other in Detroit, Michigan," I said, flipping through the file folder.

"Well, we have the *Willow News-Gazette* and the *Springfield News-Sun* on microfilm as far back as the 1890s. But we stopped getting the *Detroit Free Press* about five years ago when we had to cut our periodicals budget," he whispered like he'd just spilled a state secret. "You might be able to find that info on the Internet but we won't be getting Internet access until next year. You might try over at the college."

I really didn't need to know any more about Ricky Maynard's death. I'd already gotten all the info I needed from Timmy, Vaughn, and Ricky's death certificate. It was the deaths of Gina Parks and Joseph Porter that most interested me. I gave the librarian the dates and waited while he pulled two rolls of microfilm from a large drawer. He set me up on a microfilm reader then rushed off to help another patron.

I looked for info on Gina Parks's death first and finally found the headline TEEN DIES OF BEE STING AT CHURCH PICNIC at the end of the roll of microfilm. I printed it out and read it:

A sixteen-year-old is believed to have died from an allergic reaction to a bee sting during a church picnic at College Park. Gina Parks was taken to Willow Memorial Hospital after being discovered unconscious in her mother's car and was pronounced dead on arrival. Parks's mother, Christian romance writer Melvina Carmichael, claims her daughter had numerous allergies and wasn't always diligent about

carrying her EpiPen with her. Parks was a student at Spring-
mont High School, were she was a standout on the girls' bas-
ketball team. Funeral services are pending.

I noticed the article didn't mention how they knew she'd
been stung by a bee. If she had other allergies, then any one
of them could have killed her. I searched the entire roll of
microfilm but never found any further info on Gina's death
other than her obit, which stated that she was an only child
survived by her mother. I loaded the other roll of microfilm.
I didn't have to hunt very long for the article on Joseph
Porter's death, MISSING MAN'S BODY FOUND IN RESERVOIR:

The body of eighteen-year-old Willow resident Joseph Porter
was found in Clarence J. Brown Reservoir. Porter was reported
missing during an outing with his church on Saturday, July
12th. His grandmother, Rosalie Porter, reported him missing
when he didn't return home after the annual Holy Cross
Church barbecue. He was last seen by a member of the church,
who claimed Porter said he was going for a swim. According
to his grandmother, Porter didn't know how to swim and only
went to the picnic to help with the barbecuing. Porter was an
aspiring chef who was a freshman culinary student at Akron
University. The investigation of Porter's death is on hold,
pending the outcome of his autopsy results.

I searched further and found another article about
Porter's death a month later, titled DROWNING DEATH
RULED AN ACCIDENT.

The death of eighteen-year-old Willow resident Joseph Porter,
whose body was found in Clarence J. Brown Reservoir, has been

ruled an accident. Porter, who went missing during a church barbecue, drowned while swimming in the reservoir. His clothes were found in his car, and according to the Clark County medical examiner, his autopsy results are consistent with an accidental drowning. The investigation into Porter's death turned up no evidence of foul play.

Two suspicious deaths during Holy Cross Church outings seemed more than a little fishy to me. The fact that they were both illegitimate children of Morris Rollins, and he benefited greatly from the deaths of all three of his children, left me feeling sick to my stomach. Either Rollins was the unluckiest father alive or he had caused the deaths of his own children for the insurance money. But, in spite of my suspicions, I still couldn't figure out why Inez's death had been faked and why he would risk trying to claim the life insurance. I printed out both articles on Joseph Porter and went to the reference department. I found a copy of the Willow phone book and located addresses for Melvina Carmichael and Rosalie Porter. I'd bought a daily bus pass so I figured I might as well get my money's worth.

Rosalie Porter lived about six blocks from the library on Farley Street. Farley wasn't exactly one of Willow's better neighborhoods. It was a mix of empty buildings and old homes that ranged from abandoned and falling down to merely run-down and in need of repair. The bus let me off at what I hoped was about a block from Rosalie Porter's address. I walked down the street slowly, looking at the addresses on each house. I knew I probably looked like a confused tourist lost in the wrong part of town. But I didn't see anyone I could ask. A stray dog peered menacingly at me from underneath a rusted-out abandoned car, making me happy I'd worn my tennis shoes in case I needed to run. My ankle was still smarting from jumping off the roof, so I hoped running would not be required. I could hear loud arguing coming from one house and saw a toddler with a snot-encrusted nose and wearing a dirty winter coat playing on the sagging porch of another house. I hurried down the street looking for the Porter house, which turned out to be the last one on the block, cursing my nosiness and questioning what in the world I was trying to accomplish. I started to turn back but the next bus wasn't for another half hour so I had no choice but to make the most of my impulsiveness.

Rosalie Porter's house was one of the better-kept houses on the block but was still in desperate need of a paint job. Long strips of brown paint had fallen off of the two-story house, revealing the former color to have been white. I could hear the faint sound of a television as I walked up the creaking front steps. Before I had a chance to knock on the front door, it flew open and an elderly black woman in a tight, black, lint-covered sweat suit with fat pink curlers in her sparse white hair leaned out the door and stuck her hand in the mailbox. We both jumped at the unexpected meeting. The woman quickly recovered and peered at me suspiciously.

"Thought you was the mailman with my check. You 'bout gave me a heart attack," she said, looking me up and down.

"I'm so sorry, ma'am. I'm looking for Rosalie Porter. Is she home?"

"Rosy dead. Died last year. I'm her sister, Pearl Strong," she said, coming out onto the porch. I noticed she wasn't wearing anything on her feet but threadbare socks and wondered how she could stand the cold.

"I'm sorry to have bothered you, ma'am." I turned to go, relieved that I could get out of the depressing neighborhood, but Pearl didn't seem to want me to leave.

"No need to rush off, young lady. Don't get many visitors these days. Come on in here," she said, opening the door wide and stepping aside so I could come in.

It was stiflingly hot inside the house and it smelled, not unpleasantly, of fried food. Pearl ushered me through a dark, dusty living room, filled with plastic-covered furniture from the seventies that looked frozen in time and reminded me of insects trapped in amber, into an even hotter but much brighter kitchen. She gestured for me to sit at the lopsided kitchen table that was being propped up under one leg by a phone book to keep it level. I sat and took off my coat, hoping I wasn't being rude but too overheated to care.

"You had lunch yet, Miss, ah—"

"Clayton. Kendra Clayton, ma'am, and no, I'm not hungry. But thank you, anyway," I said, trying hard to ignore the simmering pot on the stove that smelled suspiciously like chili.

"Clayton, huh? Can't say I know any Claytons." She started to say more but my stomach let out a loud, incriminating growl. I was embarrassed to death and smiled at Pearl sheepishly.

To her credit she didn't say a word and silently dished up a large bowl of the chili and sat it in front of me along with a sleeve of saltine crackers and a glass of milk. I dug in. The chili was delicious and I was pleased to note that she put spaghetti in hers just like Mama did.

"So, why you lookin' for Rosy?" she finally asked me after I'd eaten about half my bowl of chili.

I wiped my mouth slowly so I could think before answering her. "I'm a graduate student in psychology at Kingford and I'm doing my dissertation on the stages of grief. I'm especially interested in people who've lost loved ones in accidents. I read about Mrs. Porter's grandson Joseph in the newspaper while doing my research and wondered if she'd be interested in talking to me."

Pearl's eyes filled with tears and she shook her head sadly. I felt awful. The woman had welcomed me into her home and fed me to boot, and here I was lying to her and bringing up bad memories.

"I'm sorry. I should go. I didn't mean to upset you," I said, getting up from the table.

"You didn't upset me, young lady. Sit down. I wasn't cryin' 'cause I'm sad. I ain't sad 'bout JP no mo'. I'm mad as hell, though." Her rigid body language and tightly crossed arms told me she was quite angry.

"Anger is one of the stages of grief. It's understandable that you'd be angry," I said, remembering my Psychology 101 class at Ohio State.

"Don't know nothin' 'bout that but I do know JP didn't die of no accident."

I felt my curiosity kick into overdrive and decided to press my luck a bit further. "Denial is also a stage of grief—"

Pearl threw up her hand angrily, cutting me off. "Didn't I tell you I don't know nothin' 'bout no stages of grief? I do know that my nephew couldn't swim. Rosy took him down to the Y for lessons when he was five. Couldn't never get him to even put a toe in that water. She give up after a couple a lessons. He never did learn. Now, I ask you, why in the world would he go swimmin'?"

"I read in the paper that they found his clothes in his car."

"I don't care what them police say they found. My nephew couldn't swim, you hear me?" Pearl stood up and grabbed my empty milk glass and chili bowl. She refilled my glass and sat it hard down in front of me. Milk splashed on the table. Then she opened up the fridge again and pulled out a large plastic bowl and got a clean bowl from the cabinet. She dished me up a large helping of banana pudding. It was made my favorite way with thick slices of banana, lots of vanilla wafers, and topped with a mountain of whipped cream. It was ice-cold and almost made me forget what we'd been talking about.

"The paper said Joseph told someone he was going for a swim."

"Some ole heifer who couldn't half see or hear who was helpin' out with the cookin', too. It wasn't JP told her he was goin' swimmin'. It was some other boy. But she said Reverend Rollins was the one told her it was JP. But she half senile. I don't believe he said it at all."

"So, what do you think happened to your nephew?" I asked after a few bites of the heavenly pudding.

"I think somebody musta held him under that water on purpose. That's what I think," Pearl said so quietly and calmly that I stopped eating.

"You think he was murdered? Why? Who would want to kill your nephew?"

"Hard to be tellin'. Maybe he seen somethin' he shouldn't a seen. Maybe he was someplace he shouldn't a been. All I know is my nephew couldn't swim. And they say they found him as nekked as the day he was born and he had bruises on his head and shoulders. So I'm 'sposed to believe that he decided to take off all his clothes and jump in that water? I ain't buyin' that mess for a minute."

An awkward silence had cropped up as I sat contemplating what Pearl had just told me. Even though Morris Rollins had benefited from his son's death, I still had a hard time envisioning him drowning anyone. But everything Pearl had just told me made sense. Why would someone who couldn't swim decide to take off their clothes and go swimming? Unless—

"I know what you thinkin' and you can just stop right there. JP didn't commit no suicide, either," Pearl said, reading my mind and slightly freaking me out.

"I didn't say he did," I replied quickly.

"Didn't need to. Saw it all over yo face, girly girl."

Pearl got up from the table again and disappeared into the living room. She came back a few minutes later with an ancient, red plastic family album that was cracked and almost falling apart. It had been taped in numerous places with duct tape. She pushed aside the dishes on the table and sat the album in front of me, pulling her chair up next to mine. Her mood brightened considerably as she opened the album.

"Here JP is. Musta been 'bout two in this picture," she said, gesturing towards a picture of a grinning toddler dressed in a little blue suit with a bow tie.

"He was a cutie," I said, gazing past Pearl at my half-finished bowl of pudding.

"Yes, he was. Wasn't never any trouble. Always smilin'."

Pearl flipped a few more pages until she got to another picture of a solemn Joseph, who looked about five, with an older woman who resembled Pearl.

"This was Rosy and JP on the first day of kindergarten. He was so scared. Rosy had a hell of a time gettin' him to let go a her hand," she said, chuckling softly.

She showed me numerous other pictures: Joseph singing in the choir; performing in the school play; playing drums in his high-school marching bad. I was even shocked to see a picture of him with Morris Rollins. Rollins had his arm around a teenaged Joseph who was smiling and looking quite carefree.

"Is Joseph's mother dead, too?" I asked, casually reaching for my pudding bowl.

"May as well be, far as I'm concerned."

I remained silent, hoping she would fill me in. After a minute of waiting and watching her expectantly, she shrugged her shoulders and turned the album to a picture of a slim, caramel-skinned young woman dressed in the green-and-gold choir robe of Holy Cross Church. Her long hair was pulled back from her face with a headband. She posed like a woman who knew the camera loved her.

"Here's Carla. Always was a wild one. Rosy tried and tried with that girl but she was high-minded. Nothin' Rosy ever did for her or gave her was enough. Always gimme, gimme, gimme. Wasn't never satisfied. Now, Carla was a pretty girl, and stacked. But, lord, she was lazy. Never worked a day in her life. Kept herself a man, usually a married one, to buy her whatever she wanted. Didn't care what they looked like or how old they was just as long as they had money to spend. Managed to get herself knocked up the summer after she graduated from high school. She never did take care a JP. Rosy raised him at first, then I came here to live when my husband died and we raised him together. Then, when he was about two, Carla took off. Said she was gonna go to Chicago to find herself a job and send for JP. Never came back. Rosy thought the girl was dead. Then when JP was twelve we found out she had got to Chicago and found herself a rich husband, a doctor. She never even told him she had a son. Only reason we knew what happened to her was 'cause someone at church saw her shopping in Chicago and came back and told us. We even went to Chicago and tracked her behind down.

She didn't wanna see us. Said she had a new life and a new family. Rosy was heartbroken. We never saw her again."

"Does she even know her mother and son are dead?"

"Rosy sent her a letter about JP and she never even showed up to the funeral. I didn't bother lettin' her know 'bout Rosy."

"I'm so sorry," I said sincerely. "So, what about Joseph's father? Is he still alive?" I asked as casually as I could manage. But Pearl was starting to smell a rat.

"You sure askin' a whole lotta questions. What JP's father got to do with them steps of grief you was talkin' 'bout?"

"Oh, I didn't mean to be so nosy. I just thought maybe since Joseph's grandmother has passed away and with everything that you've told me about his mother, maybe I could talk to his father for my dissertation."

Pearl stared at me for a few minutes without speaking. I tried not to squirm in my seat. I could tell she didn't quite know what to make of me and all my questions. I didn't want her to kick me out of her house. It would be embarrassing, plus I wasn't finished with my pudding.

"JP's daddy was married when he was runnin' around with Carla. I think she thought he was gonna leave his wife for her. But he never did. He always did right by that boy. Though I 'spect that was mainly cause he wanted to keep Carla from takin' his behind to court. Made sure JP had everything he needed even after Carla left town. But he was never a father to him. Had a family of his own. He ain't gonna talk to you. He just buried another loved one 'bout two weeks ago."

"Did Joseph know who his father was?" I ventured.

"If he knew, it wasn't 'cause I told him. I guess he coulda found out on his own," Pearl replied through tight lips. This was apparently still a sore point. I decided to back off.

I looked around Pearl's less-than-luxurious kitchen with the lopsided table, faded wallpaper, and chipped dishes, and wondered if Rollins had even had the decency to share the insurance money with Pearl and her sister. They'd been Joseph's parents, not Carla Porter or Morris Rollins. But I knew if I asked her she'd probably make me go cut a switch.

"Well, at least his father cared enough to provide for him. A lot of men in that position wouldn't have."

"That very well may be true. But in my book, if you cain't do the time, don't do the crime. Man had no bidness runnin' round with Carla in the first place. And him a religious man. Use to see him all the time in church with his uppity wife and daughter actin' like butter wouldn't melt in his mouth. Abusin' his power over them young people. That's why I stopped goin'." Pearl stopped talking abruptly and shifted in her seat uncomfortably. I got the impression she realized she'd said too much.

"Oh, so Joseph's father is in the church?" I asked.

"It's gettin' to be time for my show, young lady, and I need to wash these dishes first. You welcome to watch *The Golden Girls* with me. It's just a rerun but that Blanche tickles me. Cain't wait to see what she gonna do today," she said, changing the subject, and getting up from the table.

As much as I could tell she didn't want to talk about Joseph's father, I could also tell she was lonely and didn't want me to go. I decided to stay for another half hour. It was the least I could do, seeing how my stomach was full of her hospitality.

"Okay, Mrs. Strong. If you give me dish towel, I'll help so we can get done faster."

Her face lit up like a Christmas tree.

Chapter 14

It was going on two o'clock by the time I left Pearl's house. I had to run to catch the bus. Woody's girlfriend happened to be on the bus as well, sitting all the way in the back. I was worried she'd start up with me again but she looked at me like she'd never seen me before and stared moodily out the grimy window. I was seriously tempted to go home but instead found myself switching buses downtown and heading to Settler Avenue, where Melvina Carmichael lived. Even with what Pearl had told me about her nephew's death, I still couldn't wrap my head around all of the evidence pointing to Joseph Porter having been murdered, especially by his own father.

The one thing that made no sense to me was that Rollins had provided for Joseph financially. Pearl's point about him not wanting Carla to pursue him legally was a valid one. But to me it showed that he must have cared for his son on some level. Maybe I was just being sentimental, but why would he then turn around and kill him? The insurance money could be a motive only if Rollins really needed money back when Joseph died. Rollins had told me that his wife's wealthy family had been very generous to him while she was alive. Jeanne Rollins had died a few years after Joseph. So I assumed Rollins would still have had access to his late wife's money at the time of Joseph's death. I hoped my trip to see Melvina Carmichael would shed some light.

Settler Avenue wasn't just the polar opposite of Farley Street geographically, but economically, as well. It wasn't nearly as ritzy a neighborhood as you would find in Pine Ridge or Briar Creek but it was an affluent older neighborhood, the average age of its residents being upwards of fifty. I got off the bus in front of a Kroger supermarket a block away. Remembering my last encounter with the uptight Melvina, and anticipating her inevitable attitude, I went inside and bought a bouquet of pink and white carnations. I also swung by the book aisle and bought a copy of *I Will Follow Him*. I've always heard that authors have big egos. I figured showing up with an apology and a request for an autograph would be a surefire way of getting through the door.

Melvina's house was the smallest on the block. It was a shotgun-style house painted dark brick-red with black trim on the windows and front door. A butt-ugly chain-link fence encircled the yard, separating it from the neighbors on either side and most likely making her a very unpopular person. A white minivan was parked in the driveway in front of a small detached garage painted the same red as the house. I started to let myself inside the gate when I saw why the romance writer had a fence around her yard. An elderly, overweight Rottweiler quickly waddled over to the fence and started snarling and barking. Though the dog had gray in its muzzle and was wheezing asthmatically between barks, it still had plenty of teeth and looked like it wouldn't hesitate to use them on me if I stepped inside the yard. Luckily the frantic barking brought Melvina out onto her porch to see what was going on. She squinted at me from her porch then pulled a pair of glasses from her pocket and put them on. To say she wasn't pleased to see me was a supreme understatement. She visibly tensed up.

"May I help you?" she asked, charging across the yard towards me. She was wearing a jumper the color of lime Kool-Aid that gave her complexion an unhealthy greenish tint, kinda like the Wicked Witch of the West, and a black turtleneck sweater. And she sure didn't look like she wanted to help me, either. She looked like she wanted to choke me. Apparently, I still hadn't been forgiven for having been invited for a chat in Rollins's office. I stepped back from the fence, and out of choking distance, before replying.

"I'm sorry, Ms. Carmichael. I'm Kendra Clayton. Remember me? I hope I haven't caught you at a bad time. I just wanted to apologize to you for the other night at the church. I got the impression that I offended you with my question about getting published."

Melvina came closer to the fence, not taking her eyes off my hands, like she was afraid I might pull out an Uzi and fill her full of holes. Her dog had started to wag its tail when she'd come out onto the porch but continued to bark frantically at me.

"Shut up, Pookie!" she yelled, glaring at the dog. Pookie? I was expecting Killer or maybe Fang. Pookie, perhaps sensing the irritation in his owner's voice, shut up immediately. She patted his head to show she wasn't mad at him and he rolled over on his back for a belly rub. "He's harmless. He's just not used to me getting visitors," she said, bending down to rub Pookie's big belly. "Are those for me?" she asked, straightening up and coming over to the gate.

"Yes," I said, holding them out to her like an offering. "Oh, and I forgot to get you to sign my book." I was smiling at her in a way that I hoped conveyed my admiration for her creative talent but, judging by the way her eyes were narrowed suspiciously, I suspected my smile was bordering on psychotic, reaffirming my assertion that I'm a lousy ass-kisser.

"You could have just left the book with Reverend Rollins since the two of you are friends. He would have made sure I signed it for you. You didn't have to track me down at my home and disturb my writing." She took the flowers from my hand and stared at me.

"That was the last thing I intended to do, Mrs. Carmichael. It's just that I'm serious about my writing and you told me I needed to pay my dues and learn about the publishing industry. What better way to learn than from a published author? And since you're the only published author I know," I said, pausing dramatically, "here I am!"

"Yes, you certainly are," she said, not bothering to hide her sarcasm.

If I had a hard time imagining Morris Rollins in the throes of passion with Bonita Kidd, I had an even harder time imagining him doin' the do with this sour-faced, humorless woman standing before me. Bedding this woman must have been an act of charity on Rollins's part. But I knew a way to butter her up and put a smile on her face.

"You know, Reverend Rollins did nothing but sing your praises when I chatted with him after the taping. He told me what a lovely woman you are and how he really admired your determination to become a published author. He's actually the one who suggested I come speak to you."

Melvina's eyes softened and a reluctant smile spread across her face, transforming her and making her almost pretty, but not quite. Her eyes remained hard.

"Well, all right. I can spare a few minutes. But that's all. I'm on a tight schedule. My next book is due to my editor in a week and I'm not finished." She opened the gate and stood aside to let me come through. Pookie waddled over to me and sniffed my hand. I scratched him behind the ears and he followed Melvina and me into the house.

"You have a beautiful home, Ms. Carmichael," I said honestly, after stepping into the airy open foyer. I had figured Melvina Carmichael's house would be as dowdy and uptight as she seemed to be. Instead, I was pleasantly surprised to see an open floor plan that reminded me of pictures I'd seen of New York City lofts.

"A couple of years ago, one of my books was optioned by a production company that was going to turn it into a movie. The movie never got made but they paid me a lot of money and I used it to redecorate the house."

I followed her through the living room, where her laptop sat on the coffee table, over to the kitchen area and watched as she got a vase from under the sink and filled it with water. She put the flowers inside and sat the vase in the middle of the large, heavy, age-scarred wooden kitchen table.

"Have a seat and I'll make us some coffee." While she rummaged in the cabinet for cups, I took my coat off and sat down at the kitchen table. I looked around the room and something on the front of the stainless steel refrigerator caught my eyes. I got up and walked over to get a closer look. It was a picture of a tall teenaged girl in a Springmont High girls' basketball uniform. She had a basketball in her hands and was posed like she was about to make a basket.

"She took after her daddy. Loved playing basketball. He played for Springmont High, too," Melvina said in a flat, neutral tone.

I turned and watched as she poured coffee beans into a grinder. "So, was this your daughter?" I asked, coming back to sit at the table.

"Yes, that's my Gina. That picture was taken her freshman year. She was the star of the team. If she hadn't messed up her knee she could have been playing for one of those professional women's basketball teams. She was that good."

"I heard that she died. I'm sorry," I said sincerely.

"Sometimes life can be so cruel," she said softly. "Do you take cream and sugar in your coffee?"

"Just sugar, I'm allergic to dairy products," I said, unable to meet her eyes. Just because I was trying to push her buttons to get info out of her didn't mean I felt good about it.

"It's not life-threatening, is it?" she asked, looking genuinely concerned.

"Oh, no. I just break out in hives. Nothing serious. But my sister is deathly allergic to shellfish," I said, hoping to spark some kind of conversation about her daughter's death.

But Melvina turned her back to me as she fixed our coffee and I couldn't tell how my comment affected her. She didn't say a word for a few minutes and I wondered if I'd gone too far. Finally, she placed a steaming mug of coffee in front of me along with the sugar bowl and sat down on the other side of the table.

"So, what is it you'd like to know?" she asked. It took me a second to remember that I was supposed to be getting info on the publishing industry.

"First off, why did my question upset you so much? Did I breach some kind of unwritten writer's etiquette?"

"It just gets so tiresome, you know?" she began after sipping her coffee. "Of all the questions I get asked, that's the one that everybody wants to know. I get e-mail after e-mail. No one ever asks me how to be a better writer or about certain writing techniques. No, everybody wants to know how to get published, like there's some secret to it. Then when I try and steer people in the right direction, I find out they didn't really want my advice. What they really wanted was—how do you young people put it?" she said, squinting in concentration. "Oh, I know, a hookup. They just want me to hook them up with my literary agent or editor. And out of all the times I make the effort to answer them honestly, I hardly ever get a simple thank you. People these days want everything handed to them on a silver platter. Well, I'm sorry, but a little hard work never hurt anybody. Anything worth having is worth working for, right?" she asked, pausing for my answer.

"Of course it is. And I completely understand where you're coming from. But I wasn't looking for a hookup, not at all. It's just that writing is one thing, but trying for publication is something I know nothing about. I wouldn't even know the first thing about how to go about it. I imagine most people feel the same way, don't you think?"

"Some of them, maybe. But, from my experience, most of the people who contact me aren't doing so because they want me to explain how to go about getting published. The road to publication has many different paths. All I can do is share my personal experience. Then there are those who want me to read their manuscripts," she said, rolling her eyes heavenward. "I actually used to critique manuscripts before

I got so busy with my own writing. Let me tell you, people didn't really want an honest opinion. They expected me to tell them that they were the next Toni Morrison or James Baldwin and when they didn't hear that then suddenly I didn't know what I was talking about, or I was just jealous." She shook her head in disgust at the memory.

"I bet your daughter must have been very proud of you," I said to change the subject. Something told me that Melvina could talk a blue streak about anything connected to her writing and I was hoping taking the back-door approach would make her open up about Gina.

"Not really," she replied after a thoughtful moment. "Gina was an athlete and always on the go. She could have cared less about sitting still and reading anything. She was happiest when she was out doing stuff. I don't think she ever read a single one of my books."

"Didn't that bother you?"

"No. Not really. I don't write for anyone but myself. I don't really need anyone's approval. I never took it personally. Books just weren't her thing."

"Well, I bet your husband's proud then, huh?"

"Actually, I've never been married," she said, tensing up again and looking like she wanted to toss her coffee in my face.

"I'm sorry. I just seem to be offending you no matter what I ask," I said with a nervous, high-pitched laugh.

"Oh, don't worry. Most people make that mistake. Carmichael was my mother's maiden name and my middle name. I decided to use it as my pen name."

"I didn't realize that," I replied. An awkward silence cropped up and I wasn't sure how to break it. But Melvina did.

"Aren't you going to ask me?" she said, leaning back in the chair expectantly.

"Ask you what?" I said, confused.

"About how a woman who gave birth to a child out of wedlock has the nerve to write Christian romance novels. That's the next most-asked question I get."

"Honestly, it never crossed my mind and, if it did, it's really none of my business," I concluded. I was amazed I could keep a straight face telling that big ole lie. She must have seen the glitter of anticipation in my eyes because she let out a loud, humorless laugh.

"No, it isn't yours or anybody else's business, but that doesn't keep people from asking me about it anyway." A self-righteous look had settled on her face, and I realized that I truly did not like this woman. The sooner I could get what I came for and leave, the better.

"And what do you tell them?"

"I tell them the truth, of course. I'm only human. And, just like many others before me and after me, I once suffered a crisis of the spirit. I fell for a man I had no business falling for and I became pregnant with his child. I don't believe in abortion. So, I had my child and raised her on my own and was blessed with sixteen wonderful years of having her in my life before she was called home to God. I'm not ashamed of the mistakes I've made in my life. I've tried to learn from them and I hope I've set a good example for others in the same situation."

I expected to see a glimmer of tears in her eyes but they remained tear-free. "I can't even begin to imagine how hard her death must have been for you," I said. I meant that sincerely. Mama had had a child that only lived a few minutes after it was born and even fifty years later, talking about the loss of that baby still brought tears to her eyes.

"Don't you have any children, Ms. Clayton?"

"No, I don't," I said with an inward sigh of relief. I didn't know when or even if I'd ever be ready for that responsibility. Even the thought of owning goldfish made me feel twitchy.

"Then you're right. Unless you have a child you can never know the heartbreak of losing one."

"Was it hard raising her all on your own?" I asked after draining my coffee cup and putting it on the table.

Melvina shrugged nonchalantly. "Even though her father and I never married, he supported Gina financially. Money was never a problem, but she was always asking about him. I never told her who he was. He's married with a family of his own. He wasn't interested in being a father to Gina. I didn't want her getting her heart broken the way I did. But she did get to know him at church, just not as her father," Melvina said, not quite able to hide the anger and bitterness in her voice. She got up from the table and took our empty coffee mugs over to the sink. I wondered what she meant about Gina having known her father but not as a father.

"How did Gina die? Was she sick?" I figured she wouldn't mind me asking since she was being so open about her personal business, but I noticed her back stiffen before she turned to answer.

"Gina had a lot of allergies. She'd grown out of most of them by the time she was a teenager but she remained deathly allergic to bee stings. She had an EpiPen that she was supposed to have with her at all times. But she was a typical irresponsible teenager. I was always on her about making sure she had that EpiPen. We were at our church's annual picnic and I remember seeing her laughing and talking to her friends. An hour later, I found her unconscious in our car. By the time the squad got her to the hospital it was too late. The thing that haunts me the most is that I found her EpiPen in my purse. I could have sworn I'd made her put it in her pocket before we left for the park," she said. She was clasping and unclasping her hands in her lap. I wanted to hug her or squeeze her hand, but I knew she wouldn't appreciate the gesture.

"Could she have put it in your purse?"

"That's what Reverend Rollins seemed to think. He saw her playing basketball and thinks she probably put her EpiPen in my purse so she wouldn't lose it."

How convenient, I thought. Rollins had been in the perfect position to not only kill Gina but to comfort her grieving mother and wash away any doubts Melvina may have had about what happened to her daughter.

"I only met Reverend Rollins recently. He's quite a man, isn't he?" Melvina's head snapped up and she looked at me oddly.

"Yes, he is an amazing minister and an amazing man. We have quite a lot in common," she said softly, looking down at her lap.

Indeed you do, I thought. Was it possible Melvina still had feelings for Rollins even though he'd broken her heart and never wanted to be a father to their child? Something seemed odd about that to me in light of the bitterness in her voice just a few minutes ago. I also remembered the look on her face when she'd seen me sitting in his office. Was she still in love with him?

"Does anyone know why Gina was in the car?"

"She must have been changing out of her basketball shoes. I don't know why else she would have been in the car. I found her slumped in the back seat and a spilled pop can was next to her on the floor. When they did the autopsy there was a dead bee inside her clothes. It must have stung her on the neck. Her throat had swelled shut and she suffocated."

A grim mental image of a frantic girl unable to breathe, turning blue, and probably knowing she was going to die flashed before me. How had Rollins done it? I'd been to my share of picnics and knew how many bees were constantly buzzing around the trash cans and food tables. Did Rollins see Gina playing basketball and take her a can of pop with a bee trapped inside it and put it in the car with her as she was changing her shoes? Did he take her EpiPen from her as she struggled to inject herself and then put it in Melvina's purse afterward? I suddenly felt sick and didn't know if it was from the thoughts popping into my head or from all that chili and pudding I'd consumed earlier. I needed some fresh air because something else was beginning to bother me.

"Are you okay?" Melvina asked.

"Yeah," I said, slowly shaking my head to clear my thoughts. "But I've taken up enough of your time. I should go so you can get back to your writing." I stood up and put my coat on.

"We haven't even discussed your writing yet," she said, following me to the door.

"Oh, that's okay. Maybe when you have more time we can get together again." I hurried through the living room past a sleeping Pookie, and paused at the door. In doing so, I noticed a green-and-gold Holy Cross choir robe hanging on a coatrack by the door.

"Oh, you sing in the church choir?" I asked Melvina.

"No. That was Gina's choir robe. I should have given it back to the church, but I just haven't been able to," she said, fingering the folds of the robe.

"Well, thank you for your time, Ms. Carmichael," I said before walking out the door.

I was halfway to the bus stop when I heard Melvina calling after me about forgetting my signed book.

As the bus headed back downtown, I had a chance to think about what had been bothering me. I was getting some very conflicting views of Morris Rollins. When Melvina described Gina's father, she'd clearly been bitter, but when she talked about Reverend Rollins her whole attitude changed and I saw love and admiration in her eyes. I also thought about my visit to Joseph's aunt, Pearl Strong. When she talked about Joseph's father it had been with scorn and anger, but when she mentioned Rollins as someone who could have given wrong information about Joseph going swimming, she didn't believe it. Why was I getting so much conflicting information? It was as if Pearl and Melvina had been talking about two different men. So, if Morris Rollins wasn't Joseph and Gina's father, who was? And why in the world would Rollins be listed on the death certificates of children that he hadn't fathered?

I found myself back at the library, more confused than ever. I grabbed some scrap paper and wrote down everything that I knew so far about the deaths of Joseph Porter and Gina Parks: Both had died during Holy Cross Church picnics; both deaths had been ruled accidents; both Joseph and Gina had known their fathers, though Melvina claimed that Gina didn't know he was her father. Gina and Joseph's father was a member of Holy Cross Church, yet Morris Rollins was the only man's name that had been mentioned during both my conversations about Joseph and Gina's deaths. Rollins had been present during both deaths, had profited monetarily from the deaths, and he had been trying to cash an insurance policy on Inez, as well.

I wondered if Rollins had been in Detroit when Ricky Maynard was killed. How could I find out? Deciding to take advantage of the vast information resources around me, I headed over to the periodicals desk again. The same bored looking, mullet-wearing librarian from earlier was manning the desk.

"You're back. What can I help you with this time?" he said, smiling.

"This time I need to know how I can find news stories on a specific person that have appeared in the *Willow News-Gazette.* Can you help me?"

"You happen to be in luck, young lady. Two years ago we undertook a major indexing project. We've indexed all the news stories that have appeared in the *News-Gazette* for the last ten years. So as long as what you're looking for has occurred in the last ten years, you should be able to find out what issue and date it appeared in the *News-Gazette.*"

"Wonderful. I need articles from about two years ago."

He led me over to a set of alphabetized drawers where I got to work looking for articles on Morris Rollins. I had very little luck finding out news on Rollins specifically, but I was able to find a multitude of articles on Holy Cross, even one about major damage to the church's roof from a fallen tree during a storm. Finally an article that had appeared in the *News-Gazette* a year and a half ago caught my eye: HOLY CROSS CHURCH INVITED TO PARTICIPATE IN INTER-FAITH CHURCH CONFERENCE. I jotted down the date of the article, then got the microfilm from the periodicals desk so I could read it. It wasn't much of an article, more like an announcement:

Holy Cross Church has been invited to participate in the 25th annual Midwest Interfaith Church Conference being held in Detroit, Michigan, in June. Select churches in Ohio, Michigan, Illinois, and Indiana are invited yearly to participate in the conference, which is hosted by a different Midwestern city each year. This is the first year Holy Cross has been invited to participate.

There was a small picture of a group of Holy Cross Church members, including Morris and Nicole Rollins, Rondell and Bonita Kidd, and several other people I didn't recognize, that accompanied the article. The article didn't mention exactly when the church convention was being held but it still put Rollins in Detroit the same month that Ricky had been run down. I glanced at the picture and was again struck by how different Rollins and Rondell were physically. The only thing that they had in common was their height. Then something else clicked in my mind. Melvina had mentioned that Gina had gotten her basketball prowess from her father, who'd played basketball for Springmont High. I'd assumed she meant Morris Rollins, but now I wasn't so sure. I knew one way to find out.

I headed over to the reference department where I knew they kept copies of all the Springmont High School yearbooks back to the thirties. I didn't know exactly how old Morris Rollins was—somewhere in his early fifties, perhaps—so I grabbed several years' worth of yearbooks and headed to an empty table. I started with 1960. My eyes had started to cross and I was getting a headache from looking at so many bouffant hairdos and cat-eyed glasses when I finally found a picture of Morris Rollins. It was in the 1962 yearbook. Rollins had been skinny, geeky, and almost unrecognizable with thick horn-rimmed glasses and a side part in his short hair. I searched throughout the yearbook and didn't find a picture of him anywhere other than with his graduating class.

But I found other pictures that sent chills up and down my spine. While it appeared that Morris Rollins hadn't been anything special during his high school years, his half brother Rondell was a different story. Rondell Kidd had been a member of the honor society, choir, and was a standout on both the football and basketball teams. He'd also been prom and homecoming king. Unlike the overweight, poorly dressed man he'd become, his high school pictures showed that Rondell had been handsome. And while the pictures still showed him to have been a somewhat large young man, he'd been solid, without an inch of the flab that now encircled his waist, and his clothes had fit properly.

I knew plenty of men like Rondell from my own high school days. Popular, handsome guys who'd never been able to translate their high-school popularity into the real world. Guys who still tried to wear the same size clothes they wore in their glory days and never changed their hairstyles. In light of how popular he used to be, playing second fiddle to his older brother Morris must be torture for Rondell. I thought back to what Pearl and Melvina had said about Joseph and Gina's father: He had a family of his own that included a daughter and an uppity wife. The uppity wife part sure sounded like Bonita Kidd, but I hadn't heard anything about what Rollins's late wife Jeanne had been like. She could have been uppity, too. Rondell Kidd was a devoutly religious man who worshipped his wife and didn't seem like the type of man to cheat, let alone father illegitimate children. Plus, cheating on your spouse and fathering children with other women didn't make a man a murderer, just sleazy. And if Rondell had killed Ricky, Gina, and Joseph, what was the motive?

As far as I could tell, Rondell didn't seem to be showing any signs of living the high life. He and Bonita wore outdated, well-worn clothes. Their cars looked to be well taken care of but were older models. They had a nice, but hardly extravagant house. Shanda went to an expensive college yet she lived at home, saving the Kidds the expense of dorm fees. So, if the motive had been money, where was it going? As far as I could tell, the only one living in the lap of luxury was Morris Rollins. The only one who'd bene-fited from the deaths of Ricky, Joseph, and Gina, was Morris Rollins. So why the conflicting views? There were too many questions swirling around my tired brain.

I leaned forward and rested my head on the table I was sitting at and closed my eyes. I told myself it would only be for a few minutes, but soon I found myself sliding into a fitful sleep, only to jerk awake as new even-more-sinister thoughts hit me: Did Rollins kill Nicole because he mistook her for Inez? Was that the reason Inez had screamed, "Daddy, don't"? Was he hiding his daughter until he had a chance to kill her for real? It was time to get Inez out of that house and to the police before she suffered an accident like her half siblings. I called Detectives Harmon and Mercer but was told they were busy and couldn't be disturbed. I left a message for them to meet me at Rollins's house, then gathered up my stuff and headed out to catch the bus to Briar Creek.

I waited, skulking around at the entrance to Rollins's driveway for a half an hour before I got tired of waiting and headed up to the house. I should have waited for the detect-ives, but all I could imagine was a doped-up Inez being smothered with a pillow by her father. There were no cars in the driveway but that didn't mean there wasn't one parked in the four-car garage behind the house. I didn't dare knock on the front door because I knew that that bulldog of a nurse was probably watching Inez like a hawk. I walked around to the back of the house. There was a swimming pool taking up most of the backyard, and a stone deck with two levels that ran the length of the house. I peered into the house through the French doors off the patio straight into the family room. The nurse was sitting on the couch watching TV. I ducked down behind a large terra-cotta planter by the steps and waited. Finally, I saw the nurse get up and head to the refrigerator. I ran all the way up to the top level of the deck. There was indoor/outdoor furniture and a hot tub on the upper level, as well as another set of French double doors. I looked inside and saw that it was a large bedroom, probably the master suite. I turned the handle on the door. It was locked—surprise, surprise.

I wrapped my hand up in my scarf and punched through a pane of glass on the door. I crouched down, expecting a loud alarm to sound, but was rewarded with silence. I reached inside, unlocked the door, and let myself into the house. The first thing that struck me immediately was the smell of Rollins's cologne. It smacked me in the face as I crept farther into the large room. His closet door was open and I could see all of his numerous suits hanging inside. A royal blue bathrobe was laying across the large, unmade, king-sized brass bed. I tripped over a pair of his big shoes and almost chickened out. I pulled myself together and quickly headed out the bedroom door into the hallway. I recognized where I was from the last time I'd been in the house.

I hurried down the hallway past the landing overlooking

the foyer, towards Inez's bedroom. I was reaching for the doorknob when I saw it turn slowly. I took a step back as the door opened, revealing Inez Rollins. She was dressed in pajama bottoms, tennis shoes, and a sweatshirt. Her braids were wild and medusa-like, sticking up all over her head like she'd stuck her finger in a light socket. She jumped back when she saw me standing outside her door.

"Kendra?" she whispered, clearly stunned to see me. "What are you doing here?" she asked. Before I could answer she pulled me inside the bedroom and closed the door. "Never mind. Look, Kendra, I really need your help. Is my father here? 'Cause I gotta get outta this house. They've been drugging me. I only pretended to take my pill this morning. I need your help, please," she pleaded with me.

"I don't think your father is here, but that nurse is downstairs watching TV. It's okay, Inez, you're safe now. I know your father tried to kill you and killed Nicole by mistake. Come on. We can make a run for it." I grabbed the sleeve of Inez's sweatshirt, but she pulled away from me.

"What are you talking about? My daddy didn't kill Nicole. I killed her."

Uh-oh!

Chapter 15

I felt like I was going to faint. I backed away from Inez, who, sensing my sudden fear, rushed to explain.

"No, Kendra. You don't understand. I didn't do it on purpose. It was an accident. I swear," she said and started to cry.

"You need to tell me what's going on, Inez. Do you know everyone in town thinks you're dead?" I licked my dry lips nervously. I couldn't believe I'd rushed in here to play the hero and was face-to-face with a murderer.

Inez went over and sat down heavily on the edge of her bed. I joined her and patted her back until she stopped crying. She wiped her eyes with the sleeve of her sweatshirt.

"I was at work at the shop that night, minding my own damn business. I went to take the trash outside and when I opened the door, Nicole was standing there. She scared the shit out of me. I asked her what she wanted and she told me that she knew what I'd done and she was going to make sure I fixed it. I didn't know what she was talking about. Then she accused me of telling my daddy that she was having an affair. She said he confronted her about it and threatened to divorce her. I laughed and told her that I hadn't talked to my father in a month. Then I turned to go back inside and she pulled a gun on me, and told me she was taking me home with her so I could tell him I was lying. I should have gone with her. But, Kendra, I got so mad. I grabbed for the gun and tried to get it away from her. We ended up on the ground and I almost twisted the gun outta her hands when it went off. It hit her in the face. There was blood everywhere. Kendra, you believe me, don't you? I didn't mean to do it," she said, unable to finish before sobs overtook her.

Actually, if Mona Carter hadn't told me the story of Nicole attacking her nephew for spreading lies about her in high school, I probably wouldn't have believed Inez. What was it that Mona had told me about Nicole? "Little Miss Nicole takes her reputation very seriously." She couldn't have been more right. Anyone who'd confront someone with a gun over a lie meant serious business.

"Did you call your father afterwards?" I asked, rubbing her back.

"No. He just showed up. He must have been following Nicole. I told him we needed to call the police. He said he would as soon as he took me home so I could clean up. I was covered in Nicole's blood. But, when we got here, he gave me something to drink to calm me down and he must have put a sleeping pill in it or something. I woke up in this room and Daddy told me that everything would be okay. But he wouldn't let me leave. He had that nurse watching me all the time and they kept giving me those pills that made me sleep."

"Inez, your father told the police that it was you who'd been killed. He's been passing you off as Nicole. He even dressed you up in Nicole's clothes and passed you off as her at your own funeral."

"You mean that funeral was real? I thought I was dreaming. Why would he do this?" Inez asked, looking as bewildered as I felt.

"I don't know, but we've got to get you to the police so you can tell them your story. The police think a friend of mine, an innocent young man, was the one who killed you. Come on," I said, grabbing her hand and pulling her to her feet.

We left the room, crept down the steps, and were heading towards the front door when we heard the nurse's voice behind us.

"Mrs. Rollins, what in the world are you doing? Who is this person?" She apparently didn't recognize me from my earlier visit to the house. But we weren't about to stop and give her an answer.

I pulled the front door open and ran, quite literally, straight into Morris Rollins. I let out a yelp of surprise and jumped back like I'd been scalded. Inez started to cry. Rollins looked from me to his daughter and I could see the muscles in his neck tighten. Anger and rage contorted his features. He was so mad he could barely speak.

"I want to know what the hell you're doing in my house, Kendra! Where do you think you're going with my daughter?"

"Daughter? I thought you said she was your wife. What's going on here?" The nurse was looking very confused and when no one answered her she turned her attention back to me. "Reverend Rollins, I swear I have no idea how she got into the house. She must have broken in. I'll go call the police," she said, hurrying off in the direction of the kitchen.

"That won't be necessary," Rollins called out, stopping her in her tracks.

"Oh, I think calling the police is an excellent idea, Reverend. They would be quite interested to know that you've been passing your very-much-alive daughter off as your wife and trying to cash in a life insurance policy on her," I said, feeling quite smug.

"Daddy? What's she talking about?" Inez looked from me to her father while Rollins reserved his dirty looks for me alone.

"I wasn't trying to get the money for myself. I don't have the money I used to. My first wife's family cut me off after she died. The insurance money was for Inez so she could go start a new life someplace else. I will not let them put my baby in prison," he said through gritted teeth.

"Prison? Daddy, I told you it was an accident," Inez said, walking over to Rollins and clutching the front of his sweater. "Why don't you believe me? You were there, too."

"Baby girl, all I saw when I got to the shop that night was the gun go off. I know you're no murderer. But too many people know about the bad blood between you and Nicole. That's why I went back to the shop after I brought you here that night and took the gun and Nicole's wedding ring. When the police contacted me the next day and asked me to come identify a body, I lied and said it was you. I even tried to use my influence with some city officials to prevent them from doing an autopsy. I couldn't risk the police thinking you killed Nicole on purpose. They'll lock you up and throw away the key."

"But it would be okay for an innocent man to be locked

up for the rest of *his* life for a crime he didn't commit, huh, Reverend Rollins?" Now it was my turn to glare and grit my teeth.

The fact that Rollins would let someone else go to jail for something his daughter did made me want to throttle him. He must have seen the outrage on my face because he went over to the staircase, sat on the bottom step, and buried his face in his hands.

"I swear, I never thought the police would actually pin the murder on someone else. Once they did, I didn't know what to do. I've been praying and praying that they would realize that young man is innocent. I would never have let him go to prison. I would have gone to the police if it came to that."

"Well, what about your other children, Reverend? Ricky, Gina, and Joseph, what about how you profited from their deaths? You didn't also happen to rush them to their deaths, did you?"

Rollins looked like he'd been punched.

"Daddy? What's she talking about? What other children?" Inez went over to sit next to her father. He grabbed her hand but remained silent and staring straight ahead.

"We're waiting, Reverend. Your daughter deserves to know the truth," I said, walking over to stand directly in front of him.

"You think I killed them?" he asked slowly, looking up at me like a lost and helpless little boy.

"I don't know what to think. That's why I'm asking. I'm sure after the police see this folder they'll be wondering the same thing." I had pulled the folder out of my purse and was waving it in front of him.

"You got that from my office. I could have you arrested for theft." He stood up like he was going to try and grab it from me, but I jumped back out of his reach.

"Forget about that file," Inez said, grabbing her father's arm. "Who are those people she's talking about? I need to know. Daddy, please."

Rollins's shoulders slumped and he sat back down. Inez sat next to him. "I'm not a perfect man, Inez. I loved your mother but we had problems from the beginning. Your mother and I were going through bad times when you were growing up and I was unfaithful to her. I was weak and sinful and because of my actions, I fathered a child by another woman. There may also be a chance that I'm—"

"Shanda's father!" said a loud voice behind us, interrupting Rollins mid-sentence. We all turned to see Rondell Kidd standing in the open doorway. He looked like hell. In addition to his usual too-tight clothing, his eyes were red from crying, his nose was running, and his Afro was matted on one side. "How could you do it, man?" he asked, his gaze never wavering from his brother's. "You're my brother. How could you sleep with my wife? You know how much I love her, Morris. How could you?"

Rollins stared at his brother in shock. "Rondell, I'm not—"

"You're not what? Huh? Are you trying to deny that you slept with my wife? Are you trying to deny that you're Shanda's father? Huh? Is that what you're trying to do?" Rondell asked, pulling out a gun and aiming it straight at Rollins. A collective gasp went up from everybody in the room except Rollins. He remained silent, staring at his brother and the gun.

"Rondell, calm down. What did Bonita tell you?" Rollins asked, slowly standing up and not taking his eyes off Rondell.

"Calm down! You slept with my wife. You could be my daughter's father. And you want me to calm down. Man, I oughta shoot you like the lying dog you are!"

"Answer me, Rondell! What exactly did Bonita tell you?" pleaded Rollins, his voice cracking. Rondell stared at him for a few seconds, but he didn't put the gun down.

"She told me the two a you had an affair and that you might be Shanda's father, not me." Rondell was now openly sobbing.

"Rondell, I am so sorry. But, as God as my witness, it only happened once. I would bet any amount of money that you are Shanda's father. Come on, man. Don't do this. Put the gun down, please."

Rondell finally noticed Inez standing in the foyer and his mouth fell open in shock. He almost dropped the gun. Rollins crept closer to him with his hand outstretched to take it from him. But Rondell quickly recovered from his shock and aimed the gun at his brother again. "I don't believe it. The Lord gave you your daughter back and now my child might be yours, too." Rondell shook his head in disbelief.

I was too scared to move or look away. Where the hell were Harmon and Mercer? Any other time they'd show up when I didn't want to see them. I wondered if they'd even gotten my message. I heard a car pull into the driveway and I breathed a sigh of relief. But, to my great disappointment, it wasn't Harmon and Mercer who came running through the open door. It was Bonita Kidd. She screamed when she saw the gun in her husband's hands.

"Oh, my God, Rondell. What are you doing?"

"Shut up, you whore!" Rondell spat out at her.

"Don't you talk to me like that, Rondell," Bonita said, as tears rolled down her face. "You have to share the blame in this, too. You helped create this mess as much as Morris and I did."

"Me? How can you say that? You slept with my brother. I'm not stupid, Bonita. I know you've always loved him. You just settled for me. I even know you lied to him and told him

Nicole was cheating on him. I overhead you tell him you saw Nicole kissing another man. You're a liar, Bonita. You never saw any such thing. Why were you trying to break up his marriage if you didn't want him for yourself?"

All eyes were on Bonita, who had finally noticed Inez, too. "Inez? My God, you're alive! But, how?" Bonita went over to embrace her newly resurrected niece, but Inez was having none of it and moved out of her reach.

"Yes, I'm alive, Aunt Bonita. But look around. Who don't you see? Nicole's the one who died that night. She's dead because of your lie."

"Bonita, I believed you when you told me you saw Nicole with another man. I even threatened to divorce her," said Rollins, shaking his head. "Do you have any idea what you've done? Do you?" he shouted.

"Morris, I swear I had no idea this would happen. Nicole was no good for you. All she did was spend your money. She wasn't even interested in Holy Cross. With you being so much older than her, she was bound to cheat on you one day. I thought I was doing you a favor. I was trying to save you some pain down the road." Bonita buried her face in her hands and sobbed. No one moved to comfort her.

I glanced over at Inez. Her eyes were shooting daggers at her aunt. Rollins's anger had subsided and he just looked sad and deflated, like someone had stuck a nail in a tire and the air was slowly leaking out. Bonita's lie had set this whole chain of events in motion. She had a lot to answer for. But, apparently, she wasn't the only one.

"Rondell, I'm not covering for you any longer," said Rollins, shaking his head. "Kendra," he continued, turning to me. "You wanted to know about Ricky, Gina, and Joseph? Okay, I'll tell you. I fathered Ricky. He was the son I had with a woman named Vera Maynard. My wife and I were on the verge of divorce. I fell in love with Vera, but I knew I had to give my marriage one last try. She went back to Detroit brokenhearted and I didn't see her again for a long time. I didn't even know about Ricky until he was a teenager. I provided support when I did find out. I tried to be a father to him, but he wasn't interested. He was killed in a hit-and-run accident. As for the insurance, I have policies on all my loved ones. There's nothing strange about that. But I did give most of the money to Vera and I used the rest for the church."

"What about Gina and Joseph?" I asked. My voice came out in a croak because my throat was so dry. Rondell still had the gun trained on Rollins. I'm no big fan of guns.

Rollins looked at his brother. "You'll have to ask Rondell about them."

Bonita let out a strangled sob. Rondell's eyes flew to his wife. He was looking decidedly less indignant and outraged.

"Don't you have anything to say, Rondell?" asked Rollins, turning to his brother. Rondell stared at the floor.

"Bonita found out about you and Carla Porter. The night she found out you were running around with that girl, she was a wreck. She came to talk to me, and one thing led to another. It never happened again. When Bonita got pregnant, I always knew there was a chance I could be Shanda's father. We should have told you, but I just didn't want to believe it," Rollins said, shaking his head sadly. Rondell was looking from his wife to his brother. His anger was starting to return, and he opened his mouth to speak. Rollins pressed on, cutting him off before he could say a word.

"But Carla was just a teenager, man. She came to me and

told me she was pregnant by you. She threatened to drag you, Bonita, and the church through the mud. I covered for you, like always. I paid Carla child support and told her it was from you to keep her from going after you in court. I was trying to keep Bonita from finding out you'd fathered a child with another woman. She and Carla were pregnant at the same time and I was trying to save your marriage. I even tried to be a father figure to Joseph to make up for your neglect. I thought you'd learned your lesson. You and Bonita were getting along so well after Shanda was born. Then damned if you didn't turn around and do the same thing again with Melvina Carmichael."

Bonita let out an anguished moan and covered her ears like she couldn't bear to hear one more word. Instead of going to comfort her, Rollins walked over to Inez, who clearly looked stunned, and put his arm around her. Surprisingly, she didn't pull away, and Rollins continued.

"Once again I covered for you and paid support for Gina. I even encouraged Gina to join the choir so the two of you could get to know each other and maybe you would see what a special child she was in a way that wouldn't ruin your marriage. I've been cleaning up your messes ever since we were kids, Rondell, and I'm not doing it anymore. You're on your own now." Rollins sat back down on the steps.

Rondell lowered the gun but he didn't drop it or put it away. He rocked back and forth on his heels and looked nervously around the room. Bonita wouldn't meet his gaze. She was too busy staring tearfully at Rollins, who was comforting Inez.

"Morris, man, I'm sorry. I couldn't help myself. All those women wanted to get next to you. They were just using me to get to you. And Carla Porter was a little tramp. I wasn't the only one she was running around with. Her son could have been anybody's. Melvina's been in love with you for years. We started spending time together when she would hang around the church after services, trying to see you. None of them women meant a thing to me. I swear. You believe me, don't you, baby?" he asked, turning pleading eyes to his wife. Bonita still wouldn't look at him. Rondell fell to his knees and started rocking back and forth.

"Morris, I love you. I'd walk through fire for you. I helped you build Holy Cross and take it from just some wishful thinking to a reality. You have no idea what I've done for you and for Holy Cross, no idea. I always made sure you had whatever you needed for the church, didn't I? Didn't I!" he shouted when his brother wouldn't look at or answer him. Rondell's eyes had taken on a dazed, faraway look. I felt the hair on the back of my neck stand up.

Suddenly it was all clear to me. All of the bills I'd seen in Rollins's desk drawer for repairs and upkeep on Holy Cross. Joseph and Gina both being members of the church choir, thus having contact with Rondell, the organ player. Rollins had been in Detroit when Ricky had been killed, but so had Rondell. I mistakenly figured that Rollins had killed Ricky, Joseph, and Gina for the insurance money so he could support his lavish lifestyle. But, the money hadn't been for luxuries. It had been for Holy Cross.

"My God! You killed them, didn't you? Ricky, Joseph, and Gina. You killed them for the insurance money so Reverend Rollins could use the money for Holy Cross," I said, as all eyes turned to Rondell.

Rollins slowly got up and walked over to his brother. "What did you do, Rondell? Did you hurt those kids? Man, tell me what you did." Rollins was towering over Rondell's kneeling figure.

"I did it for you. I did it for the church. They were no good, Morris. They were sinners. They needed to be punished."

"Punished for what?" cried out Bonita. Rondell stood and faced his wife. He started to walk towards her, but she backed away from him in horror.

"Joseph showed me the way," Rondell began, turning to the rest of us. I looked around the room at the disbelief frozen on everyone's face. You could have heard a pin drop. It was as if everyone had forgotten to breathe.

"Morris was always after me to get to know that boy even though I knew I wasn't the only one Carla had been with. But I decided I would try. That day at the barbecue I saw him walking off towards the beach. So I followed him. I was going to tell him I was his father. But when I got down to the beach I saw that he wasn't alone. He was hugging and kissing some man. I couldn't believe it. I knew then that he couldn't be from my seed. When the other man left, I confronted him about his sinfulness. He started crying and saying he couldn't help himself. He begged me not to tell on him. I dragged him over to the water and made him kneel at the water's edge to pray with me. I dunked his head in the water to wash away his sins. He fought me, but I held on. But, then he stopped fighting. I didn't mean to kill him."

"Lord! God! Noooo!" screamed Bonita, lifting her arms heavenward.

"It was an accident," Rondell said, sighing and rolling his eyes, like Joseph's death had occurred in much the same way as a bug that had gotten accidentally stepped on.

"Then what did you do?" I ventured after a moment, since no one else seemed capable of speech. Bonita was still wailing and Rollins and Inez were hugging like they were afraid to let each other go.

"I took off his clothes and put him in the water so everyone would think he was swimming and drowned. Then a few weeks later that big life insurance check came for you, Morris. I found out you had a policy on Joseph because you were paying support for him. That money came just in time, didn't it? The church needed a new roof when that tree fell on it during that big storm. The insurance company called it an act of God and wouldn't cover the cost of a new one. We didn't have enough from donations and you didn't want to go to Jeanne's parents again for the money. It was divine intervention," he said. Rollins looked like he might be sick.

"What about Gina and Ricky?" I asked. Rondell walked over to me but I stood my ground. He still had the gun in his hand, pointed at the floor.

"Gina," he said, shaking his head. "Now, that one really disappointed me. I thought she was a good girl. She was raised right but she still turned out wrong."

Rondell's face frowned up like he had a bad taste in his mouth. More than likely he was just tasting his own hatefulness. I hoped he'd choke on it.

"She was in charge of collecting the money when the choir had a car wash. I saw her putting every other dollar in her pocket. That money was for the church's summer camp. Then a few days later she shows up at choir practice with a new pair of basketball shoes. I know she used that money she stole to buy them shoes. That was also around the time the church needed a new van and there was no money for it. We had elderly church members who depended on that van to take them to appointments, and to the grocery. I knew you had life insurance on Gina, too," Rondell said, looking at Rollins, who looked away.

"And I knew she was allergic to bee stings. I saw her go

over to her mother's car to change out of those new shoes when she finished playing ball. So I went over to talk to her. I'd bought some bee venom at the health food store the day before and put it in a hypodermic needle. I was just looking for a chance to use it. When no one was watching, I grabbed her and injected her in the neck. Then she started gasping for air and clawing at her pocket. She pulled out her EpiPen, but I took it from her and she passed out. I poured the pop out in the back seat of the car and put a dead bee in her clothes. I put the EpiPen in Melvina's purse while she was playing Bingo with the other church sisters. We got our new van a month later," he said, looking smug and proud.

"You killed your own daughter so the church could have a new van?" Inez said incredulously.

"The only daughter I have is my angel, Shanda," Rondell said, glaring at his niece.

"Shanda's no angel, Rondell. She was dating a drug dealer right under your nose and she helped him set up an innocent man for Inez's murder. She's no better than anybody else and she's looking at jail time," I blurted out like a dummy. If I got out of this without a bullet in my ass I'd be damned lucky.

"Liar!" he yelled at me, making me cringe. He raised his fist to hit me and I couldn't move. I put my hands up to shield myself but Inez jumped in front of me.

"It's true, Uncle Rondell. Shanda's been seeing my old boyfriend, Vaughn Castle. He's a drug dealer and he was seeing Shanda to get back at me 'cause I dropped his ass."

Rondell was huffing and puffing like a winded rhino. He backed away from us and turned towards his wife.

"Rondell, baby, put that gun down. Let's go home so we can talk about this. Just put the gun down, okay?" Bonita walked slowly over to her husband. She was talking to him, but her eyes never left the gun in his hand.

"Everything I did, I did for the greater good. You believe me, don't you, Bonita? I only took the lives of the unworthy. Their deaths served a greater purpose."

"And did you kill my son, too?" asked Rollins. I saw his hands clench into fists and the muscles in his neck started popping. Rondell whirled around and grinned at Rollins.

"Now, you really need to thank me for that one, Morris. That boy was rotten to the core. He was selling drugs. I knew when we went to Detroit for the Midwest conference you'd go and see that boy. I followed you and watched him loud-talk you and treat you like crap in front of all his lowlife friends. I watched them laugh at you. It was a disgrace. Then you left and I followed him around in my rental. I saw him selling that poison to people left and right. Some of them were just kids. I waited for my chance and then I saw him running after some poor guy. Yelling that he was going to kill him. So, I let the Lord work through me. I ran him down in the street just like the animal he was. And I couldn't believe it when you got the biggest insurance payout for the most worthless child. That money helped our scholarship fund, didn't it? We were able to send some kids to college. More good came out of that boy's death than in all of his miserable life," Rondell screamed.

"His name wasn't 'That Boy.' It was Ricky. And he was my son, you bastard!" Rollins cried as he lunged at his brother.

Rollins and Rondell grappled like wrestlers. They both fell to the floor and rolled around, punching each other. Rondell seemed to have the upper hand and was alternating between punching his brother and hitting him with the butt of the gun. Bonita was flapping her arms and running in circles around the two of them, like a headless chicken, pleading for them to stop. Inez and I just stared at the brawling men while the nurse, who'd been silently taking everything in, ran for the cordless phone, which was sitting on the dining room table.

Rondell lurched to his feet, kicked his brother hard in the stomach, and pressed the barrel of the gun against Rollins's forehead. Bonita let out a blood-curdling scream and threw herself on top of her brother-in-law, shielding him from her husband. Rondell looked at his wife and started to sob.

"See, man? They all want you. It's all about you." He put the gun to his own temple.

After that, everything seemed to move in slow motion. Inez raised her arms and ran forward screaming, "Uncle Rondell! No!"

Morris grabbed Bonita and threw her off him in an attempt to get to his brother before he pulled the trigger. But it was too late. A loud explosion filled the room and I turned away, but not quickly enough to miss the gush of blood and brain that splattered the foyer. I was vaguely aware of the wail of rapidly approaching sirens as I vomited in a nearby planter.

"You know, Kendra, I never would have let your friend go to prison," said Morris Rollins as we sat in his car parked in front of my duplex.

It was hours after Rondell's suicide and Rollins had given me a lift home from the police station, where we'd all told and retold our stories to the police. As it turned out, the truth had come out just in time. Timmy had surrendered earlier that day. That was the reason I couldn't reach Harmon and Mercer when I'd called. They were busy interrogating Timmy. Apparently, Timmy had been hiding in my landlady

Mrs. Carson's basement. The person I'd heard snoring the night I'd been in Mrs. Carson's kitchen had been Timmy, and not her son, Stevie, which is how Timmy had known I'd been attacked by Vaughn. Mrs. Carson had told him.

When the police had pulled up in front of my duplex earlier that morning, it was because Mrs. Carson had urged him to turn himself in. She had known him since he was a kid and used to babysit him occasionally for Olivia. She convinced him that if he were really innocent, he'd be exonerated. I was glad the police hadn't been there for me. But that didn't keep me from feeling like a complete fool for doing a tuck and roll out the window and running like I stole something.

I didn't respond to Rollins's statement. I sat staring out the window. I didn't trust myself to speak. I didn't have any children so I didn't know how I would have handled the situation if it had been me. But, thinking back on everything Timmy, Olivia, Inez, and I had been through the past couple of weeks, I was still angry.

"I hope one day you'll believe me and forgive me," he said softly, squeezing my hand.

"I'm not the one you need to be asking for forgiveness," I said, pulling my hand out of his. I started to get out of the car but stopped and turned to him. "Can I ask you a question?"

He nodded.

"Why was your name listed as the father on Joseph's and Gina's death certificates?"

"Because I couldn't stand the thought of those kids going to their graves fatherless. Rondell never did right by those kids when they were alive and he had no intention of doing so when they died. Joseph's grandmother and Melvina were too distraught to deal with all the details when Joseph and

Gina died. So I took care of everything for them, and I told the coroner I was their father. And in a lot of ways, I was. No one ever questioned it. They just figured I'd finally owned up to fathering them."

"What did you mean when you said you'd been cleaning up after Rondell since you were kids?" I ventured.

"Rondell and I are half brothers. We had the same mother. Our mother had been madly in love with my father, so I was always her favorite. But, Rondell's father was a real piece of work, a career criminal who abused her and was in and out of jail. He died in a bar fight. My mother took out all of her rage and hatred for him on Rondell. When Rondell would mess up, she'd really come down hard on him. So I took the blame whenever he screwed up because all I'd get was a lecture. Rondell got beat with whatever she could get her hands on. It was like she was afraid he'd turn out like his father and she was trying to beat the devil out of him. Even after we grew up, I never got out of the habit of covering for him. I guess I couldn't protect him from himself, could I?"

"So, now what?" I asked. He leaned his head back against the car seat and shook his head.

"God only knows," he said, closing his eyes and shaking his head.

I watched him for a few minutes. I was mad at the man for what Timmy had been through. But I felt sorry for him, too. Here was a man who had taken care of his responsibilities to not only his own children but his brother Rondell's illegitimate children, as well. That had to count for something. On impulse, I leaned over to give him a quick kiss on the cheek. He turned to say something and our lips met. What was supposed to be a peck on the cheek turned into a five-minute-long tongue wrestling match that left us breathless and staring uncomfortably at each other. We'd even fogged up the windows.

"Take care, Reverend Rollins. Thanks for the ride," I said finally, and jumped out of his car before he could respond. I ran up my steps and opened my door. I looked back before stepping inside my apartment and was happy to see he was gone.

Epilogue

was the last day of classes at the literacy center before Thanksgiving. I looked around the classroom and smiled, happy to see it so packed. Dorothy'd been back from Michigan for almost a month and everything was back to normal. Her mother still hadn't healed as fast as she'd hoped, so Dorothy brought her home to Willow to recover at her house. Inez's ex-nurse was caring for her while Dorothy was at work. Noreen retired to Florida, which was just fine by me and everybody else. It seems the students, led by Rhonda, walked out in protest after I left and refused to come back until Noreen was gone. After spending two days in an empty classroom, and getting reprimanded by the superintendent for overstepping her authority, Noreen conceded defeat and left with her tail between her legs. Touchdown, Kendra.

Inez planned to open her own beauty shop called The House of Braids sometime next year. I heard she renewed her relationship with her father. No charges were ever filed against her for Nicole's death. The police determined that she'd acted in self-defense. There was a new funeral for Nicole, which I didn't attend. I decided it was best I put some distance between Morris Rollins and myself. Besides, he had more than enough on his plate. He managed to dodge the bullet on obstruction and insurance fraud charges. But even if he hadn't, the members of his church would still see him as a hero. He was more popular than ever, still packing them in every Sunday. Donations were at an all-time high and plans were in the works for a new community center for the church. There's even talk that his show *The Light and The Way* could be headed for syndication.

All of the charges against Timmy were dropped. He passed his GED exam with flying colors and was planning to enroll in the local community college at the first of the year. He was currently taking care of Olivia, whose recovery from breast cancer surgery was going well. Luckily, the cancer hadn't spread to her lymph nodes so she didn't have to undergo chemo. I finally got Timmy to tell me what he'd stolen from Ricky Maynard. Turns out Timmy had stolen Ricky's electronic Rolodex. Timmy had been after Vaughn out of revenge for his ex-girlfriend's death from a drug overdose. But while Vaughn was very discreet in his drug dealings, Ricky ran his operation like a true businessman and had all of his drug clients' and contacts' numbers programmed into his Rolodex, including Vaughn's. Timmy had been planning on handing the Rolodex over to the police in the hopes of implicating Vaughn. But at some point while Ricky was chasing him, Timmy tripped and the Rolodex flew out of his hands into the street and got run over.

Vaughn hadn't been so much interested in revenge for

his friend after all. He'd been heavily snorting his own supply of cocaine and had become extremely paranoid knowing that Timmy was out to get him. Vaughn set Timmy up to get rid of him. It was determined that Rondell Kidd's gun was the same gun that had killed Vaughn Castle. The theory was that he'd beaten and killed Vaughn after finding out about his relationship with Shanda. But, thinking back on Rondell's obvious shock when I'd told him about Shanda and Vaughn, and knowing that Timmy was the one who beat Vaughn up, I knew that wasn't true.

Shanda was taking time off from school to care for Bonita. The strain of Rondell's suicide and the knowledge that he'd murdered three people, coupled with the realization that she was inadvertently responsible for Nicole's death, had taken a hard toll on Bonita. And even though Rollins forgave her, he also told her there would never be anything romantic between them. Bonita took that harder than her husband's death. She almost had a nervous breakdown. Shanda would not believe that her uncle could be her father and adamantly refused to take a paternity test. She also never would admit to her part in helping Vaughn set up Timmy. It was almost like she convinced herself it never happened. Since there was no evidence, no charges were ever filed against her.

Oddly enough, I was thinking about Shanda when I ran into her at the grocery store after work that day. I almost didn't recognize her. She was no longer wearing her hair in braids and had gained some weight. I had to chase her down in the parking lot to get her to talk to me.

"How's it going, Shanda?" I asked breathlessly once I caught up with her. She looked at me suspiciously and shrugged.

"Aside from my father being dead and having his good

name dragged through the mud, and my mother falling apart and spending every day crying in her bathrobe, I'm just peachy. How about you, Kendra? Still chasing down evildoers in the name of justice?"

"I'm really sorry about your parents, Shanda. And if you'd been the one in Timmy's shoes, I'd have helped you, too." I did feel sorry for Shanda over the loss of a father she loved but I wasn't about to tell her I was sorry about Vaughn. I was sure he was probably slinging dope in hell right about now. Time and the absence of Vaughn's influence still hadn't ignited any sense of responsibility or remorse for what she'd done to Timmy. She was definitely Rondell's daughter as far as I was concerned.

"Whatever, Kendra. I gotta go," she said, turning away.

"Look, Shanda. I know I'm not your favorite person but I do know how much you enjoyed working at the literacy center. I know you're taking time off from school to take care of your mom. But if you'd ever like to come back and volunteer at the center, we'd love to have you back. I know the students would love to see you."

"I'll keep that in mind," she said, turning away from me and opening her car door.

I happened to glance in her car and saw the infamous blue scarf, the one Vaughn had used to strangle Aretha Marshall, tied around the rearview mirror. The same scarf I'd stuffed in Vaughn's mouth when Timmy and I had tied him up. There was only one way she could have gotten the scarf. Shanda noticed me looking at it. She smiled and winked at me before starting up her car and driving off, leaving me staring after her in shock. I walked back to my car, determined to forget what I'd seen. Though I couldn't quite shake the images that popped into my head of a distraught Shanda sneaking out of the house with her father's gun after getting home from the hospital, going to the wooded area in back of Briar Creek, where she used to have sex with Vaughn—to see if he was there with another woman—and finding him tied up in his car. I could imagine Shanda breaking the window and pulling the scarf out of his mouth only to have Vaughn berate her and call her names, and an already fragile Shanda snapping, and shooting him. I didn't need any more drama in my life. I went home.

A few hours later, I arrived at the Red Dragon dressed to kill in a clingy, low-cut cranberry sweater dress and black, knee-high high-heeled boots. I was meeting Carl for dinner. He said he had something to tell me that he was pretty excited about. I couldn't wait to find out what it was. Carl was already seated when I arrived.

"All right, what's this big news?" I asked, snuggling up next to him in our booth and inhaling his warm scent of Obsession.

"Well, I've been thinking for a long time about ways I can give back to the community. I do pro bono work. But I've still been feeling like I could do more. Recently, I was approached about the possibility of helping provide legal aid to low-income people in need of legal assistance. And the best part is, it's an organization right here in Willow. We can spend more time together." He was so excited it was hard not to get caught up in his enthusiasm.

"So, what is this wonderful organization?" I asked. I took a sip of my water and saw someone walking towards our booth out of the corner of my eye. I looked up, thinking it was our server, and almost choked.

"It's Holy Cross Ministries. Kendra, you know Reverend Rollins, right?" Carl asked, oblivious to my discom-

fort, and gesturing towards the tall, handsome figure standing in front of us.

"Yes, I know Reverend Rollins," I said, my throat suddenly tight.

Morris Rollins looked down at me like a wolf eyeing its
prey. And I felt like a big fluffy sheep.